PEACE

Also by Shelley Shepard Gray

Sisters of the Heart series
HIDDEN
WANTED
FORGIVEN
GRACE

Seasons of Sugarcreek series
WINTER'S AWAKENING
SPRING'S RENEWAL
AUTUMN'S PROMISE
CHRISTMAS IN SUGARCREEK

Families of Honor
THE CAREGIVER
THE PROTECTOR
THE SURVIVOR
A CHRISTMAS FOR KATIE (NOVELLA)

The Secrets of Crittenden County
MISSING
THE SEARCH
FOUND

The Days of Redemption Series
DAYBREAK
RAY OF LIGHT
EVENTIDE

PEACE

A Crittenden County Christmas Novel

S<small>HELLEY</small> S<small>HEPARD</small> G<small>RAY</small>

A V O N
INSPIRE
An Imprint of HarperCollins*Publishers*

P.S.™ is a trademark of HarperCollins Publishers.

ISBN 978 1-62490-662-6

For Lesley

Though he fall, he shall not be utterly cast down:
for the Lord upholdeth him with his hand.

Psalms 37:24 (King James Version)

The best time to do something worthwhile is
between yesterday and tomorrow.

Amish Proverb

Chapter 1

The thing one needs to know about Crittenden County is that it ain't near as sheltered as one might think.

MOSE KRAMER

Crittenden County, Kentucky

Blood was dripping onto the pristine doormat under his feet. As he watched one drop, then another, and another fall to the ground, then glow eerily in the reflection of the thousand white lights adorning the rooflines of the Yellow Bird Inn, Chris Ellis felt his resolve slip.

He should never have come back, and certainly not in the condition he was in. But here he was.

He peeked into the tall rectangular window that framed the front door, his fist hovering like a nervous hummingbird over the wood. Over and over again he would almost knock, but then a bizarre pang of conscience would surface and he'd stand motionless a little bit longer. Trying to persuade himself to do what was right.

Turn around. Walk away. Never return.

But at the moment, he wasn't sure he could take even one more step forward, never mind make a complete U-turn. He was dizzy, weak, sweaty, and hot—even though it was barely thirty degrees out. Chances were slim to none that he'd even be able to remain in an upright position for much longer.

Besides, where would he go? Back to his beat-up SUV to spend the night in a vacant parking lot like he did last night? Somehow drive back to St. Louis? Lexington?

Not that he'd get very far in either of those cities. He was a target right now, given that the leader of the drug ring he'd been befriending had learned of all the questions he was asking Billy. All that mattered now was that he kept his cover until Taylor, his partner, could figure out what to do next.

So, where did a man who was beaten and bleeding go when he'd been working deep undercover for so long that even his family thought he was a person to avoid?

The only place that had come to mind was Frannie Eicher's Yellow Bird Inn. Frannie had a brisk, efficient way about her that he appreciated. She was the type of proprietor who would treat him with kindness . . . but give him his distance, too.

And he was desperate for a little bit of kindness.

But of course, even the nicest people weren't always understanding when it came to near strangers bleeding on their front porch three days before Christmas.

Before he could talk himself out of it again, he knocked. Well, he let his hand slip and fall against the smooth planes of the door. Just once. If no one answered, he'd go back to where he'd hidden his truck and drive away.

Almost immediately, the front porch lights turned on. Then a face peered through the window just to the right of the door.

But it wasn't Frannie. It was the one person he'd hoped never to see again.

He was still standing there, stunned, when he heard a dead bolt click, followed by a high-pitched squeak as the door opened.

And there was Beth Byler. His mouth went dry as his gaze ached to take in every single inch of her.

It didn't help that she was looking as perfect and beautiful as she'd been when he'd last seen her. Looking just the way she did when she appeared in his dreams. Petite and fine-boned. Smooth brown hair and bright blue eyes. Wholesome. Amish.

Chris fought to keep his expression neutral. Which was crazy of course. Like she'd care about his look of shock when he was bleeding all over the front porch.

Sure that she was about to slam the door in his face, he anxiously continued to look his fill. A man needed as many sweet pictures to store for times when nothing he was seeing was good.

Dim candlelight cast a mellow glow behind her. The scents of pine and cinnamon and everything clean and pure wafted toward him, teasing his senses. He reached out, gripped the door frame in order to keep from falling.

Blue eyes scanned his form. Paused at the cuts on his hands. At the new scar near his lip. At the way his right eye was practically swollen shut.

He waited for the look of revulsion that was sure to come. What kind of man let himself get so beaten and bruised?

"Chris?" she whispered.

"Yeah. It's me."

"Wh-what are you doing here?"

He needed someplace quiet to stay until after Christmas Day. He needed an out-of-the-way place to hide out, to recover. To heal his body and his soul. To try to remember who he was.

He was attempting to say that, to come up with a way to convince her to let him in without making a big fool of himself or scaring her, when he looked down at his boots.

Noticed the blood again ruining the doormat.

"I'm bleeding on your front porch," he muttered.

"Bleeding?" Her gaze darted away from his swollen face. Traipsed down his body. Down his jeans to his thick brown Timberlands. Then her eyes widened as she, too, noticed the blood dripping steadily on her doormat.

"You must come inside!" And then she snaked an arm out, tugged at the hand against the doorframe. The one that had been holding him upright and had stopped him from doing something foolish, like sway toward her.

She pulled him in.

Her slight form wasn't strong enough to keep him on his feet. Those three little steps took the rest of his strength, while the relief he felt at finding comfort sapped the rest of his energy.

"Beth, I'm sorry," he muttered, as the pain and his clumsy apology got the best of him. He collapsed at her feet, no doubt staining her freshly scrubbed floor in the process.

Illustrating yet again that he wasn't the man he should have been.

"Chris!" Beth cried as he slipped through her hands and fell to the floor. "Chris?"

Heart beating so hard she felt like she'd run a mile, she knelt at his side. Looked at his swollen cheek, the cut near his lip. The blood on his shirt. "Oh my goodness. Oh my goodness! Chris? Chris, what happened to you?"

Of course he didn't answer. But when the cold wind blew against her cheek and threatened to douse the flame in the kerosene lantern behind her, she focused on the present. Quickly, she slammed the door shut, then carefully bolted the deadlock. Just in case someone was after him.

Like the last time he'd been there.

Now, satisfied that he was safe from the cold and wind, at the very least, she knelt back down by his side. His eyes were closed now, making his whole appearance shift. Until that very moment, she'd never realized just how much his piercing gaze affected her. With his eyes closed, he seemed almost approachable, which was laughable, considering how damaged his body was.

"Oh, Chris. What in the world has happened to you? What have you been doing since we last met?" she murmured as she reached out and gently smoothed back a chunk of wayward honey-brown hair from his forehead.

She'd last seen him almost ten months ago. She'd offered to help watch the inn after Frannie had had a kitchen accident and had to be hospitalized. During that time, everyone in the area had been under a lot of stress, what with a body being found on the Millers' farm. At first, she'd been afraid of Chris. She'd been half afraid he was one of Perry Borntrager's drug-dealing friends.

Then she'd learned that Ellis wasn't even his real last name. And that he had no intention of telling her what his real name was. Her suspicion of him had grown and warred with her attraction to him.

Only later did she discover that Chris was a good man after all. He'd only looked dangerous because he'd been working undercover for some kind of alphabet agency. What was it again? Not the FBI . . . the DEA! That's right.

But to her shame, even before she'd known he could be trusted, there had been something about him that appealed to her. She'd been drawn to him like a fly to butter or a moth to a light or a bee to honey.

And that, of course, had been a bad thing. She was Amish; he was not. She lived a quiet existence, spending most of her days either caring for her mother or babysitting other people's children.

His life was surely the opposite of that.

And he'd been stronger than her, too. With little more than the slightest hint of regret, he'd informed her that she should forget about him. That no good would ever come from a relationship between the two of them.

But yet, he'd come back.

Now he looked to be in terrible shape. Taking inventory again, she noticed that not only was his cheek swollen, but there were also cuts and scratches along his fingers and knuckles of his hands.

And that there was even more blood staining his clothes.

After getting the lamp, she knelt and examined him more closely, pushing herself to ignore everything she'd ever found attractive about him and focus solely on his injuries.

Remembering the pool of blood under his feet, she hastily untied his boots and yanked them off. He groaned as she gently pushed up his dark jeans, one leg at a time.

When she shoved the fabric up his left calf, she saw nothing out of the ordinary, just a man's finely muscled leg.

But the right brought a cry from him . . . when she uncovered a bleeding hole in his leg.

He'd been cut badly. But was that his only injury?

Leaning close, she pulled his arms from the sleeves of his jacket and tossed it on the floor.

Then saw the other wound—a deep gash at the top of his chest. So deep, the area around the cut was saturated, and little drops of excess blood pooled, then dripped to freedom.

Fear knotted her stomach as she tried to keep her cool. "You take care of babies, Beth," she told herself sternly. "You've nursed children through all sorts of illnesses. Even helped a boy recover from an emergency tonsillectomy when his father was out of town."

Surely, she could help one man seek medical help?

Unable to stop herself, she lightly touched his shoulder before getting to her feet. She needed to go find the phone Luke insisted Frannie keep at hand for emergencies.

She'd just picked up the cell phone when Chris called out her name.

"Don't, Beth. Don't call."

"I must. You're injured. And . . . and you're bleeding, Chris. Something awful." When he merely raised a brow, she said, "Chris, this . . . this is mighty bad."

"No, Beth. You can't contact the police."

"I was going to call for an ambulance."

"Nope. Not them, either. Put that phone down, Beth. Making that call could put both of our lives at stake."

Surely he was exaggerating things? "You need help, Chris. You need stitches."

"Then you're going to have to stitch me up. You know how to sew, right?"

"*Jah* . . . but—"

"But nothing."

But everything! She couldn't sew *him*. Realizing that he was truly worried about their safety, she softened her tone. "Chris, listen—"

Looking weary, he propped himself on his elbows. Stared at her again with those unusual pale eyes. "Beth, no one can know I'm here."

The agitation that had been teasing her conscience switched to fear in the span of a heartbeat. "Why, exactly are you here? Are you in some kind of trouble?"

"I'm in trouble, but I don't know why I came here. I was driving and so tired. And then I saw the signs for Marion and I remembered the inn. I couldn't go home. I . . . I had thought Frannie could help me." As if his short speech had sapped all his energy, he lay back down on the ground.

"You wanted Frannie's help?" Oh, she hoped he wouldn't hear the pain in her voice.

"Yeah. Where is she?"

"She went to Cincinnati with her husband. With Luke. For Christmas," she added somewhat lamely.

"So they did get married." His voice turned soft.

She cleared her throat in order to hide her nervousness. In order to hide the hurt feelings she was trying to conceal. She shouldn't be disappointed that he'd come back looking for someone else besides her. She really shouldn't.

"I need to hide, Beth . . . until December twenty-sixth."

"That's days from now!" What was she going to do with him for days on end?

"I don't have to stay that long if you don't want. All I really need is to lay low for a day or two. Just until I'm healed enough to get away. Neither my boss nor Taylor can meet up with me until the day after Christmas. Can I stay, even if it's just for a little while?"

To her embarrassment, she realized she knew exactly who Taylor was. His brave and resourceful female partner. The mention reminded her of just how different that woman must be from her. How Taylor would probably know exactly what to do.

And yet, Chris came to the Yellow Bird Inn for help. "I . . . I just don't know."

He met her gaze again. Seemed to come to terms with whatever he saw in her expression. Then came to a decision.

With a grimace, he raised himself back up on his elbows. "You know what? It's okay. I'll go. I shouldn't have come here. I knew better." He shifted again, now sitting upright. "Just give me a few minutes, and I'll get out of your way."

The right thing to do would be to stand firm. To agree with that plan of action. She was only living at the Yellow Bird Inn part-time, as a way to keep an eye on things for Frannie. Never had Frannie imagined that there would be a visitor. In fact, she'd told Beth that she'd lied to two couples that she was full over the holidays so that Beth wouldn't be tasked with cooking and cleaning, two things she wasn't so skilled at.

So, yes, it would be best for Chris Ellis and his blood and injuries and mysterious life to leave. Beth had no authority to accept any guests. And it surely wouldn't be right to accept a guest without checking in with Frannie first.

And yet . . .

"Chris, are you sure you don't have somewhere else to go for Christmas?"

The look he sent her spoke volumes. "Not everyone remembers it's almost Christmas, Beth." His voice was gentle, almost as if he hated to be the one to tell her that for some people Christmas was only another day to get through. "And not everyone wants to see their family on that day."

It broke her heart. "No?"

"No." The skin was white around his mouth as he struggled to his feet, obviously favoring his right leg. "I'll be fine. Don't worry."

He wasn't going to run to his partner; he wasn't going to turn to his family. He was going to be alone. She knew it as surely as she knew that even after all this time, she still dreamed about him.

Still thought about him. Thought about what would never be. Before she could change her mind, she spoke. "Stay."

He stilled. "You sure?"

Her gaze met his. And in that instant, she knew he saw the tears in her eyes. Saw how vulnerable she was . . . at least when it came to him.

"I'm sure. Stay here until your boss or partner can come get you. I'll help you get better. I'll sew up your wound."

"Don't forget—no one can know I'm here, Beth."

"Then I won't tell anyone you are." There. The decision had been made.

"Thank you," he said simply. "Now, if you could, tell me where to go. I've only got about another two minutes in me before I pass out again."

Taking a deep breath, she wrapped an arm around his waist and guided him to the stairs. Though it was tempting to put him in the one guest bedroom downstairs, she felt it would be safer if he stayed in a more secluded spot.

Without a word of explanation, she guided him up the stairs, leading him one step at a time. Their progress was halting and painful. When they were only halfway, he was leaning so heavily on her, she wasn't sure that she could continue without a rest.

But finally they made it to his room. It was at the end of the hall, next to the bathroom. The room was smaller than most, and rather sparsely furnished, too. But it was warmer than some of the others and also held an oversized easy chair, which was perfect for a man of his size.

When she helped him lie down on top of a thick quilt patched in a crazy quilt design, he gripped her arm. "Beth?"

"*Jah?*"

"Don't forget about the blood."

"Blood? I don't understand."

His face paled as he struggled to speak. "I . . . I parked in the back, near the woods. But you've got to check to make sure I didn't bleed on the ground. Do you understand?"

Then he closed his eyes and fulfilled his earlier promise.

He'd passed out.

And left her with a terrible load of problems as well as a miserable trail of blood to remove. Why did the worst things always happen when Frannie was out of town?

Chapter 2

Some folks wonder why I watch both English and Amish kinner. But to my way of thinking, all God's children are basically the same. Especially at Christmastime. Ain't so?

BETH BYLER

Thinking he was alone in the store, Jacob Schrock crumbled his father's latest letter from prison and tossed it at the trash can. The wad of paper sailed through the air, skimmed the rim of the metal can, then promptly floated to the floor.

It seemed he couldn't even get his father's letters out of his life easily.

He was about to stride over and pick up the offending piece of paper when his wife, Deborah, bent down and snatched it up.

She glanced at the crumpled slip of notebook paper in her hand, then slowly raised her gaze to his. "What is this, Jacob?"

"You know exactly what it is—it's another letter from my *daed*."

"Did you read this one? Or were you too busy again?" Her tone held a healthy amount of sarcasm in it.

Jacob didn't blame his wife for being so sarcastic. Throwing out his father's carefully penned letters was a rather harsh thing to do. But he was justified, he was certain of that. He'd promised himself not to dwell on the past, and to him that meant moving forward after his father's imprisonment, not looking backward.

And even though they were married, this was *his* father they were talking about, not hers. After all, some things simply couldn't be shared. This was one of those things. "I did read the letter." This time, he had.

She raised an eyebrow. "Every word?"

"Almost." He'd read until his father started asking him for forgiveness. But instead of admitting that, he turned away and pretended to be very interested in cleaning out the immaculate shelves underneath the front counter of the Schrock Variety Store. Which, of course, was his family's namesake. Now, though, he was the one running it.

Still holding the crumpled paper, Deborah softened her voice as she walked to his side. "Jacob, maybe we should talk about this."

"Talking won't help. Besides, there ain't anything to talk about."

"Your mother says that every time she visits your father in prison he always looks a little worse."

"Prison is a harsh place. I can't imagine that he's having an easy time of it."

"I don't think it's only the prison that is hard for him to bear. I think he's having a hard time dealing with your anger." When he flinched, she softened her tone. "Jacob, I think you need to think about your feelings. Pray on it. You need to find a way to forgive him. . . ."

Anger flashed through him like an old, violent friend. "Deborah, he was going to let me take the blame for Perry's death. He hired a lawyer. And most importantly, he knew the guilt and pain I felt about the fight I had with Perry was eating me up . . . and he let me suffer. If I hadn't pushed him, if my mother hadn't pushed him to admit everything . . . if Detective Reynolds and Sheriff Kramer hadn't questioned him so much, pressing him to finally admit the truth, I could be the one sitting in prison." He still felt dizzy when he remembered sitting with his father at their kitchen table, and discovering that his *daed* had been willing to do whatever it took to protect himself—and keep his own actions a secret.

His wife sighed, and the look on her face told him that he was trying her patience something awful.

So he held his tongue. Barely.

"What Aaron did was wrong, and I know he's sorry for it, too," she finally said. "But he's paying the price now."

"So am I," he said, unable to keep the bitterness out of his voice.

"Jacob, don't forget that it was my brother who was murdered."

"I never—"

She held up a hand. "What I'm tryin' to say is . . . if I can find it in my heart to forgive your father, I would think you could, too. It's our way, you know."

She was referring to one of the hallmarks for the Amish faith. To turn the other cheek. To seek to forgive. To rely on God for retribution, not to take matters into one's own hands.

But while it was a commendable belief, it wasn't so easy to put that philosophy into action. At the moment, he wasn't ready to forgive, and there was no way he could convince Deborah to understand.

He didn't know how to make her understand things from his point of view. He'd already tried, but she had obstinately stood firm.

"Deborah, I know you don't approve, but you've got to at least try to see things my way. I can't change how I feel."

Setting the letter on the counter, she looked at him sadly. "Please pray about this. I know if you let the Lord guide you, your burden will feel lighter," she murmured, resting her hand on his shoulder. "Especially now, at Christmas."

"Christmas is just another day, Deb." To his shame, instead of accepting her gesture of comfort, he shrugged off her hand.

Visibly stung, she stared at him for a long moment, then walked out of the store.

Leaving him alone with his hurt and his pain . . . and now his guilt. The day he'd married Deborah had been one of the happiest of his life. He'd felt so hopeful that all the pain of the past year and the long murder investigation were behind him.

Now, six months later, he was even starting to feel like people in Crittenden County were accepting him again. They were beginning to frequent the store more, and no longer avoiding him at church.

But now this friction caused by his father's need for absolution was creating a fissure in his fragile new bond with Deborah. If they couldn't see eye to eye, he knew things were going to turn dark again.

And though it was almost Christmas, he couldn't see any way around that.

She'd done it. She'd gone outside with a damp washcloth and a bottle of cleaning solution and had wiped up Chris's blood from the sidewalk.

After that, Beth had taken the broom and carefully swept off his footprints from the driveway.

With the snow that was expected soon, the last traces of his walk to the inn would be gone.

Now it was time to tend to him.

She'd been pacing outside Chris's room for a good three minutes. It didn't feel like that, though. It felt like an eternity. The worst things in life really did seem to take the longest.

Every time she passed in front of the door, a little voice inside her head encouraged her to go inside.

And she certainly did need to.

In one of her hands was a sewing kit. In the other was a bottle of rubbing alcohol, a clean washcloth, and a couple of bandages. It was a pitiful attempt to provide adequate medical care.

However, she'd promised him that she'd do her best to tend to his needs. If she could gather her courage.

She was pacing outside the door again when she heard Chris moan. She needed no further encouragement to at last turn the door's handle and walk in.

He raised his head when the door opened, and his eyes were bleary as he watched her walk toward him. "Beth?"

"*Jah*, it is me. I'm here to try to help you." Yes, *try* was the operative word here. Crossing the room, she closed the open blind, taking a peek out the window as she did. Snow lay on the ground and more snow was expected by nightfall. Next, she turned on the kerosene light by his bed and studied him again.

Truthfully, he looked no different, except his feet were now bare.

That set her to action. She walked to the bathroom next to his room, poured water into the bowl she'd brought upstairs, then added a liberal amount of alcohol to the water. Then she soaked the washcloth before finally returning to his side with the bowl in her hands.

After getting settled, she carefully placed her palm on his forehead. He seemed feverish so she pushed aside the quilt that had covered him, trying to give him some fresh air.

He winced. "I think I might have ruined the quilt."

"It doesn't matter."

"Frannie might think so."

"I'll worry about Fannie," she said crisply.

Examining his bloodstained arm and the shirt that seemed determined to adhere to his skin like glue, she felt a fresh wave of pity toward him. He really was in poor shape.

But even under the revulsion she felt toward the cuts and blood and dirt that covered his body, he was still attractive to her.

Which, unfortunately, had been the case from the moment they met. There had been something almost tangible between the two of them that she'd never felt with anyone else.

And though he'd never said anything, she was sure Chris had felt that same way. Before, he'd been the strong one. He'd told her no good could come of a relationship between them.

Perhaps he'd been right. Now she needed to be the strong one. She needed to help him recover, offer him shelter, then send him on his way.

As if doing that would be easy for her.

What she needed to do was imagine him as one of the children she watched over. Yes, that was it! She could try to think of him not as Chris Ellis, but as four-year-old Robbie Yoder.

The washcloth was cooling, which made her stop her musings and get to work. That was what needed to be done.

Glancing at Chris's face, she saw his eyes close again and she spoke. "I'm going to undress you now."

Eyelids popped open. "What did you say?"

She was sure her face was now beet red. "I mean, your shirt. I need to take off your shirt. To help doctor you."

With a wince and a stifled groan, he sat up, then began releasing the buttons himself.

Feeling more helpless than ever, she watched him struggle. Little by little, one button was freed. Then two.

Her hands itched to take control. Yet again she

wished that he was far younger, more like the children she babysat. She wished he had baby-soft skin instead of hard muscles. Wished he looked at her with wide-eyed innocence instead of with a barely hidden heat that she didn't quite understand.

Then she could be in control.

But things were far different with a man like him. He was used to being the strong one. Used to being the protector. She could only imagine how he was handling being so helpless.

At last, his shirt lay open. Exhausted, his hands went limp by his sides.

She took charge and began carefully pulling the blood-soaked cotton away from his shoulders. "I'm afraid this shirt is ruined, Chris."

"It doesn't matter."

"I'll make you a new one," she murmured, mentally checking her storage closet at home, with the bolts of fabric neatly stacked on shelves.

He said nothing to that as she finished removing his shirt, then began carefully dabbing at his cuts with the warm cloth. Her hand shook a bit as she noticed the three tattoos gracing his chest. They were some kind of signs, and their black ink forms made his pallor more pronounced.

When she dabbed at his shoulder, he flinched and the wound there started bleeding in earnest again. Feeling a little sick, she gulped.

Chris glanced down at the cut, then met her eyes. "Did you bring your sewing kit in here?" he asked.

She nodded.

"Then you need to sew me up, Beth."

She didn't know if she could. "I know what I promised, but I simply don't know if I can give you stitches."

"There's no one else."

"I don't want to hurt you."

"You won't. You'll be healing me, Beth." Somehow he was able to summon a rakish smile. "Plus, I'm already hurt. I promise, nothing you could do would hurt me worse."

That didn't make her feel any better. "But—"

Looking aggrieved, he stared at her until she met his gaze. "Call it a gift, then, Beth. Call stitching me up your Christmas gift."

"I couldn't."

With a wince, he moved his arm, bringing forth a new rush of blood. As they both watched it run down one of his tattoos, he whispered, "It has to be done."

She wanted to turn away, but there was nowhere to go. She wanted to argue, but he was too weak. She wanted to refuse, but he had no one else.

With clumsy fingers, she opened her sewing kit and pulled out a spool of thread and a brand-new needle. "This is the worst sort of gift, Chris Ellis."

Something flickered in his eyes before he somehow found the strength to smile. "Not to me."

Chapter 3

I've learned the hard way that you've got to be careful about knife wounds and bullet holes. If they're not carefully tended, they can leave some pretty bad scars.

CHRIS ELLIS

It wasn't hard for Chris to remain motionless under Beth's shaking hands. All he had to do was imagine what would happen if he was found at the hospital . . . and what could happen to Beth if the wrong person discovered she'd taken him there.

He was hoping that the two men who'd beaten him hadn't punished Billy as well. The poor kid was just hungry for attention and when Chris befriended him, he'd opened up. But knowing the crew Billy worked with, he was probably in worse shape than Chris.

He couldn't imagine bringing that kind of trouble to Marion, but he needed a place to hide and this was the most out-of-the-way place he knew.

If his appearance at the Yellow Bird Inn brought even a bruise to Beth's flawless skin, Chris knew he'd always regret his decision to come back to Crittenden County.

As the minutes passed and her needle continued to stitch, Beth's hands shook harder. Little by little, his effort to seem aloof began to war with his sympathy for her.

As she tugged a bit too hard, he lost the battle and he winced. "Sorry!" she gasped.

"My fault, not yours."

Her eyes welled with tears. "I hate this."

"I know you do." So far, she'd placed six neat stitches through his skin, but each one had cost her. She looked to be on the verge of a breakdown.

Silently, she made another knot. Lifted the needle again, then paused.

She remained frozen, staring at her work with something that looked a lot like anguish, so he attempted to encourage her. "I bet you're almost done."

"Almost." Perspiration dotted her upper lip now. When she met his gaze, hers was apologetic. "I think you still need one more stitch. I'm sorry, Chris."

There was nothing for her to be sorry for. Actually, he was the one who owed her an apology. He ached to tell her that, but the time wasn't right. At the moment, she needed him to be quiet and still. Stoic.

Even though there was nothing he could do to help her, even though he didn't want to matter to her, he wanted to believe she was fine.

The idea that they were both just fine in each other's absence was all they really had, anyway.

"I haven't been sick," she finally answered. "I just haven't been too hungry." Turning, Beth smoothed her hands over her waist and along her hips. On another woman, the action might have been faintly suggestive. But he knew she was nervous and unsure—of both being around him, and of how he was regarding her.

Of his criticism.

Which just went to show him yet again what a jerk he was. Here she was giving him shelter and healing his wounds . . . and he was analyzing her figure and making her feel bad about herself.

Oh, but his momma would have given him what-for if she'd heard him. She'd raised a gentleman, and those manners she'd taught him were inside him somewhere—still with him, even though he'd done his best to pretend that they'd never been learned.

But here they were, and his sense of chivalry appeared to be alive and well . . . even though he was beaten and injured. And imposing on the very woman he should be staying away from.

Fact was, he didn't deserve to be in the same room with her, let alone be with her at Christmas.

Still looking out of sorts, she gazed at him. "It's getting late. I think I will leave you now."

"Please don't." He needed to make amends, to make her feel more comfortable around him.

Selfishly, he wanted to find out what she'd been up to since he'd left. Did she have a man in her life now? Was there anyone who would be visiting? And would there be anyone who would notice that she had taken in an *Englischer* for Christmas?

That sudden thought made his voice harsher than he'd intended when he spoke. "Beth, sit down and talk to me," he rasped as he tried to scoot up against the headboard. "Please. Just for a few moments."

Her eyes widened at the spot on the bed he'd patted. "I should find you a new shirt. Luke might have one he could spare. . . ."

Feeling a bit silly, he pulled the sheet up, tried to cover most of his bare chest. "I've got fresh clothes in my truck," he said in what he hoped was a more soothing tone. "I'll get them later. Sit and talk to me. Please."

"Um, all right." Reaching behind her, she curved her fingers around the top rung of the oak ladder-back chair and pulled it closer. Then, after smoothing the skirt of her dress, she sat.

Bracing himself, he sat up a bit. "So . . . quite a bit of time has passed since I last saw you."

"Almost ten months," she corrected. Letting him

know that she'd felt their separation as much as he had. "The last time I saw you, I mean, when we saw each other . . . was in March."

With a slight frown, she looked out his smallish window. "The crocuses were just starting to bloom. As were the daffodils. Now, the streets are lit with tiny white lights and the air smells like pine and fresh snow." She shrugged. "But it doesn't really matter how much time has passed, does it? All I really remember is you telling me that you never wanted to see me again."

He saw the hurt on her face. "I only said that because staying away from me would keep you safe."

"But you've come back."

"I never meant to." Of course, as soon as he said that, he ached to take his words back. He hadn't wanted to see her again because he still thought about her in the middle of the night. Or when time dragged during a stakeout.

Or when he was eating by himself in a restaurant. Or when he happened to drive by a sign with a buggy and horse on it.

"I see."

Her obvious disappointment in his answers stung. He'd been proud of himself when he'd walked away from her, and from the longing he'd seen in her eyes. He'd done the right thing for her, and that had made him feel like maybe he was a better person than he'd ever imagined himself to be.

And yet, he'd still returned.

Obviously he still wasn't the man he wished he could be. He cleared his throat. "So . . . what have you been doing with yourself? Watching children?"

"*Jah.* I've been babysitting a lot. And caring for my mother."

He remembered that Beth's mom suffered from multiple sclerosis and was confined to a wheelchair. "How's she feeling?"

"Right now, she's good enough for me to be here. Some of her new medicines are helping, which is a blessing. She hasn't seemed so tired."

"I'm glad to hear that."

"We have some neighbors who we're close to. They've been checking up on her several times a day. And my aunts . . . my aunts will be paying her a visit soon." Lifting her chin a bit, she said, "I am grateful to have people who care about us."

Against his will, a burst of jealousy shot through him as he imagined one of her "close" neighbors being tall, dark, and single. "Have you been seeing anyone?"

A line formed between her brows. "Seeing?"

"A man." He swallowed. "Has any man finally gotten up the nerve to court you?" He remembered asking her about the men in her life the last time they were together. She'd playfully mentioned that she was a little too strong-willed of a woman to be a perfect Amish wife.

But instead of smiling at the remembered conversation, she scowled. "Chris, we shouldn't be talking about that."

Jealousy—that petty emotion he had no right to feel—made his cheeks flush. "What does that mean?"

Visions of Beth riding in some mystery man's Amish buggy popped in his head. And who knew what had been happening there? Amish or not, Beth was too much of a temptation for any man to ignore.

Her voice hardened. "My personal business is none of your concern."

"Yet I am concerned." Feeling like a fool, he said, "I hope whoever you're seeing is a nice guy. And that he knows that you're a good woman."

"Good?"

"Um . . . virtuous?" When her expression stayed just as frozen, he cursed himself and his limited vocabulary. Now he sounded like a fool.

When she said nothing, merely glared at him, he backtracked quickly. "I'm sorry. You're right, and I was right months ago, too. Who you're dating is none of my business. I was simply trying to figure out if we were going to have company," he lied. "If you had a man who was going to be calling on you here."

"You don't have to worry about that."

Ironically, her good news made him sad. "I see."

"Chris?"

"Hmm?"

"Um . . . what is your real last name?"

Her voice was soft, her eyes searching. Suddenly, the air between them felt thicker, and all those months between them melted away. His tongue felt thick in his mouth. There was so much he wanted to share with her . . . and just as much that he knew better than to even mention aloud. "It's probably better if you don't know."

"I'm giving you refuge. I stitched your wound." She leaned forward, bracing a hand on the edge of the mattress. "Now you're telling me that you're worried about me receiving other visitors. I think I deserve to know the real name of the person I'm hiding. I deserve that, at the very least."

She was right. He'd already put her in danger simply by being here. Even though he didn't think anyone was tailing him, he could never be sure. And if something did happen? She deserved to know his real identity at the very least. "Hart."

She raised a brow. "Hart?"

"Yeah. Hart, like the deer, not the organ." He laughed when her eyebrows rose even farther. "Sorry, it's an old joke of mine and my brothers. Anyway, Beth, I'm Christopher Randall Hart." He was amazed at how unfamiliar his name felt on his lips. He'd been someone else for so long, he'd almost forgotten how it felt to be himself.

"Christopher Randall Hart," she murmured, as

if she were trying it on for size. "Why, that's a fine name."

He almost smiled, the comment was so like her. He wondered if she was always so generous with her compliments or if it was something she'd picked up while caring for her preschoolers. "My mother thought so, too."

"Where is your family? Where do you come from?"

"My parents and brothers, um, live in Lexington."

"That's not terribly far from here, just a few short hours' drive. Chris, why didn't you go there? It's Christmas. I bet your mother would have loved to see you."

She would have . . . if he'd been the man she'd raised. But since he was far from that, it was best to stay away. Fond memories had to be better than the stark disappointment of reality. "There are reasons I can't go home."

"Such as?"

He knew he should ignore her question. His answers weren't easy to share, or easy to think about. But he supposed he owed her something more than one- or two-word vague answers. She'd given him shelter, sewn up and tended his wounds. He knew there was little he would deny her. "I can't go home, Beth. I've had to keep a lot of secrets from my family. Years ago I burnt some bridges with my parents. I didn't come home when my mother was in the hospital. I didn't even call—I couldn't because I was deep undercover." It was amazing how regrets could still feel so sharp. "Anyway, when I did finally stop by, my brothers let me have it."

"What did you do?"

"Not a thing. There wasn't a way for me to defend myself. Even if they did know that I worked for the DEA, I don't think that would have made much of a difference. They wouldn't understand my job or my decision to put a job before family. It's too late now for our relationship to be repaired."

She shook her head. "It's never too late to make amends."

"I'm not one of your preschoolers, Beth," he retorted, his voice harsh.

When she flinched at his tone, he attempted to soften his voice. "The things I've done?" He glanced at her, then looked back at his clenched hands instead of the wide wonder in her blue eyes. "Well, suffice it to say they can't easily be forgotten. Or forgiven."

"What have you done that is so terrible?"

He noticed that her hand was still curved around the edge of the mattress. So close to his own. It would be so easy to grasp her hand. To run a finger along her knuckles, to try to ease her fears.

To alleviate his own regrets.

"Nothing good. All you need to know is that I'm a far different man from what I was brought up to be."

"I'm sure you're still the same person inside."

Her voice was so sure, so certain, it warmed him. "Maybe. But that doesn't really matter. In my world, perception counts for a lot. And their perception of me is pretty bad." Recalling the last argument he'd had with his father and two brothers, remembering the tears in his mother's eyes, he shook his head. "The worst part is that a lot of what they think about me is actually true."

"Oh, Chris."

His eyelids felt heavy; he knew he was weakening. If he wasn't careful, he was going to start telling her too much. "You know, you're right. It is awfully late. We should talk later. I'm kind of tired."

Immediately, she got to her feet. "*Jah.* Sleep would be good for both of us. Please rest. I'll come in and check on you during the night."

"Don't trouble yourself."

"It will be no trouble."

"Listen, I'm good. I just need to sleep. Thanks for patching me up." He closed his eyes so he wouldn't see her look of concern or accept anything more from her that he shouldn't.

He kept them firmly closed until he heard the rustle of her dress as it brushed against her legs when she stepped away from the bed. He caught the faint whiff of lemon and lavender before she turned and walked out the door.

Only when the door clicked shut did he dare open his one good eye. Then, he stared at the door and cursed himself for being ten times a fool. Here, against his best of intentions, he felt himself falling for Beth all over again.

Worse, he felt himself opening up to her, letting Beth hope that there was something special between the two of them.

After Christmas, he would go. And she'd be abandoned all over again.

His behavior was shameful.

He really had become everything his mother had never wanted him to be.

Chapter 4

It's not what you see that lets you know that Christmas is just around the corner. It's that special feeling of expectation that suddenly fills the air.

BETH BYLER

Despite his protests, Beth had checked on Chris during the night. But he had been as good as his word. Each time she'd slowly peeked into his room, he'd been lying on his back, resting peacefully.

While he had slept, she'd tossed and turned. Thinking about his return. Thinking about him.

Christopher Randall Hart. Finally, she had a name—a real name—for the man who'd consumed far too many of her dreams.

The fancy, three-part name suited him, she decided. Suited him far better than Chris Ellis. Chris Ellis was blunt and to the point. This new name was long and complicated, complex.

Far more like him.

Not that she should be thinking of him at all, Beth reminded herself as she pinned together the front of her blue dress and slipped a black apron over it. Chris represented everything she wasn't and had never intended to be. He was a secret government worker, pretending to be mixed up in the drug and gun trades in order to catch bad people.

And no, Chris hadn't actually revealed that, either. He'd been too secretive to ever be so forthright. Instead, it had been Frannie's husband, Luke, who'd told her so much of what she knew about Chris.

One evening, long after the investigation surrounding Perry's murder was over, she'd admitted to Luke and Frannie that she couldn't stop thinking about Chris.

After a moment's hesitation, Luke had told her what he knew about him.

But instead of that scaring her off, she'd secretly become more intrigued with the mysterious Chris Ellis. There was something about a man risking everything, even his reputation for a greater good, that appealed to her.

She'd only ever lived in Marion, Kentucky, and had only ever visited a few places. Most of her time was occupied with caring for her mother and watching other people's children. In many ways, she'd never risked anything.

Chris? It seemed he'd risked everything he had, his family, his reputation . . . his life.

Unable to stop thinking of him, she finished dressing as quickly as she could, then half listened for him to call her name while she washed her hands at the kitchen sink and put the kettle on the stove. She was wondering if he would be able to eat some eggs and toast while the tea was steeping. She was debating whether she should go check on him again when there was a knock at the back door.

Imagining the worst, Beth peeked through the sheer white curtains, then felt silly when she saw it was only Lydia Plank staring back at her, a tote bag in hand.

Not wanting to reveal too much, Beth opened the door halfway. "Lydia, what are you doing here?"

"It is *verra* nice to see you, too," she said with a bit of humor lighting her face.

While Beth warily stood sentry at the door, Lydia stomped one of her boots, making bits of ice and salt fly up. "It's pretty cold out here. Yesterday's sunshine has left us, and more snow is on the way. Are you going to let me come in?"

"Sure. Of course." Reluctantly, she stepped back. "I didn't expect to see you."

"I just happened to be nearby and wanted to check on you."

"Why?" Her stomach knotted. Had she forgotten

to wipe away some of Chris's blood on the sidewalk?

Lydia looked at her curiously. "Because I promised Frannie I would." After sitting down in one of the chairs that surrounded the kitchen table, she said, "Beth, what in the world is going on with you? You seem nervous."

"I have a new guest," she blurted. "He's sleeping and I don't want to wake him up."

"I could have sworn Frannie said she only needed you to house-sit."

"Well, he's here. And he's asleep, so we must stay quiet."

Lydia's brows rose. "I didn't realize we were being loud."

Flushing, Beth realized that she did sound a bit paranoid. Oh, she was going to do a horrible job of keeping Chris's visit a secret!

"I'm kind of surprised you've got a guest here so close to Christmas."

"It's not my place to question guests' behavior."

If Lydia was taken aback, she didn't show it. "Frannie would say it's not your place to guess what your guests are doing in their rooms. But we can still wonder about them, right? I mean that's human nature."

"Perhaps."

"So, what's he like? Is he handsome?"

Feeling like a gnat caught in a spider's web, Beth shrugged.

Since her lies weren't working, she decided to be evasive. "Let's not talk about him. He doesn't matter. How is Walker?"

Luckily, Lydia let herself be sidetracked. She smiled sweetly. "Perfect. He's doing well on his Deutch, and enjoying life on the farm." She leaned forward. "And guess what? The bishop has given us permission to marry at the end of January."

"That's *wunderbaar*!" Beth knew just how many obstacles Walker and Lydia had gone through over the past year. Not only had they both been friends of Perry's, they'd both been suspects during his murder investigation. In addition, Walker was English, while Lydia was Amish. Even after they fell in love, neither knew if they were supposed to be together.

"I'm so excited, and so anxious to start my married life with him."

"I bet. I can't wait to help you with the wedding."

"*Danke*. I knew I could count on you." Lydia stretched out her hands. "We've all been through so much, it's hard to grasp it all. I'm almost married to Walker; Frannie and Luke are married and are in Cincinnati for the holiday; and Deborah and Jacob are celebrating their first Christmas as a married couple."

"Yes, much has changed," Beth echoed, trying not to feel sorry for herself, since her life seemed exactly the same. She was alone, the only one in their close circle of friends without love in her life. "I haven't been to Schrock's lately. How are Deborah and Jacob?"

"Not so well."

"They have a lot of burdens."

"I think so. I'm not sure how they are going to get through everything. I mean, we were all surprised when they insisted on marrying despite her parents' protestations. . . ."

Beth nodded. Deborah and Jacob had had a difficult path, for sure. Not only did Jacob's father kill Deborah's brother, but Deborah's parents still blamed Jacob—and to some extent Deborah—for much of what had had happened to Perry. They were never able to see the faults in their firstborn son, despite the trouble he'd brought to the entire community.

"It's so sad. I heard that, despite it being Christmas, Mr. and Mrs. Borntrager have been ignoring them both," Lydia said.

Beth sat down next to her friend. "Though they didn't attend the wedding, I had thought their hurt and anger would have softened by now."

"The last I heard, that isn't the case."

Beth wished she had some idea of how to make her dear friends' lives easier, but she knew there was little she could say or do to make things better. Only their faith could help right now. "They're just going to have to rely on prayer."

"You're right." Reaching into the tote bag, Lydia pulled out a plastic container of muffins. "I made you and your mother these. They're morning-glory muffins." Looking pleased, she added, "Have you had them before? They're chock-full of carrots and pineapple, spices and nuts."

"They smell delicious."

"They are. Filling, too." Looking toward the doorway that led to the rest of the house, she added, "I supposed you can serve them to your guest."

"I will put them to good use." She was beyond nervous now. Chris needed her to keep his presence a secret, which meant Lydia needed to leave before he cried out in pain.

Or anything else happened.

She stood up. "I'm sorry, but I don't have time to chat. Running a B-and-B is a busy job, you know."

Lydia's brows rose but she said nothing. Instead she got up slowly. "Beth, if you start feeling overwhelmed, or have any trouble, don't hesitate to ask for help. This is the slow time at my parents' nursery."

"I won't have any trouble. I'll be just fine."

"Sheriff Kramer is doing extra patrols, too. If you get worried or scared, I bet he could stop by regularly."

That would be the absolute last thing she wanted to happen! "I won't need the sheriff here, Lydia. There's no need for him to trouble himself with me."

"I'm sure he'd be happy to check in on you. It's a big house to be in all alone."

"I'm not alone, though. I have a guest."

"Who is a stranger," Lydia pointed out.

"I will be fine." When Lydia stared at her with wide eyes, Beth tried to temper herself. "I mean, please don't send Mose my way."

"Um, okay, then. Hey, Walker and I are going to spend Christmas Eve at my house with my family. We'd love for you and your *mamm* to join us. Mamm and I have been baking for days."

"*Danke*, I'll talk to my *mamm*." Of course, she knew there was no way she was going to leave Chris's side until he left Crittenden County for good.

Firmly, she walked Lydia out. "Thank you again for the muffins."

Lydia nodded but stared at her friend hard before turning to leave. "You're welcome."

The moment she shut the door, Beth locked it, turned the dead bolt for good measure, then practically ran to the stairs.

She jerked to a stop when she saw Chris standing in the upstairs hallway, his jeans riding low on his hips. A gun was in his hand and his expression looked murderous.

"Who was here?" he rasped.

She'd thought she'd seen every expression on his face, but she now realized she'd been wrong. Standing in front of her, he looked dangerous and fierce.

He looked like no man she'd ever seen before— not even when he'd appeared in her dreams. "It was no one, Chris. No one you should worry about. Just a friend."

His hard expression didn't ease. "Who was it? You said you wouldn't have any visitors."

Her mouth went dry as she continued to stare at the gun. At his bare chest. Felt his hard gaze settle on her. And realized that there was something about him that she wasn't ever going to be able to forget.

It was starting out to be a very trying day, and it was barely 9:00 A.M.

Chapter 5

I never imagined this would be my life. It's not that I thought it would be better . . . only that it would be a whole lot different.

JACOB SCHROCK

Jacob was not living the life he'd dreamed of as a child. When he was small, he'd planned to raise horses, perhaps even move to one of the fancy horse farms near Louisville or Lexington and be a trainer, groomer, or farrier.

But little by little, his father had divested him of that dream. When Jacob was a boy, his *daed* had kept him close to his side at the store. Every day, his father would give him a lesson about running the place, and though Jacob had never been interested in being a shopkeeper, he'd slowly learned how to be a good one.

With a mixture of folksy sayings and true warmth, Aaron Schrock had made each customer feel as if he or she had stumbled into a cozy treasure trove of unique goods and practical necessities, all wrapped in a tidy knot of friendly warmth.

Jacob had often felt that way at home as well. His mother had been the practical enforcer, and although she'd kept her standards high and did her best to make sure Jacob met those expectations, she'd also been free with her hugs and jokes.

He'd been happy.

Looking back, Jacob realized he'd grown up in a cocoon of security. After he'd given up his dream of raising horses, he'd been secure in the knowledge that he would take over the store one day. Furthermore, all of his childhood memories seemed to be bunched together in a jumbled mass of happy times and laughter.

He had been blessed, and he knew that.

Now, however, he'd never felt more alone. With his father in prison and his mother off visiting their extended family in Holmes County, Jacob was left to bear all of the responsibility for the store. Though he'd spent much of his life preparing for it, the weight of the burden almost immobilized him.

What if he couldn't continue the store's success? What if everyone in the area found him lacking, or if the legacy of all that had happened with Perry Borntrager was too much to accept? What would he do then? How would he take care of Deborah if the store went bankrupt?

Here in the near-empty store, he wished he could find something to replace the confidence he used to have in spades.

"Your problem, I think, is that there are no critters in here," Sheriff Mose Kramer said as he wandered up to the counter with a plastic basket full of baking products.

Jacob pulled the basket close and started punching in the prices for chocolate, sugar, and green and red candies on the ancient cash register. "My problem?"

"Yep," Mose drawled, eyeing the store with a critical eye. "I was wandering around here, wondering what felt different, when I realized that it was altogether too quiet. That's when I realized that you don't have any cats or dogs or hamsters in cages. You should get on that, Jacob."

"The critters were my father's doing, not mine."

"Oh, I know that. Of course they were your father's doing. He always had a soft heart for animals and a keen mind for business."

"That is true."

Mose flashed a smile. "Those animals sure kept things lively. They were a topic of conversation around town, too. Folks would sit at the Marion Cafe, or Mary King's Restaurant or even at the gas station and talk about what confounded new animal Schrock had brought in."

The reminder of his father stung. "It's eighteen

dollars." When the sheriff handed him a canvas bag, he began to put the items inside. "Looks like you're doing some baking?"

"I, uh, found an easy recipe for Christmas fudge. I thought I'd give it a try."

"Good luck with that." It was far easier to concentrate on Mose in the kitchen instead of the emptiness in his heart. He felt like he was living a complete lie. This was the man who'd brought him in for questioning, then actually arrested his father, and here Jacob was talking with him about the atmosphere in his family's store.

Mose handed him a twenty-dollar bill. "So, don't keep me waiting. What do you think about my idea? A few animals might liven things up, right?"

"It's a *gut* idea, but not one I'm ready to take on. Those animals were troublesome. And their antics created a lot of work. You know, it's just me and Deborah here now," he said as he passed back the change. "Everything is different now."

Mose ignored the two dollar bills and eyed Jacob intently instead. "It doesn't have to be that way."

"It does. I can't afford any more employees right now." In addition to sales being down, they had a pile of lawyers' bills to pay. Every extra penny had to go to them.

"You might be able to afford more if you did things a bit differently."

Jacob kept his mouth shut because he didn't want to get into things that weren't any of Mose's business. "Thank you for coming in. I hope the fudge turns out."

But instead of taking his not-so-subtle hint, Mose looked pained. "Son, I've known you a long time." He rested his hands on the other side of the counter. "Maybe we should sit down and chat for a bit. We could talk about how you are doing."

"I'm fine."

"Married life agreeing with you?"

"Of course. Deborah is great."

"That she is. And how is your *mamm*?"

"I haven't seen her in a few weeks," he replied, keeping his face carefully blank. "She's staying for a time with my aunt in Berlin."

"Ah. Yes, I remember hearing about that now. Berlin is far away."

"It is."

"Is she coming back for Christmas?"

"*Nee*. She's going to come back after the New Year. But on the way back, I'm sure she'll stay in a motel near the prison and visit my father for a few days. She's done that before." He bit his lip. Would it ever get easier to admit that his father was in prison?

Would it ever get easier to admit that now he and his mother didn't have much of a relationship? She couldn't quit being her husband's greatest advocate.

And he? Well, he couldn't stop blaming his father for everything.

Mose's eyes narrowed as he nodded slowly. "Sorry, I know it's a sore subject. Have you, by any chance, gone to visit your father yet?"

"I have not."

"You might think on it. I'd even be happy to drive you out there, if you'd like. Dreams arise and problems occur, but family is always family."

But that was what he was struggling with. He didn't want to think about his father in prison, and it hurt to think about how close they used to be.

But how did a son admit that? So instead of confiding his troubles to the sheriff, he lashed out instead. "Sheriff, I don't owe you any more explanations, do I? I thought I was done being questioned."

Mose stilled, then carefully cleared his expression of all traces of hurt. "Of course you don't owe me a thing. But I'm more than just the sheriff, Jacob. I'm a friend—at least I thought I was."

Jacob felt terrible. This wasn't how he wanted to be. A sense of foreboding filled him as he realized he was slowly losing the slight, tenuous hold he had on himself.

One step at a time, a small but sure voice inside him whispered.

"I'm sorry, Mose. I don't seem to be myself lately."

Mose's gaze softened. He looked like he had a lot

to say, but instead he merely put the two dollars that had been lying on the counter back in his wallet.

Just as Mose was reaching for his canvas tote, his cell phone rang. After looking at the screen, he took the call, his expression concerned.

Jacob watched Mose's face as he spoke to whoever was on the line in a series of short, one-word answers. He looked worried when he clicked off and stuffed the phone back in his jacket.

"Everything okay, Mose?"

"You know, I'm not sure. That was a buddy of mine from Paducah. He heard word that our town might have an unexpected visitor here."

"What does that mean?"

"Nothing good, I reckon."

Unexpected? Again? Foreboding filled Jacob as he thought about once again living in uncertainty. "Is it someone dangerous?"

Most stilled. "I don't think so. But to be honest, I'm going to have to stew on this one for a bit." He paused. "Sorry, don't know why I even said a word about that call. But, Jacob, if you do hear of something unusual going on . . . or if you see someone in the store who seems like he shouldn't be here . . . let me know, wouldja?"

"Sure. I'll for sure let you know if I see something."

After picking up the sheriff's bags, Jacob walked around to the front of the counter. "Here you go,

Mose. And, thanks for asking about my family. It means a lot to me, and I know both of my parents will be glad you were thinking of them."

"I care about you, Jacob. And believe it or not, I still care about Aaron. Your *daed* was my friend for many years."

"I still can't believe he caused so much pain. I would have never guessed it."

"I'm not defending him, but I should warn ya that I've talked to many people who broke the law. It ain't always a person's intention to do something illegal. Sometimes people do things without thinking about the consequences."

Lowering his voice, he added, "I've seen the nicest men and women do some terrible things for the best reasons. You just never know what you are capable of until push comes to shove."

Jacob swallowed as his mouth turned dry. Before he learned to keep his temper under control, he'd said things he wished he could take back. But that was different from what his father had done.

He needed to continue to remind himself of that.

The sheriff's expression turned sympathetic. "Chin up now, Jacob. You have a new marriage to celebrate, and your first Christmas together, to boot. That's something not to take for granted."

"I don't. Deborah means to the world to me."

Mose rapped his knuckles on the counter. "That's

good to hear. Well, in case we don't see each other, Merry Christmas!"

"And Merry Christmas to you," Jacob murmured as the man left and the store fell empty again.

As he gazed at the neat shelves, the clean counters, and the carefully swept floors, Jacob suddenly realized that it did feel different from the way it had when his father was there.

He'd assumed the quiet was from the lack of customers. But maybe Mose had a point. Maybe the store was missing a bit of chaos that only a container of animals could bring.

As he imagined the mess and the noise and the pandemonium even a hamster could bring to the store, he winced.

He'd suddenly realized that the animals had been nothing compared to his father's presence in both the store and his life.

His father had been both a source of amusement and support. Folks in the area genuinely liked him, and his laughter could fill the emptiest room with happiness.

Yes, the store did seem quieter without those animals.

But it seemed completely empty without his father.

And, to some extent, so did his life.

Chapter 6

Turkey, ham, Christmas trees, Bing Crosby, too many presents. That's what Christmas used to mean to me.

CHRISTOPHER HART

As she gazed at her guest, Beth fought to keep her expression calm.

He was glaring at her. Looking fierce and lethal. Scary.

And afraid.

"Chris, it's still early. What are you doing out of bed?" Beth asked, inwardly wincing as she heard her voice. It sounded shrill and sharp.

Chris didn't answer. Instead, he continued to stand on the landing of the stairwell, the black gun still held firmly in his hand. His blue eyes were pale and cold. He looked like he was going into battle.

How could she calm him down? Remind him

that he wasn't anywhere near danger? He was at the Yellow Bird Inn in the heart of Amish country.

She climbed the steps slowly, each one making her feel as if she were edging closer to danger. "Chris, did ya hear me?" she asked in a conversational way. Just as if they were about to have a cup of tea. "You're sick, you know. You should go back to sleep."

He didn't move.

As she got closer, she noticed that his skin was flushed, his eyes glassy. Sweat beaded his brow. It was obvious that he was burning up with fever.

And still that gun hovered in his hand.

As she stared at the gun, old doubts began to fester. Why hadn't she ignored his wishes and called for an ambulance when he'd first arrived?

She was a capable woman. She knew better than to leave so much up to chance.

She cleared her throat and attempted to sound like one very put-upon babysitter. "Christopher Randall Hart, you need to stop pointing that gun at me. Someone could get hurt."

He blinked in surprise. Immediately, his hand lowered. Once the pistol was no longer staring at her she breathed a hearty sigh of relief.

"That is much better," she said briskly as she took

another step closer to him. "Now it is time to get you back into bed."

"Not yet. I want to know who was here." His voice was hoarse and scratchy sounding. Rough.

"It was Lydia Plank. She's just a friend. Do you remember me speaking of her?" Because he looked so on edge, she added, "Or, perhaps you heard her name from Frannie? We have been friends for a long time, you see."

He shook his head.

She stepped closer, praying for him to keep that terrible-looking weapon pointed toward the floor. "There's a story about Lydia, you know. See, she's Amish but she fell in love with Walker Anderson, who is English. We were all friends growing up, but it wasn't until Perry's murder investigation that they fell in love," she said easily.

Pure confusion entered his eyes. "She came over to see you."

"*Jah*. She brought me muffins. It's like I told ya, Chris. She is no one for you to worry about. And she's gone now, so it's just us. So, perhaps you wouldn't mind putting that gun away?"

Finally, he seemed to break out of his trance. Looking shamefaced, he fussed with his gun, then spoke. "Beth, I'm sorry. I'm on edge. And I'm so, so afraid that I've brought you trouble. I don't know what I'd do if something happened to you."

She walked to his side but hesitated before touching him. She told herself it was because she was worried about his gun, not about the fact that he was standing right in front of her, without a shirt on. "Is your gun safe now?"

His lips curved slightly as he stared at her. "It's safe enough. I'll put it in a drawer when I get back to the room."

"I suppose there's no way you'd consider locking it away in your truck?" she asked as they slowly walked back toward his room.

He stopped abruptly. "Not on your life. I would die if something happened to you."

Her breath hitched as his words hit her like a gale-force wind. Of course he didn't mean anything by that.

But never in her life had she heard talk like this before. The only way she could categorize it was passionate. The whole situation they were in felt larger than life, and she didn't know if it frightened her or made her feel like she was finally living for the first time in her life.

Awkwardly, she stood at the door while he opened the top drawer of the bedside table and set the gun in it, then firmly pushed the drawer closed.

But that seemed to take up the majority of his energy. He sank to the bed then, the skin around his lips pinched. Without thinking about the consequences, she rushed to his side. Unable to help herself, she wrapped her hands around his shoulders and back and tried to help him get steady.

His skin was hot beneath her touch. She felt him flinch from the contact with her cool hands. "Chris, you're feverish. I fear you're becoming sick."

"Not sick. Injured."

Trying to support him better—which was a difficult process since he had to weigh at least seventy pounds more than she did—she climbed up next to him on the bed.

Those light blue eyes that had crept into her dreams stared into hers. "Beth, you shouldn't be here," he rasped. "Not with me like this."

No, she definitely should not. She should not be in bed with him—not even if she was fully clothed and he was half dressed. Not even if he was injured and feverish and she was trying to heal his hurts.

Fact was, she knew she should not be harboring a man in Frannie's bed-and-breakfast. She shouldn't be trying to nurse him at all. She should have called for help, contacted a real doctor.

But most of all, she shouldn't be thinking about him the way she was. No matter how much she tried to think of him differently, Chris kept creeping in her head. And heart.

And those feelings were as dangerous to her as any

gun or knife. Being around him made her think of things she'd never considered before she met him. He made her think of a world outside Marion. A world where her heart beat a little faster and her pulse raced.

Chris made her question her life and the choices she'd made.

Worse, when he wasn't around, she felt empty.

But he was forbidden to her, and that was how it should be.

She needed him to be nothing more than a temporary guest in an otherwise outlandish situation. A mere glitch in her rather quiet existence. Anything else would only bring her pain.

"Beth?" he said again. "I can tell you're worried. I know you're afraid. Tell me, what can I do to make this better?"

Quickly, she scooted off the mattress, just as if he'd reached out to touch her.

But of course he hadn't.

She backed up and cautioned herself to remember that they were nothing to each other. Nothing more than practical strangers. Two folks who could never act on what was between them, and more important, never should.

At the moment, she was the strong one, and because of that, she needed to stay strong.

Looking him directly in the eyes, she said, "You

are sick and I am helping you. That is all." She cleared her throat. "Now, see if you can help me make you more comfortable. We need to get you covered up so you can rest."

He complied with her attempts to rearrange him, slowly slipping under the cotton sheet as obediently as if he were a young boy instead of a mature man.

But when she attempted to slip a quilt over him, he pushed it away. "I'm too hot for that, Beth."

"It's your fever that's talking."

"So? I'm still hot."

"The house is chilly. You need to stay covered. Listen to me, I know best."

Almost belligerently, he shoved the blankets off his body, forcing her to stare at his bare torso, with those strange tattoos on his chest and arms. At the way he was dressed only in faded jeans.

Her face began to heat because she couldn't seem to look anywhere else. "Chris—"

"I'll be fine."

"You're acting childish. I'm trying to help you."

"Is that right?" He scooted up against the head-board, twisted his hips so he was facing her. "Then pull up your chair and sit with me. Don't make me lie here alone."

"Right now?"

"Yeah. Unless you're too afraid," he added, his voice sounding almost like a challenge. "If you're afraid of me, then you should leave." With that, he shifted again, so he was lying flat on his back. A second later, he closed his eyes.

He almost looked as if he'd forgotten all about her, but she knew better, of course.

Lord? she prayed silently. *What do I do? What should I do?*

As the clock ticked on his bedside table, she felt her heartbeat slow, and with it, a new sense of calm eased into her.

Reminding her that with God, all things were possible.

That was enough for her.

So, even though everything that was right and true warned her against getting too close, she pushed the chair close enough to reach out and clasp his hand in hers. As she'd imagined, his palm was callused and his fingertips rough.

But still, it felt good to hold on to a small part of him.

He opened his eyes halfway and gazed at her. "Why are you holding my hand?"

"Everyone needs some hand-holding every once in a while, Chris."

"Even guys like me?" His voice was acerbic, almost teasing. But she knew better now.

She couldn't help herself, she squeezed his hand slightly. "Especially men like you."

He closed his eyes then, and she exhaled a sigh of relief. Before she knew it, he would be asleep again, then she could sneak back out and leave him in peace.

And attempt to figure out how she was going to tell her mother that she wouldn't be stopping by that day.

"Beth?"

"Hmm?"

"Talk to me, would you?"

"About what?"

"You. I want to know all about you."

"I'm not terribly interesting. What you see is what I am."

"What's that like, Beth?" he rasped. "What's it like to be the same person on the inside that the rest of the world sees? What's it like to be so perfect?"

He was wrong, of course. Most of the world saw her as a confident woman who was happy to take care of other people's children. Who never minded that her mother had been stricken with a terrible disease far too early in life.

The truth was she was a woman who was rapidly becoming an old maid but didn't have any earthly idea how to change that.

But she could never admit that. Not to herself and certainly not to him.

"You know everything you need to know about me, Chris. I'm a simple Amish woman."

"But that's where you're wrong, Beth. You're the most interesting woman I've ever met."

"I doubt that."

"You shouldn't. It's true. So, come on. Talk to me. Don't make me guess and wonder what you're really like."

It was as if he already knew. "Chris—"

"Please, honey?"

"Honey?" she echoed, certain she hadn't heard him right.

He turned his head toward the wall. "Sorry. I've been calling you that in my head. It just slipped out. Do you mind it?"

To be honest, she didn't really know. It sounded both alluring and unfamiliar at the same time. She didn't think she was supposed to like an endearment like that.

She didn't want to.

But already, she ached to hear him whisper it again.

Her heart felt like it was skipping a beat as she weighed the consequences.

Scratch that. As she pretended to make a decision. Really, from the moment she'd let him inside . . . she knew she had made her choice.

"I don't mind it," she whispered. "I don't mind you calling me a sweet name right now."

Actually, she wished he'd call her all sorts of things.

The tender words made her heart patter faster and her insides turn soft. They made her feel like she wasn't an old maid—forgotten and overlooked.

Actually, she wished she was brave enough to whisper something sweet and soft right back.

Chapter 7

*It's as hard to forget good times as much as bad. I know,
because I've really tried.*

CHRISTOPHER HART

As Chris gazed at Beth through half-closed lids, he
knew only one thing could be happening: He had to
be in the middle of some fever-induced, hazy dream.

He knew the dream well. He'd experienced different variations of it at least a hundred times.

In it, he would feel at peace. He'd feel strangely
comforted and hopeful, because he *was* safe and
comfortable.

And in each dream, there was always a beautiful,
angelic woman by his side. The air surrounding her
would smell vaguely of cotton and lemons, mixed
with the faint scent of lavender.

It was every good smell in the world combined with
a huge slice of comfort. To him, it never failed to be
completely addictive.

At least it felt that way in his dreams.

In his mind, the woman was slim. Her brown hair leaned toward golden and her blue eyes were so dark they could be mistaken for brown. But she would have a graceful way about her that he'd never felt anywhere else in his life.

Her touch was gentle, her voice softly lilting. She'd give him the briefest sliver of happiness, simply because she cared about him.

And then he'd wake up and discover that his reality was the exact opposite of his dreams.

Not this time, though. Now, unbelievably, the woman of his dreams had become his reality. She was sitting next to him and even though he should have every nerve on alert, he kept finding himself dozing off, eased by the comfort of her presence.

It seemed God had a greater sense of humor than he'd even imagined.

"I'm not used to talking about myself. I don't know where to start," she said hesitantly.

"Then don't start. Just talk to me about something easy." Vaguely, he remembered her mentioning it was almost Christmas. "Talk to me about your Christmas."

"This year?" she squeaked.

"Any year. What do you usually do?" Through the fog in his brain, he tried to recall what men gave to their girlfriends for Christmas gifts. A pain shot through his heart as he recalled the gifts his older brothers had given their girlfriends and wives. He'd never had the chance to get close enough to someone to bring them something special during the most magical time of year.

"Do you have a boyfriend who brings you roses and candy?"

"*Nee!*"

She sounded so shocked, he found himself chuckling. "Is that not what Amish boys bring to girls they fancy?"

"I don't have a boyfriend."

"Finally, you filled me in on your status. I was beginning to wonder if you ever would."

"Chris, you shouldn't tease."

"I'm not teasing," he murmured, making sure he didn't add a single trace of humor in his voice. And it was true—he was completely serious when it came to Beth. "You're so pretty, I can't imagine you not having a man at your heels, waiting for a smile."

"Well, I do not. But if I did, he wouldn't be bringing me roses in the winter. No one gets those!"

She sounded positively scandalized. He loved it. Privately, he thought if he were her man he'd find a way to bring her red roses every chance he got— even if he had to pay a small fortune for them at the florist. Only red roses would complement the way her cheeks burned when she was flustered.

"So . . . what would a proper Amish man bring you, Bethy? If you had one of those in your life."

"It's Beth," she corrected primly. "And, um, it's the Amish way to give each other gifts that would be far more useful."

"Such as?"

"Such as . . . fabric. Or a sweater or coat."

He couldn't resist egging her on. "I'm no woman in love, but I'd rather receive chocolate and red roses than a bolt of fabric."

"I would, too," she whispered, before wincing. "I didn't mean that," she said quickly.

He let that pass because they both knew differently. "So . . ."

She shifted primly in her chair. "So . . . this is all beside the point. Because it doesn't look as if either of us is going to be getting roses and chocolate on Christmas Day. No man is at my heels, and no woman besides me knows you're here."

Still anxious to learn more about her life, he asked, "What have you done in the past on Christmas Day?"

"Once, when I was younger, we went hiking in the woods while the turkey was cooking. It was great fun. Both my parents went. My *mamm* was healthy then," she explained, her tone wistful. "Another time, I visited all my friends. A few of us went ice skating. Sometimes now we all get together at each other's houses and have a Christmas potluck."

"Hmm."

"What about you, Chris? What did you used to do on Christmas Day. Before . . ."

"Before I couldn't go home? Well, most Christmases my brothers and I received too much and played too hard. We used to love to get Hot Wheels—those are little metal cars. We'd race them around the house."

"And who would win?"

"My oldest brother, of course. That's how it goes with brothers, Beth. The oldest always wins."

Because she was there, he gave himself permission to think about things that he usually made himself forget. "My mom makes a beef tenderloin for Christmas dinner. And some kind of potato casserole that probably has about a thousand calories in it, which is so good. And green beans. And squash."

She chuckled. "You wrinkled your nose at the squash."

"I don't care for it. At least I didn't use to." Now, though, he imagined that he'd probably lick his plate clean, he'd be so grateful for the comfort of a familiar meal. For the life of him, he couldn't remember the last time he'd had a meal like that. A homemade Christmas meal served on china.

"What else?"

Since Beth seemed so interested, Chris continued, his voice warming at the fond memories in spite of his best intentions to forget his past. "My mother gets out her fancy wedding china and we eat at the dining room table, trying not to break anything or spill gravy on the white linen tablecloth. But of course, we always do." He chuckled. "My father's the worst. He can't keep a tablecloth clean to save his soul. He always apologizes and my mother always looks irritated but pretends it doesn't matter. We all try to use the manners she taught us, but it all goes out the window about five minutes after we say the blessing. Next thing you know, we're arguing and giving each other grief."

"Your Christmas dinner sounds *wonderful-gut*," she whispered.

"It is. I mean, it was. I haven't been there for dinner in a long time. I wish . . ." Hating to sound so weak, he let his voice drift off.

But of course Beth prodded. "What do you wish?"

"I wish I could see it all again one day." But more than that, he wished he could take her to his parents' home for Christmas dinner.

He'd be so proud, bringing her in through the front door. Instinctively, he knew she'd love the tree in their living room and the bands of garland wrapped around the banister with wide silver ribbon. She'd love the big marble fireplace decorated with stockings, lights, and yet more garland and ribbons. She'd enjoy his mother's pecan pie and almond tarts and would no doubt love Beasley, his parents' old English sheepdog. Beasley was too big and too furry and, worse, he loved to sit on the couch and cuddle and get dog fur and dog slobber all over everyone's clothes.

He was a wonderful dog.

Just as important, he knew that his parents would love her. After all, who wouldn't love Beth? And his brothers? Well, they'd probably curb their cussing and become almost gentlemanly. And when she wasn't in the room, they'd most likely jab him in the ribs and ask how a beautiful woman like her would ever look twice at a guy like him.

Yes, if he brought someone like her home for Christmas? He would feel like he had finally done something right. Getting a woman like her to love him would mean as much as bringing down a whole gang of criminals.

She leaned forward. "You should call your parents, Chris."

Just like that, his daydream bubble burst. "Beth, I can't—"

"All you have to do is call and let them know that you're okay. You don't have to tell them where you are."

Her naïveté about how modern technology worked made him wish that things really were so simple. "It's not that easy."

"I know! You could call them on your cell phone."

"Cell phones can be easily tracked. Besides, I don't have one. I dumped mine hours before I got here." He didn't want to scare her, but he was pretty sure that his parents' phone lines were being tapped. "I promise, what we're doing right now? It's enough. Even talking about my family is more than I've let myself do in years."

"But I'm sure they're worried about you. I'm sure your *mamm* would want to know if you were sick and in bed. Covered with bruises and fighting off a fever. At Christmas, no less!"

"I doubt they even think about me much anymore." He didn't want to sound so maudlin, but the simple truth was that she probably had no concept of what it was like to be so alone. Tempering his voice, he said, "Beth, at the moment, I'm tucked away in a lovely inn, sitting next to a beautiful woman." After debating for a bit, he tried to smile. "If this is the best thing that happens this Christmas I'll count myself lucky."

He was just about to say something else. About to say too much, about to tell her something she wouldn't be able to handle—like that he loved her—when a sharp rap at the front door startled them both.

Beth jumped to her feet. Eyes wide, she whispered, "What should I do? Do you think someone's found you?"

"Um, I don't think they'd be knocking at the door if they had. At least, not like that. We'd better go find out."

Her hands clenched and it was obvious she was attempting to hide her fear.

He hated that. A thousand recriminations hit him hard. "I'm sorry, Beth, but you're going to have to go answer it. I'll be right behind you, though." Then he tried his best to concentrate only on his gun and his quick inspection of it.

Pulling on a shirt that she'd left on the end of the bed sometime during the night, he followed her downstairs in his bare feet.

Just as the knock came again. This time much, much harder.

"Beth?" Mose Kramer called out.

"It's the sheriff," she whispered to Chris. "What should we do?"

If the sheriff was here, Chris knew he couldn't embroil her into his mess any further. "You don't need to do a thing. Go sit down in the kitchen. I'll deal with him."

"I'm staying," she said obstinately.

"Beth? Hello?" the sheriff called out again, this time accompanying his call with a jangle of the doorknob.

He was out of time. "Suit yourself," Chris murmured as he turned the dead bolt to the right and finally opened the door with a new, desperate feeling of doom. "Hello, Sheriff," he said.

"You," Mose said, staring at him with a healthy look of disdain. "I should have known."

The frigid air burst into the entryway and onto his bare feet. It was so cold he immediately felt the chill. "Want to come in?"

Mose stepped right through the door, not sparing Chris a second glance. Instead his gaze seemed to be fastened on Beth. "Are you all right?" he asked as he walked toward her, bringing salt and ice onto the wood floor with him.

"Mose, take off your boots," Chris said.

"My boots are the least of your worries, pup."

"You're tracking snow and ice onto Beth's clean floor." To Chris's pleasure, the sheriff immediately hunched over and started unlacing his boots.

"Chris?" Beth mouthed.

He attempted to smile, glad the little task was buying them both some time. Beth looked like she was about to faint from worry. And him? Well, he needed to decide just how much to tell the sheriff.

Once his feet were clad in only white socks, Mose turned to Chris. "Looks like I'm staying for a while. Have a seat and tell me what in the world you're doing here. And by the way, you look like you were on the losing end of a good fistfight."

"I was," Chris said dryly.

Beth was hovering by his side. "He should be in bed, Sheriff. He has stitches. And a fever."

Mose raised his eyebrows. "Stitches?"

Chris was thankful that he'd let Beth's fever comment slide. "They're nothing to worry about."

"Not now. But they were before I stitched him up."

Mentally, Chris shook his head. Now she was happy about the stitches?

"If you've got Beth stitching you up, I'm guessing you didn't go to the hospital. Care to tell me why?"

"I couldn't risk it."

Mose leaned back, like he was settling in for the afternoon. "Hmm. It looks like I got here just in time. You'd best start talking."

Chris made his decision. He was going to have to trust Mose. "My cover was blown two days ago."

"Which is why you're looking like you do." Leaning forward, resting his elbows on his knees, he said, "Keep talking. I'm confused as to why you're here instead of somewhere safer. I would have thought you fancy DEA agents would have had a better system for trouble."

"We do, but I've been ordered to stay in the area until after Christmas."

"Why?"

He shrugged. "They wanted me out of the way so they could pursue all the leads without me being there. I'm a liability now."

"You still haven't told me why you came here and not someplace else."

Chris hated revealing how weak he felt—and how alone he was. "I could barely drive. As you can see, I was beaten up pretty good. This place, it's just about in the middle of nowhere, Mose. At least to most outsiders."

"These people you've been dealing with, are they working around here? 'Cause if they are, I need to know."

"They're not. They're farther south. Near Tennessee."

Mose stared at him, then at Beth. "Beth, surely this isn't what you expected when you agreed to look after the place for Frannie and Luke. Are you afraid? Do you want me to get him out of here for you?"

Chris felt like closing his eyes in despair. Of course she was afraid. Anyone who looked at her could tell she was. And of course it would be best for her if he agreed to leave with Mose.

But though all of that made sense, something inside him rejected the idea. Quite simply, he didn't want to leave Beth. Their time together was going to be short enough. Selfishly, he wanted to stay by her side as long as possible.

"I'm not afraid with Chris here."

"He's the reason you should be afraid," Mose said gently. "I don't want to scare ya, but this man attracts some of the worst folks you can imagine. They're desperate, and not a one of them has anything to lose."

"He has a gun."

The sheriff turned to him and glared. "Well, of course you do. Why wouldn't you be armed in a country bed-and-breakfast?" Looking irritated enough to spit nails, Mose got to his feet. "Mr. Ellis—or whatever your name is—I think it would be best for everyone if you came along with me. I can put you up at my place. There's a room up in my attic that you can have until you can be on your way."

Wearily, Chris got to his feet, too. "I'll get my gear."

Beth stepped in between them. "*Nee.* I want him to stay."

"You don't know what you're saying, Beth," Mose warned. "This man is dangerous."

"Not to me." She looked at him beseechingly. "Tell him, Chris. Tell him that you'd never hurt me."

He ached to reach out to her, to take her into his arms and soothe her fears. "Of course, I'd never hurt you," he said quietly. "But I can't promise that no harm will come to you. There's a difference."

To his amazement, tears formed in her eyes. "Please, don't leave me alone." Turning to Mose, she said, "There's a chance those men, those drug dealers might already know he's here, *jah*?"

"Yes."

"Then there's a chance that they could come here. I don't want to be alone if they show up."

Mose stared at her. "What else is going on, Beth? What are you not telling me?"

"Nothing is going on. It's just that I simply know what I need to be doing—and that is taking care of Chris. He can take care of me if something happens."

Mose sat back down. "Beth, what is your mother going to say?"

"Nothing, because I'm not going to tell her."

"This will come out sooner or later. You know it will."

Beth looked at Mose with a schoolteacher glare. "Nothing good will come from telling my mother about Chris, Mose. You know that as certainly as I do. Besides, in a few days this will only be a memory."

The sheriff stared at her hard before glancing his way. "Chris, I hope you know what havoc you've created."

"Believe me, if I felt like I had a choice, I would have stayed far away from here." Knowing that some things had to be shared, he turned to Beth. "Would you please get me a sheet of paper and a pen? I need to write some names and numbers down for the sheriff."

When she left, Chris turned to Mose. "You have every right to ask me to go, but I'm asking you to let me stay until the twenty-sixth. By then I'll be well enough to get around better and my boss will have been able to send someone out to run interference."

"Interference my foot. You've got a terrible problem here."

"I swear, I don't think anyone will find me here. I wouldn't have come otherwise."

Mose shook his head slowly. "I ain't talking about your drug-dealing buddies, Chris Ellis." He looked at him meaningfully. "She's a good woman with a kind heart. I'd hate for you to stoop so low as to start taking advantage of an Amish woman's kindness. Or make her think that something could ever be possible between the two of you."

Beth's return prevented him from replying. Instead, he took the paper, and wrote down two names. "If something does happen, call Taylor King. She's my partner. Or, you can call Ryan Holditch; he's my direct report and is in the Chicago office."

Mose took the paper, studied the names for a minute, then stood up with great reluctance. "I can't say I'm real pleased about this, but since it's out of my jurisdiction and no crime has been committed, I guess it don't matter much what I think." Turning to Beth, he waved a finger. "Don't forget to visit your mother. And don't forget to use Frannie's cell phone and call me if you change your mind about things."

"I won't forget."

After he slipped on his boots and tied the laces,

Mose glanced at Chris one more time. "You really do look poorly, Chris. You might consider taking a long rest."

"I'll do that. Thank you."

Mose tipped his hat, scowled at him one more time, then let himself out.

When the door closed behind Mose, Beth heaved a sigh of relief. "Oh, Chris, I was so worried that he was going to make you leave."

Before he could reply, she sat down next to him and treated him to a perfectly beautiful smile of triumph. "Everything is going to be just fine now. I know it."

She would stay safe. He would do anything it took to make sure of that.

But as he counted the hours until he left her forever, nothing felt "just fine." Of course, what did it matter if his heart was breaking?

Needing some time to collect himself, he said, "Beth, why don't you go see your mother for a little bit? Mose was right. You should probably reassure her. We don't want her sending anyone else over here to check up on you."

"I don't want to leave you alone. Your fever could get worse."

"I appreciate your concern, but I took some ibuprofen. And all I'm going to do is take a nap. I really do think a visit to your mom is a good idea. When you get back, I'll make us a fire and we can sit here on the couch. How about that?"

"I think that sounds *gut*. But don't you start thinking you got anything over on me, Chris. I'm still intent on looking out for you."

"I'm planning on it," he murmured. When she hopped up, he followed, only much more slowly. His body was exhausted and his brain felt like mush. He wasn't going to be able to do another single thing until he got some sleep.

"See you in a bit," he said as he headed toward the stairs. And, he hoped, sweet oblivion.

Chapter 8

Every Christmas, I get my mamm *a new set of cozy flannel pajamas. She used to get them for me, you see. Now it's my turn to treat her.*

BETH BYLER

A surprise greeted Beth when she stopped by her house to check up on her mother. Two of her aunts were in her mother's sewing room, sitting on either side of her mother's wheelchair. From the looks of it, all three seemed to be in deep conversation over a pile of fabrics.

Her mother and aunts had spent many hours designing, piecing, and stitching quilts for the annual Amish Country Quilt Show. Four years ago, they'd even earned an honorable mention. From their intent expressions, Beth was sure they were getting ready to enter again.

"Uh-oh," Beth teased. "Are you three planning a new prize-winner?"

Practically in unison, all three jumped, then looked at her with pleased expressions.

Aunt Josephine was the first to recover. "Beth!" she said as she got to her feet and trotted over to give her a hug. "Aren't you a sight for sore eyes!"

"I could say the same about you. I didn't know you were going to pay Mamm a visit today," she said after she hugged Jo, Aunt Evelyn, and finally her mother. "Seeing the three of you together is a *wonderful-gut* surprise."

"Were your ears ringing?" Aunt Jo asked with a sly wink. "We were just talking about you."

"Oh?" Carefully, she kept her face expressionless. "I can't think of a reason why."

"Oh, Beth," her mother chided. "You are always so standoffish."

"I'm not." She was simply private. Taking a seat across from her mother, Beth attempted to look carefree, though her insides were churning. She'd come over to check up on her mother, grab a few personal things, then hurry back to Chris's side.

With her aunts here—especially given the way they were looking at her as if *she* were the new project instead of the quilt—getting in and out of the house in a timely manner might be harder than anticipated.

"Don't look so worried, daughter. I was simply telling Jo and Evelyn here that you've been working too hard. And on Christmas, too."

"Imagine our surprise to hear that you were helping out at the Yellow Bird Inn," Aunt Jo said. "We didn't even think you could cook."

Although she might be a rather private person, her inability to bake well was one thing that she had never been able to hide. "I'm learning to cook better. And Frannie left a lot of things in her freezer for my suppers." Smiling mischievously, she added, "I'll have you know that I've become mighty *gut* at thawing frozen food."

"Which is quite an accomplishment, to be sure." Aunt Evelyn chuckled. "Don't fret, Beth. We're only teasing ya."

"My only concern is that you're spending too much time working and not enough time enjoying yourself," her mother said. "Here it is Christmas, and instead of enjoying some time with other young people, you're taking on another job."

"I don't mind work." Hoping to move the conversation along, Beth said, "I didn't know you were expecting company today, Mamm."

As she hoped, her mother's expression brightened. "I didn't know it, either. Seeing my sisters has made me mighty happy."

"We came over to surprise Patience. And you, of course," Evelyn added politely. "And to offer another surprise. We want you both to spend Christmas in Charm."

"Who is in Charm?" Beth asked.

"My daughter Martha and her family," Evelyn explained. "They have a big house, with plenty of room for Patience's wheelchair to move around in."

"*Jah*, no one should be home alone for Christmas," Jo added. "My husband's cousin Jim isn't Amish, so he has a car. He's offered to drive us there, since it's on the way to Cleveland."

"That's where Jim's wife's from," Evelyn added helpfully. She paused. "Forgive me. That was probably far more information than you needed to know. But anyway, please do come. We want you both to join us."

Looking at her mother, noticing how much younger she looked in her sisters' company, Beth felt like cheering. Her aunts' offer was an answer to her prayers. "What a wonderful idea, Mamm. I hope you will go."

"I would like to go." Looking at Jo and Evelyn with a fond expression, her mother added, "But Beth, you'll come, too, *jah*?"

"I'm afraid I can't."

"But Beth, it won't be the same without you." Evelyn frowned.

Beth gazed at her Aunt Evelyn and thought about how her aunt always had a kind word for everyone. She was guileless and sweet. Just as sweet as her sister Josephine was peppery.

She would have liked to spend some time with them, to watch her mother laugh like she used to. But there was no way she could leave Chris, even if she'd wanted to. His injuries were still too severe.

And his mood seemed fragile, too, as if he would be very hurt if she, too, abandoned him.

"There's a guest at the Yellow Bird Inn. I need to be there to watch over things." To her embarrassment, her cheeks started to burn at simply mentioning him! She hoped her blush wouldn't betray her strong feelings.

"But it's Christmas," Aunt Jo said.

"It is. But it will still be Christmas even if I'm not with you," she said lightly.

"That is not what I meant, child."

Aunt Josephine glared at Beth. "I don't understand why you'd be putting the inn before your family. Christmas is a time to be together, not to be apart."

"I know that, but this year will have to be different, I'm afraid. I made a promise to Frannie that I must keep." Gently, she added, "Mamm, I am glad you will be in Charm with Josephine and Evelyn and their families. I want you to go."

"Frannie should have closed the place for the holidays, not accepted guests," her mother said. "And if she did have guests, she should have tended to them herself. Not left them for you."

"Frannie didn't think she was going to have any

guests," Beth said quickly, anxious to defend one of her best friends. "This one came as a surprise." But of course, as soon as she said that, she wished she could take it back.

Because she'd just opened the proverbial can of worms.

"Oh?" Evelyn asked. "Who, exactly, showed up unannounced? Anyone we know?"

There was no way she could share the truth. That would be asking for trouble, and would practically guarantee a long conversation and debate about whether Beth should be anywhere near a man like Chris.

Thinking quickly, Beth blurted, "The woman who is staying at the inn is not from these parts."

"You should have told her you were closed for Christmas," Josephine said with a raised brow.

"Umm . . . Well . . . I would have, but she's a nice lady who is having a bit of a hard time of it."

All three women leaned forward. "What do you mean by that?" Evelyn asked eagerly.

Out of the air, the fibs continued. "Divorce," she whispered, thinking that was just shocking enough for her mother and aunts to not question why a lady would be traveling alone at Christmas.

Immediately, all three women leaned back with stricken expressions. As if divorce could be catching. "Oh, but that is a shame," her *mamm* murmured.

"Indeed," Jo added.

Feeling like a bit more explanation was needed, Beth said, "Yes, she, uh, wanted to get away from her troubles for a bit."

"It's also a shame that the only way she could do that was by bringing you more work!" Aunt Josephine said. "You'd have thought she could find comfort in her own family at a time like this."

"Or to have tried to get back together with her husband," Evelyn said with a reproving air. "Marriage is not to be entered into or gotten out of easily, you know."

"I feel blessed to be able to help her through this difficult time," Beth said piously. "She doesn't seem to have anyone else."

"I wonder why?" Jo asked. "Is she mean and rude?"

Beth was in a deep hole and for some reason, she seemed to keep digging that hole deeper. "Not at all. She is polite."

"I hope so. Would you like us to visit with her? Or perhaps just me? I could counsel her. I'm *gut* at giving advice." Looking at her sisters, Evelyn said, "I could walk back with Beth now and you two could come get me when Jim comes to pick us up."

"*Nee!* I mean, that would not be a *gut* idea. Frannie likes to give her guests privacy. She would be mighty upset if she discovered that I was gossiping about Mrs. Jones."

"Mrs. Jones is her name?" Evelyn asked.

"*Jah*," she replied recklessly. In for a penny, in for a pound.

"Well, Beth, I suppose that you must stay. *Got* must have had a reason for you to be with this Mrs. Jones over Christmas. But if you do let her stay, you'll be alone for Christmas. I had best stay here," her mother said.

Evelyn frowned. "Oh, Patience. We would certainly miss you."

"*Nee!* You mustn't stay here," Beth said quickly. Seeing the ladies' looks of shock, Beth said, "I mean, I want you to go to Charm, Mamm. There's no reason for you to be alone in this house over Christmas." She didn't dare say anything more specific. Not a day passed that her mother didn't mention how much she missed Beth's father.

Funny how their family hadn't seemed too small when it was three of them. Now that there were only two? Some days, it felt as if they were two lonely people simply passing time.

"But what about you, dear?"

She thought quickly. "Well, Mrs. Jones is going to keep me mighty busy. You know what? I'll go visit everyone after Christmas. It won't be for the holiday, but things will be calmer. We can have a nice relaxing visit."

Jo and Evie looked at her mother and then

shrugged. "If you think that is best, Beth. Of course, we would love to have you visit any day of the year."

"That's settled then. I'll look forward to visiting in January." She turned to her mother. "Mamm, would you like me to pack your suitcase?"

"Don't worry about that, Beth," Evelyn said. "We'll take care of your mother."

"I'm going to go get some of my things then. I don't want to leave my guest alone too long."

"She will notice you missing?"

"There's always a chance that she will," Beth said before trotting off to her room. She was afraid to say anything else for fear of inventing even more lies!

But as she walked back to the Yellow Bird a little less than an hour later, Beth had to admit to herself that she wasn't only anxious to get back to her job.

She was anxious to get back to Chris.

So much so, she almost walked right past the black Suburban with the dark windows parked on the side of the street without noticing it.

Jacob wondered if his wife would never stop laughing. "It ain't that funny," Jacob protested as Deborah, Walker, and Lydia all exchanged amused glances. "It really isn't."

The four of them had decided to go to Mindy's for dinner and had ended up lingering over slices of pie. First, Walker had shared several stories about life on his grandfather's farm. Then Lydia had filled them in on her family's news. Then, eventually, the conversation had turned to Schrock's Variety Store.

That was when Jacob had made the error of mentioning that he'd been giving Mose's idea of selling pets some thought. Which the other three thought was amusing. Mighty amusing.

It had obviously been a mistake to bring it up. "I don't see what is so funny," he protested. "I really do want to hear your opinions."

"It's funny because ever since I've known you, you've hated selling pets," Walker said.

"*Hate* is a pretty strong word for how I felt," he mumbled, feeling more embarrassed about his past behavior with each new comment.

"You certainly haven't liked them!" Lydia said, her pretty face flushed with amusement. "All you've ever done is complain about their noisiness."

"And their messes," Deborah pointed out.

"And fetching their food."

"You didn't even like the Dutch bunnies, and they were the cutest creatures ever," Lydia added.

Jacob winced. The Dutch baby bunnies had been cute. Color-blocked in black and white, they were soft and shy. They were so small, you could hold them in one hand. They had been the gentlest of animals, too. But his father hadn't been able to make a proper hutch to save his soul.

Because of that, Jacob had been constantly on a rabbit hunt around the shop. "I liked those rabbits. I just didn't like picking up their droppings. Or chasing them."

On his right, his bride kept chuckling. "Oh, Jacob," she gasped when she came up for air.

"What do you think, Deborah?"

"How about you tell me what brought this on, first."

"I was talking with Mose earlier today and he mentioned how quiet the shop was. I started thinking that he probably had a point about that."

"Your father did keep things lively," Walker said. "And I do have to say that folks did often stop by to see what animals your *daed* had gotten a hold of." Sobering, he added, "Everyone knew how much your *daed* enjoyed those animals, Jacob. That was part of the charm of your father keeping the pets."

"He was fond of them," Jacob allowed with a reluctant smile.

"*Nee*, he loved having animals in the store," Walker corrected.

"Remember the guinea pigs? He really liked those guinea pigs," Deborah teased.

"I remember the parrot Mr. Schrock had two years ago," Walker added. "He was a good bird, for sure. That parrot could mimic the customers like nobody's business."

"I never thought I'd see the day when we sold that parrot. He loved to make fun of my mother." Jacob shook his head. "Gosh, what was his name? I can't believe it's slipped my mind."

"Penny," Deborah reminded him. "The parrot's name was Penny."

"How could I have forgotten that?"

"Because you didn't care for it, Jacob," she said as she took a dainty bite of peppermint cream pie. "I think you tried to ignore her as best you could."

"Penny was pretty, but he was an angry bird, too."

"Penny was a *female*," Walker said, laughing again. "That might be why she never cared for you, Jacob." With a wink at his fiancée, he said, "Women don't like to be ignored, you know."

"So, do you think I should try selling some animals?"

"Nope," Lydia said.

"Truly?"

"*Jah*. It wouldn't be the same, Jacob," Walker said, his expression now serious. "I fear it would only make your days harder. Making the store like your father's won't help things."

"We need to make the store the right place for us, Jacob," Deborah said softly. "Having animals without your *daed* wouldn't be the same."

"Just give it some time," Lydia murmured. "Things

will liven up on their own. For what it's worth, my parents think you're doing a *gut* job. The shop has never been so clean and neat."

That was something, Jacob supposed. But what if sales didn't improve? What if he lacked the charm his father had, and that was why everyone was staying away?

How was he ever going to prove that he was a good shopkeeper, even if he was never going to be the gregarious man his father was?

You mean is, his conscience murmured. *He still is that way.*

He stewed on that as they finished their coffees, said good-bye, and then walked home on the shoveled sidewalks.

Yesterday's glimmer of sun was long forgotten. Thick clouds had rolled in, promising snow.

It was cold out. Maybe too cold to be walking. But with Deborah snug in her black cloak next to him, with her mittened hand curving around his elbow, Jacob was glad to have her company.

She made everything better. As did breathing in the fresh, pine-scented air and seeing the many lights and garlands that decorated the shops and houses they passed. When a buggy passed them, the horse's red harness festooned with tiny brass jingle bells, he grinned.

"What are you smiling about?" Deborah asked.

"Oh, nothing. I was just thinking about how fresh everything feels out here. It's cold, but there's something about Christmastime that makes me feel like there's hope in the world."

Deborah squeezed his arm. "There is always hope, Jacob. I know it's hard, but try not to worry so much. Things will work out, I feel sure of it."

"Really?"

"*Got* came to save us in the form of a tiny baby. If He can do that, why I bet He'll be able to help us do all sorts of things, too. We just need to believe. Faith is a wonderful thing."

Jacob nodded, believing Deborah's words to have a lot of merit.

He just hoped he'd remember them in the middle of the night when he was lying awake worrying and sleep seemed as unattainable as a relationship with his father.

Chapter 9

Christmas cards hanging over the mantel make large rooms feel homey and festive. That's important in an inn, you know.

FRANNIE EICHER REYNOLDS

"Chris? Chris!" Beth called out as she ran into the inn and climbed the stairs at lightning speed.

She heard a thump, followed by a door clicking open. And by the time she got to the landing, Chris was standing in the upstairs hallway facing her, gun in hand.

"You're all right. Oh, thank the good Lord," she exclaimed.

He stepped closer. "What's wrong, Beth?"

"There's a black truck parked outside."

Little by little, some of the panic that had been in his eyes cooled. It was obvious he'd been worried she was hurt. He relaxed as he slowly descended the staircase. "What did it look like?"

Whether it was because he was taking her seriously or because it looked like he had deliberately adopted a calm manner, her pulse slowed, too.

She took a moment to collect her thoughts. "Well, um . . . like I said, the truck was a dark color."

"You said it was black. Is it black?"

"*Jah.* It had dark windows, too. It's parked just across the street. I've never seen it before, either. Oh, Chris, I thought maybe they'd already come in here. I was so worried someone had found you!"

The corners of his lips lifted slightly as some of the gravity left his gaze. "Did you run in here to rescue me, Beth?"

Now she felt a bit of a fool—as if she could do a thing to truly protect him. "Maybe," she allowed.

Those blue eyes of his warmed, becoming almost a true blue. "Thank you," he murmured before turning and walking back into his room.

She was somewhat taken aback. She'd been ready to be teased, to be mocked. Instead, he was treating her like his equal.

And thanking her for looking out for him!

Feeling more empowered, she followed on his heels. "What are you going to do now?"

"Looks like I'm going to have to investigate."

"Would you like me to go with you?"

"Definitely not."

Remembering his stitches and the fever, she feared

he wasn't in nearly as good shape as he imagined himself to be. "Are you sure?" she asked, then halted in his doorway as she watched him slip on boots and a coat. It was then that she'd noticed he had on fresh clothes. "You changed."

"Yeah. After you left, I went out to my truck, grabbed my extra set of clothes, and even took a shower." He rubbed a hand across his short hair. "I'm on the mend. Finally."

"It hasn't been long enough. . . ."

"It has to be. Though that truck may be nothing, I want you to stay safe."

When he checked his gun for ammunition and then turned back around, she felt her heart race. "You really do believe me. About that truck being worrisome."

"Of course I do." He paused. "Why would you think I wouldn't?"

She thought of the men she'd known before him. They wanted her to keep her feelings to herself. To not speak her mind. "I . . . I thought when you smiled, you might have been thinking that I was overreacting."

"If I smiled, it was because you want to save me."

"I know I'm not very big or strong. But—"

"No, no, it's not that. It's just that it's been a long time since anyone thought I was worth saving."

That made her sad. She ached to question him

about it, to ask him again about his family. To pry into his past. Surely a man as handsome as he had had his share of girlfriends? More than that, she ached to reach out to him, let him know by touch that he meant a lot to her.

But it certainly wasn't the time or place.

With effort, she tried to sound a bit detached. "What are you going to do, Chris?"

"I'm going outside to see what's going on."

She was gratified he was taking her seriously, but now a whole new set of worries claimed her. "Chris, they might see you."

"I bet they will."

"But then they'd know you're here for sure."

He started down the stairs. "If someone is parked outside watching the inn, they already know I'm here."

His words were thrown over his shoulder, stated as if he hadn't a care in the world. "I think we should wait for them to knock on the door," she argued.

"We?"

"*Jah*." She followed on his heels, almost matching his pace on the stairs.

"I might have come here for shelter, but I certainly didn't come here to put you in danger. You are going to stay hidden."

"But—"

He stopped just before they reached the entryway

and turned to her. "Beth, if someone has come here to gun me down, they're not going to be knocking on my door."

His jibe hurt. "I'm not a fool, Chris. I don't expect them to be polite. But perhaps you should be a little less obvious."

They stood next to the front door now. Only a thick piece of wood separated Chris from people trying to hurt him.

As she gazed at his bruised face, at the way the skin around his eye was black and blue and swollen, she corrected herself: from the people who were trying to hurt him some more.

"I don't think you're thinking straight," she said quickly. "Perhaps you have a concussion."

He smirked. *Smirked!* "I don't."

"Or your stitches? They could come loose. Maybe torn. I'm not that good of a nurse, you know. You could hurt my handiwork."

He rolled his shoulder. "I'll be careful of my stitches."

As he reached for the door handle, Beth couldn't resist grabbing his free hand.

When he glanced at her in surprise, she knew there was nothing to say but the truth. "I couldn't bear it if something happened to you. Please don't go out there, Chris."

Finally, her words seemed to penetrate his

thoughts. After a gentle squeeze, he pulled his hand from hers. But only to reach up and gently run the backs of two fingers against her cheek. "It's no wonder I can't stop thinking about you."

She was spellbound. Not just by his touch, but by his words, too. No man had ever looked at her this way. Certainly no man had ever spoken to her like this.

Just as she gathered her courage to ask him about why he'd been thinking about her, they heard heavy footsteps on the sidewalk.

Followed, ironically, by a brisk, forceful knock.

Chris's eyebrows rose. "It looks like you were right," he murmured. Staring at the door, he said, "I don't think Mose is back. This time, let's not take any chances. Go upstairs, Beth. Now. Go into my room, take the ladder up to the attic, and hide."

She didn't know how he'd found that ladder. But she certainly didn't want to go up into that dark, cluttered room by herself.

She also didn't want to leave him alone. "But—"

He was still staring at the door. "Do it now," he ordered in a tone that held no room for argument.

But still she did. "Chris, maybe—"

"I promised myself that no matter what happened, you would stay safe. Now go."

Feeling like everything that she cared about was about to be pulled from her hands, she turned, hurried up the stairs, down the hall into his room, and then climbed up the rickety ladder that she pulled down from the ceiling. With a sinking heart, she made her way into the attic of the Yellow Bird Inn. As the blackness and the cold surrounded her, her fear heightened.

She was far enough away that she couldn't hear what was happening below. And because of that, she felt more alone than ever before.

All she could do was guess what was happening and try to be patient.

It was too dark in the attic to even see shadows. Too dark to do anything but kneel on her knees and pray. Pray for them all.

When the knock came again, this time the knuckles pounded the wood, making the wood shudder.

Chris waited another second or two more, just to be sure Beth had had enough to time to hide.

He felt curiously empty inside. He was out of options. All that really mattered was that he keep Beth safe.

And that, he realized, was the truth. His life had only one focus: Beth. It didn't matter that they weren't in an actual relationship. The point was that he cared for her so much that she was already in his heart. And, he realized, she would always be there.

It didn't matter if nothing ever happened between them. She would be always be his, even if she never felt the same way.

With a renewed sense of conviction, Chris opened the door. And received the surprise of his life.

"It's about time you got your act together, Hart," his boss said scathingly. "I've been standing out here looking like a vagrant, knocking on the door and freezing half to death. Do you have any idea how cold it is out here?"

"I'm beginning to get an idea," he said as the frigid air fanned his cheeks. "Ryan, what are you doing here?"

Without being invited, his boss, all five-foot-nine inches and one hundred and seventy pounds of him, strode through the door with a fierce scowl. "What took you so long? I was about to shoot the lock! Who the heck did you think it was?"

There was no reason to lie. And every reason to defend himself. "Who do you think?" he asked as he closed the door behind Ryan and secured the dead bolt. "I thought it was Hager or one of his buddies who tried to kill me two days ago."

Ryan grinned and briefly patted his arm in an almost tender way. "Just for the record, I am glad you're alive. The word was that you were in pretty bad shape."

"I was. But I'm healing. So, why are you here? I

was told to sit tight until December twenty-sixth. Has something else happened?"

"Yeah. Listen, we need to talk." As Chris led him to the living room Ryan looked around him with interest. Chris could see him taking in the arrangement of Christmas cards over the mantel, eyeing the arrangement of glass ornaments in a wooden bowl, and smelling the scent of cinnamon and spice in the air.

As he fingered one of the thick quilts lying on the arm of the overstuffed couch, Ryan turned back to Chris. "Where are we, by the way?"

"In Amish country." Somewhat caustically he added, "Welcome to the Yellow Bird Inn."

"It's homey. And, ah, festive."

"It's more than that. It's off the grid. No one comes here unless they know about it."

"I had a tough time tracking you down, that's for sure. Taylor thought you might be out this way. We finally called the sheriff and only got information out of him after we pretty much told him our whole life story."

"That sounds like Mose Kramer. He's a good man."

"So, who owns this place? Can you trust him?"

"It's owned by a woman, a Mennonite woman. But she's out of town. Her friend is watching over things, and I bet she's scared to death. I've got to go get her."

"Where is she?"

"I sent her upstairs to hide." Already imagining Beth's tears, Chris was anxious to get to her. "Listen, have a seat. I'm going to go get her. I'll be right back."

"Actually, I think I'll join you."

"Do you not trust me? Or are we still in danger?"

"Let's just say I'm not eager to let you out of my sight right now."

That sounded cryptic. But since Chris had no choice in the matter, he shrugged. "All right. You can come with me. But try not to look scary," he said as they climbed the stairs to the second floor, then walked down the hall.

His boss said nothing as they made their way into his room, then pulled the ceiling trap door and ladder down leading up to the attic.

He remained silent as Chris's pulse sped up. He was sure she would have said something by now.

"Beth?" Chris called out. "You can come down now. It's safe."

He heard a snuffle. "Chris? Is that you?"

Beside him, he felt Ryan's body tense with interest. Unbidden, a pang of jealousy tore through him at the thought of Ryan checking Beth out. She might not be his but she was his to take care of. At least for the time being.

Climbing up the first two rungs, he said, "I promise, everything's okay, you can come on down."

Chris felt his cheeks and neck go red as he heard

the tone he was using in front of his boss, but he steadfastly ignored the way his boss was eyeing him.

"Are you sure it's safe?"

He had to smile. If he were really in trouble and had come to retrieve her, he knew he'd have no choice but to say whatever it took to get her to comply.

"I'm sure."

He climbed up the rest of the rungs and poked his head into the narrow crawl space where she was hidden. Realizing how dark it was, he started to worry about her. "Where are you? It's bigger than I thought. Do you need me to find a flashlight or a candle or something?"

"Candle?" Ryan murmured.

"You'll understand soon," Chris said under his voice. Far more concerned about taking care of Beth, he climbed up another rung. "Hey, how about I come up to get you?"

"There's no need," she said after a moment's pause. "I can come down. If . . . if you're sure we're safe."

He hated that she was so frightened. He hated that he'd done this to her. "I'm sure." With a bit of surprise, he realized he had an endless amount of patience where she was concerned. He didn't mind her nervousness. Didn't care that she needed a lot of assurance.

All he cared about was her well-being.

When he saw her face peeking out, half hidden

in the attic's dark shadows, he saw that it was tearstained. "Everything is all right," he said as calmly as he could. "Come on down. It was just Ryan, by the way. He's my boss."

As she shuffled toward him, Chris started down the ladder.

As he reached the floor, he held out his hand to offer it to Beth. To his surprise, he felt himself half holding his breath as she descended. Her safety and care was his main concern now.

As her black flats, then dark blue skirts came into view, he had to stop himself from reaching out to embrace her. And when she turned to stare at Ryan with wide eyes, he saw her eyes were distrustful.

"Like Chris said, I'm Ryan. Ryan Holditch," his boss said as he held out a hand.

She ignored it, looking at Chris in concern instead.

This time he did give in to temptation. Stepping to her side, he rested a reassuring arm around her shoulders.

It seemed he was beyond subtleties now. "He's a good man, I promise."

But instead of looking relieved, her expression grew more uneasy. "Why is he here?" she whispered.

After a quick glare in Ryan's direction, effectively stopping any comment he was about to make, Chris guided her toward the hallway. "How about we talk downstairs?"

For a moment, he was sure she was going to refuse to budge. But then she walked down the steps, her head high.

"Wow," Ryan murmured before following Chris down the stairs.

He understood what his boss meant. Beth was lovely. There was something else about her, too. Something that made a man want to take another look at her. There was little that was weak or fragile about her. Despite her tears, there was a silent strength that was intoxicating.

He knew right then and there that he would do anything in order to protect her from harm.

He just hoped it wouldn't come to that. There were countless reasons why his boss would show up, unannounced, two days before Christmas. But none of those reasons were good.

Chapter 10

Christmas comes but once a year. Thank the Lord for that.
CHRISTOPHER HART

When the three of them were sitting, Chris next to Beth on the couch, Ryan perched on an uncomfortable-looking chair across from them, Chris spoke.

"Tell me why you're here. This isn't proper protocol."

"Billy Ivester is dead."

It took everything Chris had to take the news in a calm manner. "When did you hear?"

"About two hours before I started the drive." He paused. "His throat was cut."

Guilt hit Chris hard. He'd done everything he could to earn Billy's trust . . . all so he would spill secrets. He tried to speak, but too much emotion clogged his throat. Billy's death was his fault.

Suddenly, Ryan's face looked more haggard. "I don't have to tell you that this changes everything."

Though he hated to drag Beth further into his world and problems, it was obvious that he had no choice. Though it pained him to speak, he forced himself to admit what he'd done. "Billy was . . . a kind of inadvertent informant," he told her, practically choking on the word *was*. "He was barely twenty-one."

"I'm so sorry," she said.

"Me, too." He meant it, too.

His boss shook his head in a derisive way. "Don't waste your sympathy on him. He was a dealer for years, and a snitch, too. Neither of those occupations guarantees long life, Chris. This was no naïve kid."

"Yeah, I know." The words were true, but it didn't really matter to him. All Chris could think about was when he'd met the fresh-faced kid for the very first time. It had been at the back of a crowded bar in downtown St. Louis. When Chris had first seen him, he'd wondered how the kid had even gotten past the bouncers.

Billy was short for his age, had freckles. Skinny. At first glance, he'd looked like the most innocent twenty-year-old on the planet.

But then Billy had started talking. Within seconds of hearing his profanity-laced speech, all twisted up in a husky voice—due to years of chain-smoking unfiltered cigarettes—anyone would know that it had been a very long time since Billy had been a child.

"But even though he was a tough kid, he sure was too young to die."

"We found out he told Hager what you guys had been talking about . . . all the stuff he shared with you. That's why they went after you."

Chris shook his head. That kid . . . just desperate for someone to pay him mind, not realizing his mouth could get him, well, killed.

"Yep. Your cover is completely blown. But the good news is that Billy's death was messy enough to track down Hager. Taylor collared him."

"That's great," he said, though disappointment for his own failures was almost choking him. "Taylor's a good agent."

Ryan leaned forward, his elbows resting on his knees. "Taylor is. She did a good job with Hager. We've been after him for years."

A new, worrisome thought entered Chris's mind. Was he about to be replaced? Was that why his boss had trekked all the way out to Crittenden County so close to Christmas? "Did you come for my resignation?"

"Of course not." Looking vaguely uncomfortable, he said, "We've known each other a long time, Chris. I know that kid meant something to you." He shrugged. "I wanted to tell you in person before you got picked up and taken to your next assignment."

"Thanks for that." Not wanting to talk about Billy any longer, he switched topics. "So, you're moving me."

"Yep. On the twenty-sixth."

"I'll be ready. I'll be healed up fine by then."

"All of this happens, just like that?" Beth asked, her voice sounding slightly indignant.

"I'm afraid so," Ryan said, having the grace to look slightly embarrassed. "Moves don't always happen this quickly, but structures are in place in case the need arises. We try to keep our men safe." He paused, eyeing Chris with a bit of chagrin. "It's a dangerous job, though."

Standing up, he reached into his suit jacket and pulled out a phone. "Use this if you need to, my contact numbers are already programmed in. I also brought you some more clothes. They're in a sack by the front door."

"Thanks."

"No problem. We'll be taking your truck today. Do you have any personal items in it that you need to retrieve?"

"No."

"All right, then. Taylor or someone from support will bring you your new vehicle and papers on the twenty-sixth."

"Understood." They'd been through these types of conversations many times. There wasn't room for emotion on either of their parts. Chris had a job to do, and Ryan's job was to make sure he did it.

Unwanted warnings or doubts had no place in their work.

But Beth was staring at the two of them like they were creatures from another planet.

Ryan put his hand out. "Beth, it was nice to meet you. Now, though, I need to get on my way." With a wry smile, he added, "Christmas is coming, you know."

Chris walked him to the door. "Thank you for coming to tell me in person," he said simply. He ached to add a hundred other things. To apologize for the mess he'd made of the case. To ask Ryan about what the higher-ups really thought. To get a hint about where he was going to be assigned next.

But this wasn't the time or place. Besides, if Ryan had wanted him to know something, he would have already said it.

"Merry Christmas," he said instead.

Ryan held out his hand and shook Chris's gravely. "Merry Christmas." Glancing at Beth, who was standing by the couch, still looking lost, he added, "To both of you."

The moment Chris opened the door, the black Suburban pulled up, followed by his beat-up truck.

Within minutes, both were out of sight.

After picking up the sack of clothes, Chris closed

the door and locked it behind him. "So, this means you're safe. No one is going to be attempting to break in. At least not because of me. Now all we have to do is get through Christmas. Then I'll be out of your way soon after."

Beth's eyes widened but she said nothing.

It was all too much. Billy's death. Ryan's appearance. The knowledge that he was about to be someone else, probably somewhere very far away.

It was overwhelming.

"I'm going to go upstairs, Beth."

She walked toward him. "Are you sure you don't want to talk about things?"

"No, I'm not ready to talk about any of that." Billy most of all. That kid had been a felon and a drug addict, but in spite of all that, Chris had hoped that one day the kid would want to change, and that Chris's presence in his life would provide him with an avenue out.

Now, because he'd gotten so beaten up, he hadn't been there to look out for Billy. And because of that, Billy would never get the chance to lead a different life.

"At least let me get you something to eat."

"Not right now, Beth. I need to be alone. And now that I know that I don't need to keep watch, I need to get some sleep."

"All right."

He forced himself to start walking before he got too tired and started telling Beth about all the doubts he was wrestling with. Ever since he'd left the Yellow Bird Inn months ago, he'd been struck by how much of his real life he missed.

He missed his parents. He missed his brothers and regretted not getting to know their wives. Most of all, he'd missed having a decent reputation. He was tired of constantly having to pretend to be someone he would never want to know.

Most of all, he had spent too many hours thinking about Beth. Wishing there was a way that they could have a real relationship.

Since those wishes were far from coming true, it was definitely best to push them aside. No good would ever come from sharing them with Beth.

"I'll see you later, Beth," he murmured before going to his room, turning off the light, and lying down.

Only then did he close his eyes and let the tears flow. For Billy, for his failures, for his life.

And because, although he no longer felt like his sacrifices were worth the gains . . . he still didn't feel strong enough to give it all up.

Chapter 11

My mother used to say that it was far more important
to be the right person than to find the right person. Good
advice, that.

MOSE KRAMER

As the hours passed, there seemed to be nowhere
to go.

Beth stood in the middle of the inn's entryway,
feeling the leftover chill from the door opening.
Feeling the chill of Ryan's departure.

What a curious tumble of events had just occurred! In the span of only an hour, she'd been
huddled, frightened half to death in the dark of
Frannie's attic. Then Chris's unassuming boss had
appeared.

For the first few seconds, she'd let her imagination get the best of her—she'd feared that Chris had
been taken hostage and was helpless.

She'd been sure that it was going to be up to her to save the day!

Next had come Ryan's revelations. Her heart had gone out to Chris as she'd watched him attempt to remain stoic. Then, almost as soon as he'd arrived, Ryan had left.

But not before sharing the news that Chris would be on to another job very soon. And then? He would be gone from her life forever.

All that would remain would be a series of vivid memories and devastating feelings, all mixed up with the knowledge that she, too, would need to move on.

"And move on from what?" she mumbled to herself out loud. "You have no special relationship. Not really."

If she ever confided in anyone, she knew they would tell her that she needed to accept their differences and move on with her life. She needed to look around at the men in her community. It was time to be married and start having children of her own.

She needed to accept her way of life and the place she would have in it.

And so what if she wasn't thrilled about her future? Being giddy and happy didn't mean much, not in the grand scheme of things. Being content was what counted.

Her mother had taught her that.

Her sweet mother had been dealt a hard blow but she never complained. Beth had never heard her ask why she had been the one to live most of her life in a wheelchair. She'd never seemed overly frustrated by the limits on her life.

Beth had a perfectly healthy body, and a good mind, too. She had a mother who loved her, friends who were genuine and caring, and a community that she thought was the prettiest ever.

She was a selfish girl to wish for anything more.

Feeling as if she were in a daze, she walked to the kitchen and put the kettle on to heat. Instead of busying herself in the kitchen, heating soup for Chris or attempting to bake bread, she sat and looked out the tiny kitchen window above the sink.

Frannie, in an obvious flight of fancy, had hung a piece of green garland over the sink and tied bright red ribbons on the ends, and it sent a faint scent of pine into the kitchen. The touch of Christmas in the warm kitchen was very like Frannie.

When the whistle of the kettle blew, Beth got to her feet and made some orange-cinnamon tea, then sat back down and watched it steep.

And realized that tomorrow was Christmas Eve. She had nothing prepared for the meal and she had no gifts to wrap or to look forward to. Furthermore, she'd sent her mother away to be with her sisters. All because Beth had chosen to remain by a dangerous man's side. A man whom she'd never see again after a few days' time.

The day was sure to be a bittersweet one.

And then she looked at the phone and realized that there was one thing she could do.

It would likely win her no favors with Chris. He might even be very upset with her. But she knew that if she tried hard enough, she could figure out how to give him a special gift on Christmas Day.

That is, if she was daring enough to do it.

Leaving her mug, she picked up Frannie's cell phone and dialed information. And when the operator answered, Beth made her decision. "I am wondering if you have the number for the Hart family of Lexington, Kentucky," she said. "Hart is spelled h-a-r-t. Like the deer, you know."

"One moment."

And then, she was being connected. There was no turning back.

"Jacob, we are going to be so busy tomorrow," Deborah said as they put away the delivery of bread that had just arrived.

He paused his careful stacking of rolls. "Only in the evening, right?"

Though he wasn't all that excited about it, he had told her that he'd be willing to share Christmas

Eve dinner with her parents. Things between them were still strained, and he imagined they always would be.

But if they were willing to move forward, he certainly could, too. He'd do anything for Deborah, but he didn't want to be there all day!

As she wiped down a tabletop, Deborah murmured, "Don't forget, we also said we'd visit Walker and Lydia in the morning."

He looked at her curiously. Something was on her mind, and it wasn't their Christmas Eve schedule. "I am looking forward to seeing them. It's for brunch, yes?"

"*Jah.*"

"Well, it will be a lot of eating, but it shouldn't be too busy, Deborah," he said with a smile. "Since the store will be closed, I might even take a nap in the middle of the day."

She stopped her wiping and looked in his direction. "Well, I hope it won't be too much activity, because"—she paused and bit her lip—"well, Jacob, I asked Sheriff Kramer to take us to see your *daed* on Christmas day."

He froze. "You did what?"

"I stopped by his office to talk to him about visiting hours and such. He said he'd be happy to take us." Not meeting his eyes, she said, "It's all arranged."

"I think not."

"You need to visit your father, Jacob. You'll regret it if you don't."

She was probably right, but he wanted to do this in his own time. "Deborah, I'm not ready."

Looking resolved, she shook her head. "That is why I took things out of your hands. Mose and I already called the prison to let them know that we would be coming up to see your father. And I'm not going to back down, especially since Mose was so kind as to offer to take us on Christmas Day of all days. Oh, Jacob, what a gift that will be to your father!"

"It's a gift I'm not ready to give!" Though he hated raising his voice, the frustration—and fear—he was feeling overruled his best intentions. "Deborah, you have overstepped your place."

"Don't yell. I'm doing this for you, Jacob." More quietly, she added, "For us, too. Before you know it, the visit will be over. You can see how you feel then. But it's important to take this first step."

"What if it doesn't go well?"

"Then at least you'll have visited. Jacob, I love you, and I want to be a *gut frau*. I try to follow your advice on most everything. But this time, you need to trust me to know what is best. And you need this. You need to see your father and find some peace more than anything."

Though his teeth were practically grinding, he

knew she was right. And though he didn't expect any miracles, he knew that the sooner he crossed this bridge, the better. "Fine." Somewhat roughly, he set down the last of the loaves of bread on the table. He turned around, "But Deb—"

"You don't need to say anything, Jacob. I don't care what happens now." She grabbed his hands and gave them a squeeze, her warm eyes saying everything she wasn't.

Her gesture humbled him. She loved him so much, she was willing to risk his anger to do what was right. She was willing to visit a prison on Christmas Day.

"So, Mrs. Schrock, have you already made us plans for this evening, too?"

A new light entered her eyes. "As a matter of fact, I have."

He braced himself. "And what are we going to do?"

"Have a nice supper here at home. Just the two of us."

"Really?"

"Well, we are newlyweds . . . I think it will be *wunderbaar* to be alone with you on the eve of Christmas Eve."

"Now that is something we can agree on." He leaned close and kissed her cheek.

Laughing, she pushed him away as a pair of customers walked in. "You mustn't be kissing me in the middle of our workday. Now, off you go. Go help those folks. I have the rest of these rolls to organize. And a special supper to make."

Smiling at her enthusiasm, he greeted the women who already had shopping baskets in their hands. "May I help you?"

The older of the two shook her head. "Thank you, but we won't be long. We had to pick up a few last-minute Christmas gifts."

"My sister and her family were able to make it here for Christmas after all," the other woman added. "Isn't that just like it always is? No matter how prepared one is for the big day, something unexpected always occurs."

"I've had a few unexpected surprises myself," Jacob murmured.

The older lady placed three Amish dolls and a box of cookie mix into her basket. "But that's what makes this season so *wonderful-gut,* don'tcha think? Christmas truly is a time of blessings . . . and wonderful surprises."

"I couldn't agree more," he murmured as he walked slowly back to the counter. Christmas truly did bring them all some surprises . . . and a reminder of their blessings, as well.

Chapter 12

Do you ever wish things were different? I used to.

BETH BYLER

Could ten seconds ever feel longer? Beth's pulse raced and she kept glancing over her shoulder, afraid she was being spied upon.

On the other end of the line, the line clicked as the operator connected them. Then the rings began. One. Two. Three . . .

Four.

What she was doing was wrong. Chris's private life was none of her concern. He certainly wouldn't thank her for meddling. What she should do was hang up.

Ring number five. She held her finger over the button, ready to end the connection . . .

"Hello?" The voice was brusque but friendly. Out of breath.

It was now or never. "Yes. Hello?"

"Yes?" The lady sounded more impatient now. Like she was about to hang up.

"Is this the Hart residence?"

"Yes? May I help you? And listen, if this is a telemarketer, I'm on the do not call list . . . "

Beth had no idea what kind of list that was. All she did know was that she'd better say something meaningful, and quickly. "I'm calling about your son."

There was a sharp intake of breath. "Which one? Is something wrong? Did something happen?" she blurted, her voice now sounding nervous. "And who is this?"

"My . . . My name is Beth Byler. I'm calling about Chris."

"Chris?" The woman's voice seemed to rise a whole octave. "Oh my gosh, Chris. Hold on." There was a rustle and a clatter as the receiver was set down, followed by a muffled call. "Tim! Come here quick."

When the woman got on the phone again, Beth had finally composed herself. It was strange, but just knowing that she'd called the right house and was actually speaking to someone who cared about Chris, too, put her at ease. "Is this is his *mamm*?"

"Mamm? Uh, no. I'm his mother," she said hesitantly. "What, ah, what do you know about Chris?"

Beth decided the best way to begin was with the

basic information. "I live in Marion, Kentucky. Your son, he is a friend of mine."

"Have you seen him lately? Is he okay?"

"He is okay, I suppose," Beth said slowly. "He is resting here. I am looking after a bed-and-breakfast." Realizing how choppy everything was sounding, she bit her lip. This wasn't going too well.

"Tim?" the woman said again. "Tim, this woman says Chris is with her."

There was another click, then a deep voice spoke. "Hello?"

"Hi," Beth said. One more time, she introduced herself. "My name is Beth. I am a friend of your son Chris."

"Yes?" The man's voice sounded even more wary.

"Um, well . . . because it's Christmas, I wanted to call and let you know that your son is all right."

After the briefest of hesitations, he said, "He hasn't been all right for a long time."

Beth was stunned until she remembered that his family didn't know what he truly did for a living. Oh, but she wished that she had thought things through before she had called them. It was a difficult thing, trying to figure out what to say to clear Chris's name without giving away his secrets. "Chris is a mighty *gut* man," she finally said. "The best."

"Miss, where are you from?" his mother asked. "Did you say Kentucky?"

"*Jah.*"

"You sound strange."

"I'm Amish."

"You're Amish?" the man repeated.

Right on his heels, the woman asked, "Our Chris is staying with an Amish woman in a bed-and-breakfast in Marion?"

"Yes. He was injured, you see. But he is better now."

"Injured? What happened?"

"He was in a fight with some bad men."

Chris's father chuckled, but it wasn't a happy sound. Instead it sounded bitter. Harsh and disappointed. "I don't know how to tell you this, but Chris has been lying to you. He's the bad one."

"*Nee.* That is not true!"

"What isn't?" Chris said from behind her.

She turned so quickly, she almost dropped the phone. "Chris!"

"Chris is there with you right now? Can you put him on?" his mother said urgently.

Chris stared at her. "Beth, who are you on the phone with?" As he saw the answer in her eyes, the color drained from his face. "What have you done?"

"I'm giving you a Christmas present." Abruptly making up her mind, she thrust the phone at him. "I've been talking to your parents, Chris. But I fear I've been doing a poor job of it. You . . . you should talk now."

He shook his head even while his left hand grabbed the cell phone.

With a look of pain, he held it up to his ear. "Mom?" he asked. "Dad? Yeah, it's me."

Beth felt like crying. Even though it was hurting him, she knew she had made the right decision. Turning, she grabbed one of the kitchen chairs, dragged it to where Chris was standing, and gently guided him into it.

"Dad, Mom, there's a reason I couldn't contact you. A very good one. Uh, no, Dad. That is actually not what I was doing," he said quickly.

Standing off to the side, Beth watched him bite his lip, then shrug. Just as if he'd made a decision. "The truth is that I've been working for the DEA for years undercover." He paused, then spoke again. "Yes, the Drug Enforcement Agency."

Just as she was edging away, Chris reached out and grabbed her wrist. "Don't leave," he mouthed, just before he spoke out loud again. "I know I looked scary, Mom, but that's kind of the point."

To her bemused surprise, his lips curved up. "I'm not hurt too badly, Mom. Just a little banged up." He sighed. "It's nothing, I promise. Stitches."

Little by little, Beth felt her anxiety settle as she felt Chris's whole mood lift. As he continued to talk, asking about his brothers, she watched him run a hand through his hair.

Then, wonder of wonders, he chuckled.

"I know, Mom."

Danke, Got, she silently prayed. She truly hadn't been certain that this had been the right thing to do. All she had felt was a real need to make things a little brighter for him while he was still with her.

Now, all she had to do was pretend that she wasn't going to miss him terribly when he left the day after Christmas. . . .

"Beth?"

Realizing her mind had drifted, she stared at him. "Yes?"

He handed her the phone again. "My mother wants to talk to you."

Feeling awkward, she took the phone from him and put it up to her ear. "Yes?"

"Thank you," his mother said, her voice thick with emotion. "Thank you for calling us. I don't know if you'll ever know how much it meant to me to hear Chris's voice."

Gazing at Chris, noticing the change that had come over his features just from the five-minute phone call, Beth realized that she might have some idea about that. Tears filled her eyes.

"I'm just glad you answered the phone," she said.

"I hope one day we'll get to meet."

"Yes. Um, me, too," she murmured. "I would like that." Of course, it wasn't likely. From what Ryan had said, in two days Chris would leave Marion, would most likely leave Kentucky. He was going to get a new name. Get a new identity. And then he'd be gone from her life all over again.

When she handed the phone back to Chris, he said a few words, then hung up.

Then he turned to her, his face a mixture of bewilderment and admiration. "I can't believe you did that. You took me completely by surprise."

"I know." She was secretly pleased with herself. He was a man used to being constantly on alert. She considered it almost a badge of honor that she was able to catch him off guard like that.

"You shouldn't have called them without asking me." His voice was raspy. But was it from anger or something else?

"I know you are upset with me, but I cannot regret this." She was just thankful he wasn't asking her why she'd done it, because she really didn't know. It had just seemed like the right thing.

She stared at him. Gazed into that curious shade of blue and green and gray. Then, to her surprise, he yanked her close into a fierce embrace.

All of a sudden, she was surrounded by Chris. By

his tall, muscular build. By his clean scent. By his warmth and his strong personality.

His hands were firm on her back and head. He was pressing her close, not in a scary, hurtful way, but as if he couldn't get her close enough.

As if he was trying to commit that hug to memory.

In response, she wrapped her arms around him and held him close.

Because she knew exactly what he was trying to do. After all, she was trying to do the same thing.

Chapter 13

Some moments, some memories, are so special, it's hard to give them up.

Christopher Hart

The next morning, Chris found himself reliving those brief moments when he'd held Beth tightly in his arms.

She'd felt so right.

Chris hadn't wanted to ever let her go. He'd yearned to imprint to memory the way she felt in his arms. So much so that years from now he'd still be able to recall everything about that moment.

To remember how it felt to be held by the woman he loved.

Just as his chin had begun to lower, as his body stirred, wanting more from her, wanting to kiss her lips, he had thankfully stepped away. A fierce hug was one thing. But kissing her? That would have been a huge mistake.

After checking his stitches and getting cleaned up, he found Beth in the kitchen.

"*Gut matin! Kaffi?*"

"Coffee sounds good. Thanks." Chris wondered if she even realized she was speaking Pennsylvania Dutch. As he eyed her, he noticed she was in a pretty raspberry-colored dress, and that her cheeks were rosy and her eyes glowed. "You sure are happy this morning," he teased.

"It snowed last night," she said happily. "So we will have a white Christmas after all."

Glancing out the window at the shimmering blanket of freshly fallen snow, he had to admit it looked beautiful.

Almost as pretty as Beth did at that very moment.

Oblivious to his thoughts, she set a filled cup in front of him and chattered away. "I'm *verra* pleased about the snow. But I also can't stop thinking about your phone call, Chris. All morning, I've been thinking about how happy your *mamm* sounded on the phone. I'm so glad you talked to them."

"You gave me quite a Christmas present. I'll always be grateful."

"All I did was make the call," she reminded him as he sipped his coffee. "Your parents wanted to talk to you. Your mother was overjoyed to know that you were okay."

Beth had done something that he'd been afraid

to do for years. Though it was tempting to chastise himself for causing them so much pain, he pushed it aside. He'd have plenty of time for recriminations after he left the Yellow Bird Inn and was living by himself in some rundown apartment once again. "I can't wait to see them. I hadn't realized until I heard their voices how much I've missed them."

"I hope you'll get to see them one day soon."

Her smile faltered, right in sync with his plummeting feelings. Here was yet another thing that he wasn't going to get to do.

"Maybe. I hope so."

Shaking away that burst of melancholy, he summoned a smile. "So, it's Christmas Eve. Is there something you want to do? I bet it would be safe if you wanted to spend some time with your friends now."

"I'm not going to leave you."

He made himself laugh. "My stitches are fine and my fever has broken."

"It's not that. Chris, I don't want to leave you today."

The honesty shining in her eyes made him want to be completely honest, too. "Good, because I really don't want you to leave."

"Would you like to help me make dinner? I know cooking isn't man's work, but I'm not a very good cook."

"You're not a good cook at all, Beth," he said with a grin. "But I do okay."

"If you know how to cook at all, I'm sure you can help me."

"I'd like that very much." He followed her into the room beyond the kitchen that was Frannie's oversized storage area. Against one wall was a large freezer.

"I'm not sure what we can make," she said as she pulled open the door.

He stood by her side, reading labels of frozen casseroles, looking at the packages of chicken and hamburger. In the back he saw one pork tenderloin. Reaching for it, he pulled it out. "How about this? Do you like pork?"

"I do, but I don't know how to make that."

"I do. My mother used to roast it with a cranberry glaze."

"Chris, it's frozen like a rock."

"We've got all day to figure out how to thaw it." He gestured to the neatly lined and labeled casserole dishes. "What else do you see?"

"Here's a potato dish." She brightened. "And some frozen corn. I do know how to make a corn pudding. You know what? We might actually have a *wonderful-gut* supper."

"I hope so."

Carefully, she pulled out the two containers and

led the way back to the kitchen while he followed, holding the end of the roast like it was the end of a baseball bat.

Hands on her hips, she proclaimed, "We should make a cake, too."

"A cake? That's a bit beyond my skills, Beth."

"Frannie has a recipe for a chocolate cake. I think that sounds *gut*. We need something to help us celebrate. Christmas is Jesus's birthday, you know."

It had been a long time since he'd even heard a Christmas carol, let alone taken the time to really reflect on what Christmas is all about. "I suppose you're going to get flour everywhere. And I'm going to have to clean it up." He chuckled, thinking of the first time he'd met her. She'd been in this very kitchen, trying to clean up a very big mess.

"Probably." She sighed, but she couldn't hide her amusement.

"So what do you want to do first?"

"You figure out how to thaw a roast. While you do that, I'll find the cake recipe." Holding up an apron, she said, "Would you care for an apron?"

"I'll help you in the kitchen, Beth. I'll even clean up your mess. But real men don't wear aprons."

Looking very amused, she murmured, "I'll keep that in mind."

"*Danke.*" Of course, he probably butchered the pronunciation. But it didn't seem to matter to Beth.

Because when he glanced at her again, she was blushing and smiling softly at him.

And the picture she made was so dear, it took just about everything he had not to take her in his arms and kiss her.

Pulling his hat farther down on his head in a weak attempt to block the wind, Jacob walked along the empty expanse of the far fields of the Millers' farm.

As he walked along, taking faint notice of the fresh snow underfoot and the bare branches in the woods beyond, nestled in between bright green spruce trees, he shook his head.

The Millers' farm had always been an intriguing spot. The Millers had never liked folks traipsing across the land, but for as long as he could remember, everyone he knew had done it anyway.

He even recalled his parents saying that they used to cut across the land on their way to each other's houses when they were teenagers.

Some things never changed, he guessed.

The Millers' land lay right in between the store and half of the town. Whether a person was in a hurry, or just too lazy to walk around, the option of walking across the empty land was almost too tempting to ignore.

Lately, Mr. and Mrs. Miller had stopped protesting quite so much about all of the trespassing. They, as much as anyone, he supposed, had begun to real- ize that enforcing their wishes was futile.

And, well, it wasn't like they'd used the land in decades. Instead it had lain empty.

Of course, lately it had also been the center of scandal in their community. Abby Anderson had discovered Perry Borntrager's body in an abandoned well when she'd been smoking near it with two other *Englischer* girls.

Perry had taken to hanging around there, and had even met Frannie there a time or two when they'd briefly dated.

And, of course, the last time he'd been there with Frannie they'd argued. Which had led to Frannie crying and Jacob going after Perry to talk some sense into him.

The rest was history. He'd argued with Perry, which had led to a fistfight. Perry hit his head on the side of the abandoned well and passed out.

Which was where Jacob's father had found him . . . and then had ended up hiding Perry's body in the abandoned well.

Just a few months ago, the Millers had filled the well with cement and laid a plaque on the top. All it said was *Hope*.

As a whole, their community had thought the sentiment was well placed.

Now, as he stood before it on Christmas Eve, running his palm along the carved letters, Jacob thought it was especially meaningful.

It was now obvious that holding on to bitterness, regret, and pain wasn't doing him any good. The negative emotions, combined with the true ache he felt for Perry's passing and his father's incarceration, were threatening to change the person he was.

If he wasn't careful, Jacob knew he was on the verge of becoming just as bitter and alone as Perry had been.

He believed in Deborah, and believed in her strength and common sense. He knew it was time to finally take a step forward and see his father. He needed to reach out to his father even if it took everything he had.

It was the right thing to do. But a voice inside him was urging for more. He needed to do more than grudgingly visit his father . . . he needed to forgive him.

After laying his hand on the plaque again, he closed his eyes and said a small prayer. For Perry. And for Deborah and Perry's parents.

And, finally, for his parents and himself. He had so much to be grateful for. All he needed to do now was decide how he wanted his life to be. Either filled with hope and peace—or filled with anger and despair.

Put that way, there really was only one clear choice.

It was time to visit his father. It was time to reach out to him again.

The Christmas Eve supper had been as awkward and strained as Jacob had imagined it would be. Though Deborah promised her parents no longer held him responsible for Perry's death, he wondered if that was actually the case.

Not that he blamed them. If he were in their shoes, he had a feeling he would respond the same way. After all, it was Jacob's father who had ultimately killed their son Perry, though some would say that Perry had long since brought much of the pain on himself.

And still others would say that Jacob had a part in Perry's demise as well.

But though he tried to see their point of view, they seemed intent on only remembering Perry's best qualities.

And Jacob, not feeling like he could defend his *daed*, simply sat there. It was not his place to speak ill of Perry. And it certainly wasn't his place to excuse his father's actions.

But it made for a long evening.

At the moment, he was sitting in the *sitzschtupp*, the formal living room, with Mr. Borntrager. Deborah and her mother were in the kitchen cleaning up. Of course, they'd refused his offer to help.

Men did not do dishes in the Borntrager household.

So Jacob and Mr. Borntrager sat in silence staring at each other. Even on Christmas Eve.

Jacob looked out the window and wished the snow would start falling again. If the weather turned worse, they could make their excuses and leave and the agonizing evening would finally be over.

"What are you doing tomorrow?" Deborah's father asked, breaking the silence.

"Not too much." There was no way he was going to tell him they were going to the prison to see his father.

"Your mother didn't want to see you?"

"She is in Ohio, in Holmes County. We both agreed that it would be best if she didn't try to travel back and forth this week. It's not a quick journey, you know."

Mainly for something to say, he added, "I can't go too far, either. The store will reopen on the twenty-sixth."

Mr. Borntrager's stare was piercing. "I haven't been into your store in ages. Does anyone still shop there?"

"Some."

"Hmmph."

Jacob silently willed Deborah to leave the kitchen. His jaw was starting to ache from clenching his teeth and keeping his silence.

At last, she entered the room, carrying a tray filled with four cups of hot coffee. Her mother followed carrying a tasty-looking apple pie and four dishes with small scoops of vanilla ice cream.

Jacob jumped to his feet. "Deborah, let me help you."

"I've got it."

Still yearning for a lifeline, he said, "Beth Anne, may I help you?"

"Of course, Jacob." She smiled at him, but it was as strained as the conversation had been. Jacob took the tray and set it on the coffee table.

After a brief word of thanks, coffee and pie were passed around and quietly consumed.

Sitting beside him, Deborah glanced his way worriedly.

He knew she was concerned about him. She didn't like it when her father got on one of his high horses and began blaming Jacob and his family for everything.

But luckily, that hadn't happened yet.

At last, they were finished and he and Deborah got to their feet. "It is time for us to go," she said. "Thank you for having us over for supper, Mamm."

"We are glad you came. Aren't we, Abraham?"

Beth Anne asked, giving her husband more than a subtle nudge.

"We wanted to see how Deborah was getting on," he said.

Deborah looked like she was about to start crying, and Jacob took a deep breath, trying to remind himself that they were still suffering the loss of their son. Of course it would be hard.

"I brought you both something," Deborah said, scurrying over to her neatly wrapped gift. "Merry Christmas."

Her mother took it. "*Danke*, Deborah. We will open it tomorrow."

"Oh. All right. Yes, please do that."

They stood there awkwardly for another second, while Deborah realized that they had no gift for her, that they weren't even going to wish them a Merry Christmas. Seeing the hurt on her face, Jacob couldn't remain another moment.

Not caring what her parents thought, he wrapped a reassuring arm around Deborah's shoulders and guided her to the back door. Then, as she visibly held off her tears, he helped her fasten her cloak and handed her the rest of her things.

Then he opened the door, and walked her to the barn.

Their horse was in one of the stalls. He wasn't happy to be leaving the warm barn and pile of hay to get hitched to the buggy. But with a bit of prodding, he went easily enough.

And though it wasn't Christian, Jacob found himself cursing under his breath. His wife was so sweet, and only wanted to be accepted and loved. None of what had happened to her brother was her fault.

Over and over she hoped and prayed that her parents would one day remember that they still had her, even though they'd lost a son.

But time and again Deborah was disappointed.

When the horse was hitched, Jacob lit the portable heater and shook out the wool blanket for them to place over their laps. Only then did he walk to the barn, take her arm, and help her into the buggy.

When they were snug and at last driving on the road back home, Deborah's tears started to fall.

"I'm sorry," he said. "I'm so sorry."

"I can't do this anymore."

"You can't do what?"

"I can't go on pretending that things will get better. They aren't going to get better. Not ever."

Her sudden loss of hope had the opposite effect on him. "They might," he said, fairly amazed that he could sound so optimistic.

"They won't." She swiped at a tear. "It's not like things have ever been that good, though. And that hurts, too."

"I know it does."

"Jacob, more than ever, I'm glad we're seeing your father tomorrow."

If he hadn't been holding the horse's reins he would have flinched.

"In spite of everything, I love your father. I want to see him, Jacob. I feel like we've already lost my parents. We can't lose your parents, too."

"Listen," he said, turning toward her. "Please don't expect too much from one visit."

"No, you listen," she interrupted quickly, her voice hard and urgent. "I know going to the prison to see your father will be hard. I know it will be difficult to talk to him face-to-face. But these visits to my parents have been hard for me, too. If I can do this over and over, you can go to see your father on Christmas Day. And you can try to be optimistic about it, too. Please?"

Maybe if she hadn't been crying, he might have fought back. But right now, she was the only family he had, and he wanted her to feel safe and secure with him, at the very least.

"All right," he said at last.

In the dark of the buggy, she wrapped her hands around his right arm and hugged him tight. *"Danke, Jacob."*

And then, to his surprise, he felt himself smiling as a curious sense of relief filled him.

And a bit hopeful, too. It had been the most difficult year of his life. But it had also been the most miraculous. Having the love and support of a woman like Deborah was like the North Star in the sky, forever guiding him home.

Chapter 14

I never learned to cook; I never wanted to take the time. My mother said I would regret that one day. She was right, of course.

BETH BYLER

Their supper had been edible, Beth mused. She supposed that was something, at the very least. But since neither of them knew what they were doing, it had been a case of the blind leading the blind. The potatoes were still cold in the center. And the pork?

It had been so well-done, a knife could hardly get through it.

Actually, the only thing that had turned out well was the chocolate cake. It, now, was a thing of beauty. And if the sneaks of cake batter and frosting were any indication, it was going to be delicious.

Glancing over at Chris, she had to stifle a smile. He was currently washing their dinner dishes. Next to him was a stack of bowls and measuring cups. Spoons and spatulas. They'd made quite a mess.

"I'm grateful for your help cleaning up," she said.

He raised a brow. "Beth, it's the least I could do. We have to be the two worst cooks ever to grace this kitchen."

"You may be right," she said as she grabbed a dish-cloth and started drying one of the bowls. "You'd think it would be easier for us to clean up after our-selves."

"I'm surprised we didn't burn the place down."

She chuckled. "I'm excited to try out our cake, though."

He smiled right back at her. "Me, too."

He looked so content, having his hands in hot soapy water, the tension for once gone from his body, she gave in to temptation and touched his arm. "I had fun, though."

"Oh, Beth, so did I. At the risk of sounding pretty pathetic, I have to say that this has been one of the best nights I've had in a long time."

His words fairly broke her heart. "Things have been that bad?"

He loosened the plug on the sink and let the water drain. She could tell he was attempting to weigh his words. Finally, he spoke. "Yeah. Things have been that bad."

She admired the way he usually tried to gloss over

his pain. Whether it was emotional or physical, he always seemed to want to shield her from the worst of it.

She imagined he'd probably been like that with most people. Shouldering the burdens so others didn't have to face them.

"Let's go ahead and eat the cake in Frannie's hearth room. While I fix our plates, would you go light the fire?" she asked.

"Sure."

It was a small, quiet little room in the back of the house. The ceiling was a bit lower and the floor was covered in a patchwork of bricks. On top of them were a pair of handmade rag rugs. Also in the room sat a pair of cozy couches covered in a dark denim fabric that framed a big stone fireplace. Oak bookshelves lined the walls.

It was a private room. Beth rarely sat there, knowing that it was Frannie's special place to relax when the inn was full of guests or her husband, Luke, was working late.

But it was in a corner of the house and well hidden from the street. She wanted to sit there with Chris, to offer him a room that didn't feel like a wide-open area.

She wanted to give him a place where he could let his guard down.

When she entered the room a scant five minutes

later, she felt like she was entering her own private daydream.

Chris had a blazing fire in the fireplace, and it cast a warm glow over the small sitting area. He was standing in front of it, looking like he always did to her—handsome and lonely. Stalwart.

She made herself sound especially cheery. "Chris, I think this might be the crowning achievement of your visit."

He glanced at the cake, then smiled in appreciation. "It almost looks like it could be served to other people."

"Frannie is going to be impressed."

They sat on the couch together and took tentative bites. And to her surprise, the cake really was as good as she'd hoped it would be.

Chris ate his down in five large bites while she took ladylike ones, hoping to make it last.

As he watched her, a look of amusement lit his eyes. "I'll bring you another slice, Beth."

"I couldn't have seconds."

"Sure you could. No one would know."

"But still. One piece is enough I think."

When she finished and set her plate on the coffee table in front of them, she felt a little awkward. Here, she'd set them up in this cozy room, with a warm fire and the golden glow.

But now it almost felt too private. Too close.

He looked at her in concern, then pulled up the quilt behind him and shook it out. "Come here, Beth."

"What? Oh, I couldn't . . ."

"Come here and sit next to me."

"I shouldn't."

"I won't try anything." He held up a hand. "I promise."

The problem was that she wanted him to hold her. She wanted to kiss him. She wanted to sit in the dim light and enjoy an evening with him, pretending he was her man. Her boyfriend.

Pretending that they had a future. That he was her fiancé. Her husband.

But if she gave in to those fantasies, she knew she'd feel wicked. Guilty, too.

The silence stretched between them.

"Beth, I know you don't know what to make of us. So you don't have to say a word. But I'm going to tell you something because you need to know it. I've liked you for a very long time. And all those nights that really weren't very good? I would try to make them better by imagining that we were sitting somewhere like this. I know one day you'll be sitting in your own hearth room on Christmas Eve. Who knows? Maybe you'll be with someone special next year at this time.

"But I know I won't. You're it. And even if we aren't meant to be together, because I've done too much and you've done too little . . . let me sit here with you, would you?"

"I don't know what to say." Probably because so much of what he was saying had been the way she'd felt, too.

"That's good. Because you don't need to say a single thing. All you have to do is trust me. I won't make some move on you. All I want to do is put my arm around you and hold you close."

She had a lump in her throat, which rendered her mute for what else she intended to say.

And she was glad about that because, Lord help her, she wanted the same thing that he did.

Which was why she sat on the couch, scooted close, and let him lay the quilt over the both of them.

It was why she didn't protest when he wrapped an arm around her shoulders and held her close. It was why, when she ended up resting her head on his shoulder, and she heard his steady heartbeat, she didn't move away.

Because sometimes it didn't matter what a person's head wanted. All that mattered was what was in her heart. Chris was warm and solid and smelled like chocolate cake.

He was everything she remembered and so much more.

Afraid to speak, afraid to ruin the moment, she braved her fears and cuddled closer, sighed when he brought his other arm around her and linked his hands.

She felt her body conform to his as they shifted. And as she stared at the flames in the fire, she felt something that had been missing from her life for quite some time—something that everyone had thought she had but had been missing for almost forever.

Peace.

She felt loved and happy and content and peaceful.

It was almost too good to be true. And almost too hard to believe.

Chapter 15

I've thought about selling Christmas decorations in the store, and I've thought about selling hamsters, too. But neither of those things felt right. I'm trying to find my own way, you see.

JACOB SCHROCK

Jacob had debated whether to let his mother know he was going to the prison to see his *daed*. In his heart, he knew she'd want to know that he was finally giving in and paying him a visit.

She would be mighty glad about that.

But he figured with that gladness would come a stern lecture about how he should have gone to see his father before now. And along with that lecture would come a gentle reminder about being the person she and his father had wanted him to be. A man who obeyed the tenets of their faith and practiced forgiveness above all other things.

He was not ready to listen to those words.

Deep inside, he still had mixed feelings about his father's guilt and his hand in it. No number of motherly lectures was going to change his feelings.

No, it was going to take time and a willingness to move forward.

For Deborah, he was willing to do that.

He hoped the visit would go well. But as he stood in front of the window, watching for Mose's car to pull in the driveway, he wondered if he hadn't gone crazy. He was nervous and scared.

"He's not late. Not yet," Deborah said when she walked over to stand beside him.

"I'm not worried about that. I know he'll get here when he can."

"Aren't you going to get your coat?"

"Oh. *Jah*, sure." He did as she suggested, his mind in a fog. After slipping on his coat and putting on his black felt hat, he noticed the scarf Deborah had knitted him for Christmas. It was black and plain. But the yarn was especially soft and thick. He knew he'd wear it often, especially when he elected to walk around town instead of going to the trouble of hooking up the buggy.

He'd given her a vacation to Pinecraft. They'd never gone on any sort of vacation after their wedding, and now spent most days working in the store. He was determined to call in some favors from

Walker and other folks who had worked in the store from time to time and have them watch it while they went away.

Deborah had had tears in her eyes when he'd presented the gift to her. Her happiness had made him feel ten feet tall.

Now, though, he realized he had nothing to give his father.

By the time he reached Deborah's side again, it was weighing heavy on his mind. "I don't have a gift for my *daed*."

"Do you think he'll expect one? I don't even know if you can give inmates gifts."

"I didn't think to ask." Now he felt foolish. What had he been thinking? That the guards were going to suddenly let his father wear a wool scarf with his prison uniform?

She patted his shoulder. "Here is Mose. I know it's difficult, but I think you should try not to worry so much, Jacob. This visit seems like a good enough gift."

"Perhaps." Privately, he wondered how they would be received. Maybe his *daed* would be upset that Jacob hadn't visited before.

"Okay, then." She gave a little sigh, then grabbed his hand and pulled him toward the door. "Let's go, husband."

To his surprise, he found himself smiling on his way out to Mose's truck.

"You brought your truck," he said.

"You didn't think I'd make you travel in the back of my cruiser, did ya?"

"To be honest, I was so grateful for your help, I would have ridden in the squad car happily."

"Well, no man needs to ride in the back more than once, I'm thinking." Mose winked at Deborah. "Merry Christmas, Mrs. Schrock."

As she usually did whenever someone called her by her married name, Deborah gave a little happy smile. "Merry Christmas to you, too, Sheriff Kramer."

After buckling up, Jacob said, "I sure hope we didn't mess up your whole day."

"I didn't have anything planned, if you want to know the truth. Now I do." His smile was tight. Strained.

Jacob felt sorry for the sheriff but refrained from saying anything more. No man should have to explain his family—or lack of one, he thought.

But Deborah wasn't of the same mind. "You don't spend any time with your family?"

"No."

"But they live nearby, don't they?"

"Yes. In Murray." He shrugged. "When I decided to become a sheriff, it didn't go over real well."

In spite of himself, Jacob said, "Did they shun you?"

"No. Not shunned. But I'm not welcome. My parents—all my relatives, actually—would rather

I didn't take a job in law enforcement. They can't overlook the gun, you know."

"But you're such an important part of the community."

"Yes, but you know how it is. By and large the Amish don't care to have much to do with the police. My family is no different."

"You need a special woman," Deborah said quietly. "Everyone needs a partner in life."

Jacob couldn't agree more, and knew Deborah was speaking from experience. For most of her life, she'd lived an almost solitary existence. Growing up, Perry had needed constant attention and guidance. It had seemed he'd yearned for it, though one would never know. Rarely had he ever shown any appreciation for his parents' efforts to bend over backward to make him happy. Deborah had been expected to sit quietly in the background.

Later, when Perry's behavior had become more erratic and puzzling, eventually leading him into a world of drugs and damaging consequences, Deborah's good qualities had gotten even further overlooked.

And after his death, she'd been practically shunned, especially since she'd chosen to marry Jacob over her parents' wishes.

Jacob felt like he was finally able to give her the attention she deserved. And while he agreed with her comment, he wasn't about to step into Mose's personal life. But he did give in to impulse and gently squeeze her hand.

Oblivious to the undercurrents between the two of them, Mose chuckled. "I agree that everyone needs a mate, but I don't think my time for courting has come yet."

"Are you sure?"

"Positive. One day it will be the right time for me. It just hasn't happened yet."

"I hope it happens soon."

Mose chuckled. "Deborah, you sound just like Frannie. She's always after me to start dating." Turning serious, he said, "Anyway, love didn't work out so good for me. I tried it once, and it ended badly."

"Don't give up," Deborah whispered.

"I won't. But I fear I'll expire if I keep holding my breath for something good to happen. I seem to be out of luck in the romance department." He shrugged. "But let's not dwell on me any longer. I'm not sad about things, so you certainly shouldn't be. I've had a long time to get used to the way things are. Some things can't be changed, and it's a waste of time and trouble wishing differently."

"You're right about that, Mose," Deborah said. "But still, I do feel for you."

"And I'm grateful for your concern."

Mose's voice had turned uncomfortable, and Jacob

knew it would be rude to continue to press him. Everyone had a right to privacy.

Besides, Jacob had plenty to worry about.

They'd just passed a bright green sign announcing that they were a mere twenty miles from the state prison. In no time, they'd be seeing his father.

But he'd also be bringing his wife into a place neither of them had ever intended to see. A place filled with criminals and violence and the darkness of pain and regret.

He knew she was worried about walking inside those doors.

Almost as worried as he was about how he'd react when he finally came face-to-face with the most important man in his life.

Chapter 16

It is a wonderful-gut *night. A holy night. Ain't so?*

Mose Kramer

It was snowing again and Chris felt at peace.

"When was the last time you felt that way, Hart?" Chris mumbled to himself as he turned away from the frosty window he'd been staring out of for the last few minutes.

He didn't even need a second to know the answer. It felt like it had been forever since he'd felt so calm inside.

Usually, he woke up in a daze, blinking furiously as he forced himself to remember who he was currently pretending to be and where he was. He'd learned the hard way that forgetting his cover for even a second was hazardous to his health. The slightest hesitation or mistake meant that months of hard work could vanish in an instant.

Now, though, he was merely himself. That was all. He should have felt curiously bare. Stripped and vulnerable. Instead, he felt free.

With one ear to the door, he changed out of the old pair of sweats he'd been sleeping in and put on a clean pair of jeans, white T-shirt, and wrinkled chambray shirt from the bag Ryan had brought. He'd lived in clothes like this when he was in high school and college. The fit was familiar. Comfortable.

Only now did he wonder where his boss had gotten the clothes. Had he asked Taylor for help? Had he simply guessed his sizes? Was there some secret file that the powers-that-be kept on each employee? He wouldn't put it past anyone at the DEA.

Which brought, of course, everything full circle. Tomorrow someone from the agency, most likely Taylor, would arrive. They'd pick Chris up and whisk him away into oblivion.

He'd be back on the job with a new identity. It was sure to be someone grungy or depraved or at the very least someone down on his luck and desperate.

And then, little by little, he'd have to force himself to become that person. He'd slowly change his speech patterns, change his dialect. He would once again do things he abhorred around people he disdained.

And inside? He'd block the pain of losing himself with the knowledge that he was doing something that needed to be done. For the greater good.

Unfortunately, he didn't think that would let him sleep at night. Not anymore.

"Chris?"

Trotting to his door, he pulled it open, then blinked at the picture Beth presented.

She was bright with happiness. "It's Christmas," she said with a smile. "Merry Christmas!"

"Merry Christmas to you, too." He couldn't help smiling back. With effort, he willed himself to keep both of his hands at his sides. If he wasn't careful, he'd find himself reaching for her and pulling her into a morning hug. A sixth sense told him that she would welcome it, too.

Then they'd have even more to regret when he left tomorrow.

He forced himself to keep his manner a little distant. "How are you this morning?"

Her bright smile dimmed. "Oh. I'm *gut*." Little by little, her stance mirrored his. "I'm sorry to bother you, but I was wondering if maybe you wanted to try to cook some breakfast with me? Or would you rather I let you know when it's ready?"

"I'll come to the kitchen with you. Last night was fun. And you're in luck, Beth. I can actually cook eggs and bacon."

Her smile eased. "I can, too." She turned and started walking down the hall, down the stairs.

He followed on her heels, realizing about halfway

down the stairs that she had on a different dress. This one was blue with a white apron. She looked as pretty as a picture. Wholesome and innocent.

Which, of course, was what she was.

When they got to the kitchen, he poured himself a cup of coffee, then followed her directives. Soon he was in charge of the bacon, Beth the eggs and toast.

There was little of the teasing, romantic banter that had lingered between them the night before. He knew it was his doing. She'd come to his door in high spirits.

After eating in near silence, then washing the dishes side by side, Chris knew he had to say something. It wasn't fair to keep her on pins and needles. Not when she'd done so many things for him.

Not when she'd given up Christmas to watch over him.

When the counters were clean and too much coffee had been drunk, he knew there was little left to do but be honest.

"Beth, let's light a fire and sit in the hearth room again."

"That's not a *gut* idea."

"I know. But let's do it anyway. I want to talk to you."

Her eyes looked a little wild. "We can talk here."

"Not like I want to." Lifting up a corner of his lips, he reached for her hand. "Please?"

She pulled her hand from his. "I don't understand what game you are playing with me."

He knew she didn't. But what she likely didn't understand was that he wasn't playing a game. He was just as confused about what he wanted from her . . . and what he didn't want. "Please, let's go sit down."

To his surprise, the hearth room already had a fire lit. It was cozy and warm and comforting there. After she sat down on one of the couches, he sat across from her on one of the wooden chairs in the corner.

Today, she sat very still and stiff. "What did you want to say?"

"That I am sorry for ruining your Christmas."

"We've already gone through this." Scorn filled her gaze. "Why can't you simply be honest?"

"You don't want my honesty."

"I do. I certainly do. I want to know what you think about me."

"I think you are the finest woman I've ever met." Her eyes widened. "I care for you, Beth, but after tomorrow, it won't matter."

"Is that what you think?"

"Well, yes."

"You're wrong, Chris Ellis—ah, Chris Hart—whatever your name really is."

"I told you the truth about my name."

"Yes, you finally did." To his surprise, she jumped

to her feet, looking as irritated and out of patience as any of the women he'd met on the streets. The ones who felt like their chances were few and their futures were already decided.

A little shocked, he leaned back and let her speak.

"You may know a lot about fighting crime and apprehending criminals, and drugs, Chris, but you know nothing about feelings."

"I agree with you."

"You just hush for a minute."

Slightly stung, he sat back. "Okay . . ."

"Chris, when you left me the first time, you fairly broke my heart." She held up a hand when he started to speak. "It doesn't matter that you didn't mean to do that. It happened." She sighed. "For the last few months, all I've done is mope around and wish that things were different. I ached for you to return so I could say everything I wanted to. But I never thought I'd see you again."

He was so crushed by her words, by the pain in her voice, he said what he shouldn't. "Beth, it was hard on me, too. I missed you. I thought about you all the time."

"And you did come back."

He now realized that the pain he'd felt a few months ago was going to be nothing compared to the pain he'd feel when he left her again.

And he should know better than to force a conversation like this. "You know what? You were right. Sitting here together was a mistake."

Now she was the one who looked so sure. "I don't think so. I think you came back because you knew that I was the person you needed to be with. Most of all."

"You're right," he whispered, finally giving in.

"What?"

"You're right. You're right about that. About everything," he said quietly. "The truth is that from the moment we met I've been attracted to you. And not just your looks, Beth, even though I think you're just about the prettiest thing I've ever had the good fortune to set eyes on. There's something about you that I can't ever ignore. You glow. You bring me happiness just by smiling. You make me happy just by being you. So much so that it's all I can do not to grab your hand and pull you to my side when we talk."

Gazing at her, he continued with a small, bitter laugh. "And do you want to know the rest of it? I want to do a whole lot more than hold your hand, Beth. I want to wrap my arms around you. Kiss you." His gaze burned. "And more."

She gasped. He knew he'd shocked her.

It didn't matter if most everyone else in the world would roll their eyes at the tender, oh-so-chaste thoughts. Most people were bombarded with cable and movies and video games and shiny ads full of people barely clothed.

Most of the people he'd known while he was playing the part of Chris Ellis didn't even blink an eye at a scantily dressed woman or a man intent on satisfying his darkest urges.

But here, in the prim and pretty Yellow Bird Inn talking to sweet, clean, precious Beth Byler, his words felt shocking. Almost shameful. But that was the point, wasn't it? Though he knew he shouldn't be telling her these things, he didn't regret it. He ached to share with her his true self.

"I'm not a saint, Beth," he rasped, feeling like he was laying the worst of himself out for her to see. "Rarely have I even been considered good."

"You're being too hard on yourself. I know you."

"You don't know me well enough."

"I disagree."

"Listen. I can promise you this. I am going to do something decent for once." His resolve made his voice sound firmer. He was glad of that. "From now on, I'm going to leave you alone. And tomorrow, I'm finally going to leave you forever."

Pure dismay lit her eyes. And, something darker that he couldn't quite discern. "It sounds as if you've figured everything out."

He was glad she was starting to see things from his point of view. "This isn't a sudden decision, Beth."

"I see." One delicate brow arched. "And you have no need to ask me how I feel?"

"Beth, I'm doing what is right. For both of us." At last, he paused for a breath. Staring at her, he steeled himself, waiting for her rejection. For her tears.

Anticipating the pain that was about to come when he saw just how harsh his words had sounded to her. Almost welcoming the feeling, almost glad to know that he had made yet another mistake that he couldn't repair.

Instead she stood up.

Her gaze was hard. Her lips slightly parted.

"Even though you haven't asked me for my opinion, I'm going to give it anyway."

"What do you have to say?" He half dreaded yet yearned to hear her words.

She stepped forward. "I think you are forgetting something, Christopher Hart. I'm not a naïve Amish doll. Or some young innocent girl. I'm a grown woman who lost her father at too young an age, and has been nursing her mother for years now. I even stitched your wounds." She waved a hand. "I also have a job. A real job. Many, many families count on me to take care of their children. There's no greater responsibility."

"I never thought that you weren't a worthy, wonderful woman, Beth."

"But you are treating me like I don't know my own mind."

"I'm treating you like you deserve someone who is going to stick around."

"I dare you, Chris. I dare you to treat me as an equal." She stepped forward. "You know what I am saying. Do something that you said you wanted to do. Hold me close. Hold me too close. Wrap your arms around me." Her chin lifted. "Kiss me," she whispered. "That is . . . if you still want to."

His throat was dry. His body frozen. This was not going like he'd planned. She was supposed to be running from him, looking at him in disgust. Instead, she was practically propositioning him. Daring him to do something he so desperately wanted, but was so afraid to give in to.

"I don't think we should . . ." he began again as he rose to his feet, his voice sounding suspiciously like he had a frog in his throat.

To his dismay, she rolled her eyes. "I suppose I must do everything," she murmured.

Just before she lifted her hands, curved them around his neck, and then raised her lips to his.

And kissed him. Just as he'd imagined, her lips were sweet and soft. Perfect.

All he could do was close his eyes and hold on tight.

And, to his shame, kiss her back.

Chapter 17

Folks have told me that one day Deborah and I will start our own traditions. Perhaps we already have.

JACOB SCHROCK

"Jacob, I'm going to tell you a few things," Mose said when they got within sight of the prison. "I know you didn't ask for advice, but I wouldn't feel right if I didn't offer you some."

The nervous flutter in his stomach told him that he needed all the help he could get to survive the next few hours. "I'd appreciate anything you can tell me."

Mose took a deep breath. "This is going to be a scary situation. Life inside the prison walls? It's difficult. It's going to be difficult for you to experience, and it's going to be difficult for you to see your father experience it, too." He glanced sideways at Jacob. "You have to be prepared to hold yourself in check."

"All right."

"First thing is we're going to park, and check in. Then we're going to have to take a bus to the actual prison."

"Why?"

"Security, Jacob. Both for them and for you. Once we get to the main facility, we're going to have to walk through scanners, like in the airports. Or at some monuments or attractions."

"I've been through those before," Deborah piped in.

Mose relaxed a bit. "*Gut.* Now, you can't bring anything inside, other than a few dollars for the vending machines. Do you have any dollar bills?"

Jacob shook his head. "*Nee.*"

"That's fine. I picked up a couple yesterday." His voice turned more businesslike. "After you get through all the security, they're going to take you to a big room. Inside are a bunch of small tables and chairs. Listen to the guards. Sometimes they tell you where to sit. Sometimes they let you choose."

"All right."

"Then, and only then, will they walk your father out to join you."

"So there won't be glass in between us?"

"I don't think so. Once, years ago, I had to do some hours here on Christmas Day. Things could have changed but I don't think so. Anyway, then you'll get to spend about two hours with your father."

The mention of hours caught Jacob off guard. "They don't restrict visits to minutes?"

Mose gave him a funny look. "For dangerous criminals they do. But not at this facility." He tapped his fingers on the steering wheel. "Jacob, don't you want to spend some time with your father?"

"I do. I mean, I think I do. But I wasn't planning on being around him for so long. I had thought maybe a half an hour at the most. If we're going to be sitting together for more than that, I have no idea what we're going to do."

"They have games. Scrabble, Yahtzee. But something tells me you three might have a lot to talk about. While you're together, you can use the dollar bills and get a soda or a snack."

"And when it's time to leave?"

"About ten minutes before your time is up, the guards will announce it." Mose frowned. "It's going to be hard, Jacob. I can promise you that. You're going to be sad, and it's going to be strange to see your father go away with the guards when your visit is over."

"I'm nervous," Jacob admitted. "I think I've been pushing any thoughts of what he's been going through out of my mind. I didn't want to think about his daily life in a prison cell."

"That's understandable. You've been hurting, Jacob."

"But I think it was easier for me to pretend that I was the only person living with regrets."

"We all live with regrets. Some are heavier than others. But the fact of the matter is, it's a difficult thing, moving on after something like your families have been through. It's difficult to move on and find a way to continue. There's no right way or wrong way to do it, either."

They pulled into the parking lot and Mose parked the car. As he turned off the ignition, he turned to look at Jacob. "Are you ready?"

"Yes. I mean, I have to be."

"Sheriff, are you going to go in with us?"

"Nope. The visits are for family members. Besides, you don't need me, you'll be just fine. There's a coffee shop not too far from here. I'm going to sit down, read the paper, and have some breakfast." Quietly, he handed them his business card. "That's my cell phone right there. When you're done visiting with your *daed*, give me a call."

Jacob stared at the card, thinking of Mose sitting alone in a coffee shop on Christmas morning. "Mose, though I'm very grateful, I don't know how I can ever make this up to you."

"There's nothing to make up. Taking you to see your father on Christmas Day?" He shook his head. "I do believe I'd call that time well spent."

"I think we should go now," she said, looking ready for anything. "The shuttle bus is on its way here."

As they scooted out, Jacob gave in and took one last look at Mose. "Wish me luck."

"I'll do better than that. I'll pray for your strength. And for the lot of you." He smiled slightly. "You can do this, Jacob. It will be hard. Sure it will be. But you've been through much harder things in your life. Don't forget that."

Mose's words served as a steadying balm. He was right. Discovering Perry was dead and that he hadn't simply run off, like most people assumed, had been a shock. Being called in for questioning, fearing that he was going to be sent to prison had been hard, too. So had fearing that he'd lost Deborah forever.

Though this was mighty difficult, the Lord had already shown him that he was stronger than he realized. Feeling more secure with himself, Jacob exhaled, closed the truck's door, then waited by his wife's side.

It was time to move forward instead of only regretting the past.

After that kiss, Beth had scurried to the privacy of her bedroom. She had wanted to hug tight the bittersweet memory of Chris's embrace in private.

All her life, she'd been a caregiver. She'd taken care of her friends and had looked after children in their area. In school, she'd gravitated toward being the teacher's helper. Often she would miss recess because she'd be sitting with someone in the school who needed special help or attention.

Soon after she'd left school, her mother had been diagnosed with MS. And then her father had passed away suddenly and she'd become her mother's main provider.

She'd been happy to care for her mother. She gave thanks for her mother's even temperament and words of wisdom. Those things made taking care of her that much easier. When her mother's health improved enough for her to stay home by herself for extended periods of time, Beth had used her natural talents to care for other people's children.

She'd always been a strong person. The one who took care of things.

Until this morning, when she'd been in Chris's arms. All it had been was a hug and a kiss. Okay, a long, tender hug and a few kisses.

But that was all. And in those precious moments, she'd felt as if she'd been at his mercy. She'd felt protected and comforted.

Almost loved.

She wasn't very worldly, but even she knew that chances were slim to none that another man would ever affect her in such a strong way. She didn't know if Chris felt the same.

After those few brief moments of pleasure, he'd

pulled apart from her with a stricken expression. "I'm sorry, Beth," he'd said, then had quickly turned away and gone to his room.

She hadn't protested. She knew him well enough by now to know that there was nothing she could say to change his way of thinking about what they'd done. He was going to place all the blame on himself . . . even if she hadn't thought they'd done anything wrong.

Determined not to ruin the whole day, she pushed all her worries to one side and strode back to the kitchen. She started humming to herself. A silly Christmas song about wanting a hippopotamus for Christmas that one of her English *kinner* loved to sing.

She'd just made a fresh pot of coffee and was thinking about making fudge when she felt his presence. Turning around, she saw him standing in the doorway, gazing at her with a bemused expression.

"Hi," he said.

"Hello, Chris." She made certain she kept a slow and easy smile on her face.

He cleared his throat. "It looks like you're thinking about doing some cooking."

"Fudge. I've, ah, actually made it before. It's nothing fancy, but it's good and I do know how to make it," she teased. "That counts for something."

His lips curved before he turned solemn again.

"Listen, Beth, I think we should talk about what happened."

"I'm only going to have regrets if you can honestly tell me that I mean nothing to you."

He looked as if he'd been taken completely off guard. "What?"

"Chris, how do you feel about me? Do I mean something to you? Anything at all?"

His gaze darted off to the side as if he were afraid to look directly at her. "You know what I'm going to say, Beth."

"I truly do not," she replied. Inside, she was almost cheering. She knew he felt something special for her. She knew it. And she knew that he was doing all he could to not let his guard down.

But just as certainly, she knew he needed to let it down. After all, she was already taking that chance.

"You're going to have to tell me the words, I'm afraid," she prodded. "Chris, how do you feel about me?"

Finally, he stared directly at her.

His blue eyes looked pained as he visibly struggled to talk to her.

As he fought for control, the silence stretched. And the tension that filled the kitchen nearly made her regret she'd said anything at all.

Yet again, it seemed she was acting the fool. In her naïveté, she was placing him in a terrible position.

And very likely preparing herself to be hurt. Badly.

Chapter 18

My mother's apple pie was Perry's favorite Christmas treat. That's why she doesn't make it anymore.

DEBORAH SCHROCK

With another *click* and a *snap*, a new line of men entered the visitors' room. From his seat next to Deborah near one of the windows facing a fenced-in park, Jacob found himself anxiously scanning the faces, looking for his father. They'd been waiting several minutes already.

Deborah tensed next to him. "Jacob," she whispered. "He's here."

Whether it was excitement, nerves, or habit built from years of respect, Jacob jumped to his feet. He glanced at the line of men.

And then saw his father.

Dressed in an orange jumpsuit, his father looked strange and unfamiliar. For some reason, Jacob had never really stopped to think about his father not being dressed Plain. Jacob knew if he had been asked to wear an outfit like his father was wearing, he would feel half unclothed.

Forcing himself to look away from the glaring outfit, Jacob skimmed over his father's face.

To Jacob's dismay, his father didn't look too good. His skin seemed a bit paler, looser too. Obviously, he had lost some weight. There were more lines around his eyes. His beard was grayer and seemed shorter, as well.

But when he met Jacob's gaze that same spark, that look of pride mixed with remorse and something altogether hesitant came over his face.

That look gave Jacob hope. Perhaps everything wasn't going to be as terrible as he'd thought. A lump formed in his throat. Suddenly, all of the hopes and regrets he'd felt over the last few months faded away, leaving only the two of them standing there.

His father stood frozen. His eyes continued to search, to scan. It felt as if he were drinking in the sight of him for safekeeping.

Jacob knew he needed to say something— anything—but all he could utter was the one word that filled his head. The only word that seemed to matter. "Daed."

"Son," he finally whispered, his voice hoarse with emotion.

The guard standing nearby looked as if he was about to lose patience with his frozen father, but after a second's consideration, he held his tongue and merely remained by his father's side. Almost as if he was trying to give his father support.

With heavy steps, Jacob walked toward his father. He stared at him in wonder. Then, realizing that his father was not going to make the first move, reached out and hugged his *daed*.

"Jacob," his father said. "I can hardly believe you're here. It's like a dream has just come to life."

Both his words and his incredulous tone shamed Jacob. He'd been so awful to keep his distance.

Jacob patted his father's back and hugged him a little harder, fending off tears. His father's body felt thinner, weaker.

Older.

Why had he waited so long to visit him?

Why had he been so focused on his own pain that he'd neglected to fully consider how his father was faring in such a place as this?

"Merry Christmas, Daed," he whispered.

"Merry Christmas to you," his *daed* muttered right back.

When they broke apart, his father turned to Deborah and lightly hugged her, too. Jacob noticed that she was far more contained than either of them. But she, too, seemed to be holding back tears.

After they broke apart, the three of them looked at one another. Awkwardness and worry settled in again as they stood there together.

"We, ah, got us a table and chairs, Daed," Jacob said weakly.

"Ah. *Jah*. Yes, let's sit down."

Awkwardly, they sat down and stared at each other. Aaron's eyes watered a bit and he brushed off the tears with his right hand.

Now that they were together at last, Jacob had no idea what to say. As he weighed and rejected possible topics, Deborah smiled sweetly.

"Aaron, would you like to hear about the store?"

A spark of life entered his gaze. "Of course. How goes it?"

That was something Jacob could talk about. That was what they had between them, what they'd always had in common. Memories of being a little boy next to his *daed* filled him again. Over the years, no matter what else had been going on in their lives, there had always been one thing that united them: the store.

It was their lifeline. Their bond. No matter what else they had or didn't have, they would always have that.

And suddenly, nothing seemed hard at all.

"Well, believe it or not, I was actually thinking about bringing some animals in to sell," he said.

As he'd hoped, a small smile played along his father's lips. "Is that right? What kind of animal were you thinking of?"

"I don't know." Quickly, he said the first thing that came to mind. "Ferrets?"

"Ferrets? Now that's an animal to consider. Ain't so?"

And so the conversation had begun. For the next few minutes, they discussed the pros and cons of ferrets, his father becoming more animated by the second.

So much so, Jacob knew if he closed his eyes, ignored the smell of antiseptic and men and smoke, he could be back in Crittenden County. At their store.

Before everything that they'd known had disappeared.

Chris felt his neck flush as Beth waited for his reply. He hated feeling so awkward and gauche. Hated feeling like he was a kid again, trying to ask his first girlfriend to the middle-school dance.

As he looked into her eyes, he was tempted to evade her question. Or worse, lie.

But he couldn't do that. Not to someone who had taken him in, given him shelter, and patched his wounds.

But most important, he couldn't do it to Beth. She was far too special to him to lie to. Far too important to him now to evade.

Feeling like he was free-falling, he said what he knew he shouldn't say. "I've fallen in love with you, Beth."

She looked jarred. "Truly?"

Her dismay, which so matched his own, made the conversation almost bearable. "You know I wouldn't make that up. You're special to me, Beth. I like how you're so much tougher and stronger than everyone thinks. I like how you keep trying even when you're not sure. I like how you can't cook anything edible but you keep trying. But most of all, I like how you have made a man like me feel as if there's something more to me than my faults. All that equals love, I guess."

She shook her head. "I'm nothing special."

"No, you're everything special. You're special enough that I'm willing to tell you all this, even if it means embarrassing myself, or worse, embarrassing you."

"I'm not embarrassed."

"How do you feel?"

"Like the luckiest woman in the world."

He was torn between pulling her into his arms and running away from her just as fast as his feet could take him. He settled for reaching for her hand.

"Well?" he asked. "Are you going to tell me what you're thinking?"

"I don't know if I'm that brave."

"Why don't you just try?"

"I've fallen in love with you, too, Chris," she said at last. "For better or worse, that's how I feel about you."

Her words had to be the best Christmas present he'd ever received.

And the scariest.

As if she'd read his mind, she looked at him solemnly. "What do we do now?"

He wished he knew what to say.

But what could he say? "Nothing. There's nothing we can do."

Instead of regret, pure amusement lit her eyes. "That doesn't make me feel any better."

"Maybe we should take things one day at a time. One moment at a time."

"And only think about today?"

"If you're willing to give that a try, I am, too. I'm here with you on Christmas Day. And even though I don't have any red roses or candy to give you, I want you to know that you still mean the world to me."

"I don't need any roses. And as for the candy? Well, I'm thinking about making some."

He stepped to the counter. "If I help you, your fudge might even turn out."

"There's always a first time," she teased with a smile.

Yes there was. This was the first time he'd had

a sweetheart on Christmas Day. This was the first time in years that he'd felt content.

This was the first time he'd ever been in love.

Reaching out, he grasped her hands. "I don't mind that it's the first time at all," he murmured, talking about so much more than candy. "Sometimes it's the best."

Beth smiled. "I would agree," she said softly. "I would agree wholeheartedly."

Chapter 19

One Christmas Eve years ago, Perry and I stayed up until midnight. Hiding out under the covers in his room, we counted the moments until Christmas. It was a wonderful-gut night. One of best.

DEBORAH SCHROCK

"Ten more minutes," the guard intoned to the room at large. "Wrap things up."

Jacob winced. "This visit has gone by so fast. I wish we had more time."

"It's been so good to see you," Deborah said.

Aaron's gaze wavered and it looked as if he was attempting to retain his composure. "I feel the same way, Deborah. It means a lot to me that you came with Jacob."

"He means a lot to me." She smiled at Jacob.

Inwardly, Jacob shook his head. He wasn't sure how he'd gotten so blessed to have Deborah as his wife, but he knew he'd be giving thanks for her yet again in his prayers that evening.

"Five minutes."

Jacob scowled at the guard. "He is certainly forceful."

His father chuckled under his breath. "That's their job, I think." Then he shrugged one shoulder. It was a vintage movement that Jacob had seen him do a hundred times—and one he had missed recently. "Don't fret though, Jacob. I'm used to being told what to do."

The words made Jacob feel even worse about things. Though he'd disagreed with what his father had done, he couldn't help but hate that his father had to live in this way. In most ways, he was a gentle man. It had to be very difficult to constantly be watched and told what to do in such a harsh manner.

Around them, people were hugging and saying good-bye to each other. Jacob knew it was time to do the same but he couldn't quite bring himself to do that yet.

As if he read his mind, his father stood up. "It's time to say good-bye."

"I wish we could be here longer."

"We can't always get what we wish for. But that's okay, you know. I heard that there are several other groups of folks trying to see each other today. It's only right to give them their chance."

The couple behind them separated, the woman leaving in a flurry of tears. The inmate she left behind looked to be on the verge of tears himself. He was now standing near the exit with a haunted, resigned look on his face.

His father's eyes looked just as desolate.

"Daed, what will you do now?"

His father looked taken aback. "I'll go to my cell, of course."

"Is it terrible, living there?" The moment he asked the question he ached to take it back. What was his father supposed to say? That he liked living in such a place?

"Living here?" He paused, then nodded. "*Jah*. It is bad. But it ain't bad every minute of every day. Luckily, my cell mate is a decent sort. Some ain't got that."

"What's his name?"

Again his father looked at him strangely. "Chuck," he said at last. "He's a big man, and African American, too. And younger. Only twenty-three."

"You're very different."

"We are. He's had a hard life. Sometimes when we talk, I realize that I've had many things to be thankful for that he could only dream about." He paused, then added as an afterthought, "He likes hearing about the Amish."

"I'm glad he is nice to you. I hope your days don't go too slowly."

"Son, you haven't been reading my letters, have you?"

Too ashamed to meet his father's gaze, he tucked his chin. *"Nee."*

"Ah."

There it was. No recriminations. No guilt. No hurt words.

Which made Jacob feel all the worse. "I saved them, though. And I'm going to read them all when I get home."

"Will ya now?" His father paused, then added, "If you do that, you'll find out much about life here. You might find it interesting. Now that you've stepped inside, I mean."

"I should have read them before. I don't have a good excuse, Daed."

"I think you just might." He pursed his lips. "Please don't worry so. Everything will be all right. One way or another, we'll all survive. One must make peace with one's life. Ain't so?"

"Line up," the guard ordered.

Now there was only time to quickly hug and join the other people exiting through the door they'd entered. Jacob barely had the chance to do anything more than glance at his father one last time before the heavy steel door slammed shut behind them, effectively putting the emotional visit firmly in the past.

As they were shuttled through yet another metal detector and inspected, Jacob stood silent, barely aware of Deborah's presence beside him.

Ten minutes later, they were near a pay phone. Without a word, he crossed to it, entered the coins and dialed Mose's number.

"You done, Jacob?" he asked.

"*Jah.*"

"I'll be right over. Take the shuttle to the parking lot. I should be there by the time you get there."

"*Danke,*" he said softly. After he hung up, he turned to Deborah. "Let's get our coats and your purse. Mose will pick us up soon."

She nodded and followed him to the locker they'd been assigned.

Only after they'd taken the short ride to the parking lot did she speak. "Are you sorry we came, Jacob?"

"*Nee.* I'm only sorry I've been such a fool."

"You haven't been—"

"No, I have been," he said quickly, cutting off her words. "Deborah, my father made a terrible mistake in a span of fifteen minutes. But I've been nursing my pain and disillusionment for months now. I've acted like a child. My behavior, it has shamed me."

She gazed at him softly. Then, to Jacob's surprise, she merely took his hand and squeezed it, just as they saw Mose pull up in his shiny silver truck.

"You aren't going to say anything?" he asked, wanting to get the worst of her recriminations over before they joined Mose.

She smiled in a bittersweet way. "Let's go home."

Yet again he was in awe of his wife. She'd said exactly the right thing at exactly the right time. Going home, back to where everything was familiar and comfortable and peaceful, that was what his heart needed.

The day's visit had been nerve-racking and hard. But in a strange, surprising way, it had been good, too. Here, in a concrete building filled with a thousand lost souls, he'd found his father once again.

Chris had just brought in more firewood when the front doorbell rang.

Wary, Beth turned to Chris. She was getting used to following his directions when visitors came, but it didn't make it any easier. "Do you want me to hide again?"

His expression looked grim and more than a little confused. "You know, I don't think so. Stay here while I go see who it is, though. Just to be safe."

Wrapping her arms over her chest, she nodded, standing still as she watched him cross through the kitchen, then approach the door.

She pursed her lips, trying to remember if he had

his gun. What if he didn't? Her mind spun as she heard him gasp.

"Beth? Beth, come here!" he called out as he unlocked the door and opened it.

Without a second's hesitation, she rushed to the front. Half curious as to who would have come, half incredulous at how completely dumbfounded Chris sounded. Who would make him like that?

Then she heard a rush of laughter and voices. So many voices, the majority of them deep and masculine.

When she got to the entryway, she practically skidded to a stop. There stood Chris, surrounded by a trio of men and two women, one about her age, the other quite a bit older. The older woman looked like she was laughing and crying, all at the same time.

And then, one by one, they each quieted and stared at her.

Chris disengaged himself and walked to her. "Beth, this is my family," he said.

"Oh my!" Feeling suddenly shy, she glanced at his family. "*Wilcom*," she said.

He reached for her hand, linked his fingers with hers, and then tugged her to the little group. "This is Beth," he said simply. "Beth, please meet my parents, Tim and Meredith. And my brothers, Mike and Kevin. And Kevin's wife, Becca."

Right away Meredith pulled away from the men

and approached her. "Hello, Beth," she said with a happy smile. "I hope you don't mind, but as soon as we heard Chris's voice, we knew we couldn't stay away another second. We had to spend Christmas Day with him."

Beth glanced at Chris. He looked dazed, as if he had just seen the most wonderful thing but wasn't sure if it was real or not.

Kind of how she'd felt when she'd opened the door two days ago.

"I think you have made him very happy," she said finally.

Yes, it was an understatement, for sure.

But it was also very true.

Chapter 20

I used to think I could handle anything, anytime, any-where. Then I grew up.

CHRISTOPHER HART

In the field, Chris liked to think he was pretty adept at anticipating almost any altercation. He had quick reflexes and a keen sense of timing.

The only time he'd been at a disadvantage was when he was outnumbered. And even then, when he'd been held down and beaten, his mind had carefully been planning his next steps.

But right at this moment? He might as well have been a rookie kid on his first job. Or a high school freshman on his first date. Or . . . he didn't even know.

He was at a complete loss.

Nothing in his experience had prepared him for this moment. Before Beth had called them, he hadn't thought he'd talk to his family ever again.

Even after the phone call, he certainly hadn't thought he'd be able to see them anytime soon. Yet here they were.

Kevin, his eldest brother, came over and shook Beth's hand. "You're going to have to tell us all about Chris," he said gently. "The guy we used to know would never be caught dead at a place like this."

As her eyes widened and she looked at him doubtfully, Chris attempted to laugh it off. "You don't even know what kind of place this is, Kev."

"It's too nice for you."

His father approached. "Beth, we're indebted to you. Now tell us about the inn."

"Hold on. What should we do about everything in the car?" Mike asked.

"What did you bring?"

"Food, gifts . . ."

"Food?" Beth asked with wide eyes. "I don't understand."

"It's Christmas, dear. We want to have a Christmas dinner, just like we used to have. Since Chris wasn't going to come to us, we decided to come to him."

"It's all in the car," his father said. "Actually, the car is filled up. Come on, boys, let's go unpack it."

After taking two steps toward door, Kevin looked over his shoulder. "You coming, Chris?"

"What? Yeah."

Beth still looked worried. "Chris, be careful about your injuries."

"I'll be fine."

Kevin narrowed his eyes. "Your face looks bad, but what else is wrong?"

"He has stitches in his shoulder," Beth said quickly.

Now Beth wanted to talk about those stitches? Chris felt his cheeks color as both of his older brothers eyed him. He shrugged off his pain. The last thing he wanted to do was appear weak in front of them. "I'm fine. Mom, stay in here with Beth, would you?"

"Of course, dear." Just as he walked out the door, he saw his mother beam at Beth.

Feeling relieved, knowing his mother could make anyone feel at ease, he turned and followed his father and brothers down the walkway and to a pair of SUVs. "Are these Mom and Dad's trucks?"

"One is Dad's. One is mine," Mike said.

"Ah." Chris felt like he was in some weird daze. He knew these people, knew them well. But in other ways, they were strangers. They were like characters in a book or play that he'd read about.

Only when they were out of sight of the inn did his brothers stop and look him over. "Okay. Now you can be honest," Mike said. "How are you really?"

"Fine."

"You don't look fine. You look pretty bad," Kevin

replied. "How tough has this job of yours been?"

"It's been a tough couple of days," Chris allowed.

"It's been a tough couple of years," his father corrected, then enfolded him into another bear hug. "You've got a lot of talking to do. A lot of catching up. We want to know everything."

"Just go easy on Beth, will you?"

"What is she to you?" Mike asked.

At the moment, it felt like she was the most important thing in the world. She was his link to everything good. But after tomorrow?

She was going to be yet another something in his past he was going to have to force himself to forget as quickly as possible.

"She's my friend," he said finally.

"You two close?"

"Yeah. But nothing will ever come of it."

"Because y'all are too different?"

Because of a lot of things. And because she was Amish. And because there was a very good possibility that he was going to be killed sooner rather than later. Or that he would become so tainted by what he did and saw that he wouldn't ever want to expose her to that person. "Yeah. Because of that."

"Well, she's really pretty."

"Yeah. She is really pretty."

His father gazed at him for a long moment, then pulled out a key ring and pressed a button. A sharp, shrill beep sounded. "Car's unlocked. Let's get to it, boys. And Chris?"

"Yes, sir?"

"Watch your stitches. I don't want your girl upset with us."

"I don't want her upset, either, especially since she's the one who sewed me up."

Mike's eyebrows rose. "No way."

"Way. It was pretty intense," he said. Thinking that that was probably the most honest thing he'd said since his family had arrived.

As the men brought in things, Beth took Mrs. Hart—Meredith, she insisted—and Becca on a brief tour of Frannie's inn.

"Are you sure it's not going to put you out if we stay here with you?" Becca asked.

"Yes, we'd be happy to pay for the rooms," Meredith added.

"I wouldn't even know how to go about charging you. But I have a feeling Frannie would want you to stay here as her guests. Each of you will have to pick your rooms."

"I think we're all going to want to be as close to Chris as possible." She rolled her eyes. "I suppose you think I'm being silly."

After sharing a quick smile with Becca, Beth

shook her head. "Not at all. I think your visit is *wunderbaar.*"

"Wunderbaar," Meredith repeated. "Oh, I like that word. What does it mean?"

"Ah, something really, really *gut.*"

Meredith nodded. "That is exactly how this visit feels."

Below them, the door opened with a shove and a bit of groaning. "Mom?" one of the men called out. "Mom, what do you want to do with everything?"

Becca groaned. "They can be so helpless. Meredith, you stay here. I'll go deal with them."

"No, I think I had better see if I can help." Turning to Beth, she smiled. "Come on, dear, you'll need to show us where the kitchen is."

And so it began. In no time at all, a completely cooked turkey and ham were in the kitchen, covered casseroles littered the countertops, and three more of the guest rooms were occupied.

Chris's family was a unique combination of gregariousness and good manners. They were loud and teased a bit, though Beth noticed that each of them kept taking quiet, searching looks at Chris.

For his part, Beth thought he seemed a little skittish and unsure. Seeing him this way was somewhat of a surprise to Beth. Even when he was lying on the floor and bleeding he'd emanated a kind of masculine confidence that made her feel like nothing fazed him.

204 • Shelley Shepard Gray

Now, as his brothers teased him, he looked as if he was having to try extra hard to be the kind of man they wanted to see.

When he darted upstairs, supposedly to get something from his room, she took a chance and followed him.

Her heart went out to him when she saw him sitting on the side of his bed, his head resting in his hands. She was standing there, watching him, debating whether to keep him company or leave him in peace, when he spoke.

"I'm pretty pathetic, huh?"

"Not at all."

"I feel pathetic. Here my whole family has come to see me and I hardly know what to say to them." He raised his head, and the pain that was buried in his gaze almost took her breath away. "It's like it's become easier for me to talk to drug addicts and degenerates than my own flesh and blood."

"Maybe it is," she murmured.

He nodded, not disputing what she'd said. "Why is that?"

"It's hard to meet expectations. I feel that way with my *mamm* sometimes. She sees me as the daughter who hasn't married, who spends too much time watching other people's *kinner*." With a wry smile, she brushed a hand over her dress. "I haven't even accepted my faith. I haven't been baptized yet. I know I'm a disappointment to her in a lot of ways."

"You could never be that. Beth, you've taken care of her for years. You take care of everyone."

"That's been easy. It's easier to try to help other people and fix their needs than to focus on mine." She took a breath, then dived in. "Maybe that is what you've been doing, too, Chris. You've been playing a part, sacrificing your soul and your body for the greater good. And though that's commendable, it also makes it a little bit easier to ignore your own needs."

Standing up, he walked to the mirror over the dresser, grabbed a towel he'd left on a chair and rubbed it over his face. When he dropped the towel, she was tempted to smooth back his hair, ease the lines that were tightening around his mouth.

But since that would be too personal, too tempting, she eased him with words. "They are good people, Chris. Give them a chance to know you again."

"What if they don't like the person I've become?"

"How could they not? You've become a mighty *gut* man, Christopher Hart."

Little by little the stress eased from his face, only to be replaced by a look of sadness. "How am I going to leave you tomorrow?"

She didn't know how she was going to survive watching him leave once again. Her mouth went

206 • *Shelley Shepard Gray*

dry as she ran out of optimistic platitudes. "I don't know," she said quietly.

When she heard footsteps, she turned quickly and opened the hall's linen closet and clumsily pulled a trio of white towels into her arms. Just in the nick of time, too.

"Beth, I hope you aren't going to any trouble for us," Meredith said as she got closer.

"Not at all. I was just getting you some fresh towels."

"Have you seen Chris?"

Beth pointed to the open room directly across from her. "He's right here."

Meredith smiled weakly at her, then walked into his room. "Christopher, are you okay?"

"I'm great, Mom."

Beth quickly turned away and walked down the hall before she eavesdropped any more. She hoped the good Lord would shine on Chris and his family and help them connect in a way that would encourage them all.

Just as she hoped He would give her the comfort that she needed to let Chris leave.

Chapter 21

*What's so special about Christmas? About this Christ-
mas? Why, everything, of course.*

MEREDITH HART

His mother acted as if there was nothing unusual
about her sitting next to him on his bed. Just like
she used to do when he was in middle school, she
grabbed one of his pillows and propped it on her lap,
hugging it close.

Then sat quietly for a moment.

And just like back when he was thirteen, he slowly
let himself lean against her. She smelled like she
always had—a mixture of familiar perfume and
soap. And something else that he could never put
his finger on; it was simply, essentially, Mom.

It didn't matter that he was twenty-nine or sitting
in a guest bedroom of an Amish bed-and-breakfast.

At last, he'd come home.

"Care to tell me how you're really feeling?" his mother asked after another long moment.

"Not really, but I will."

"Ah, reluctant honesty," she teased. "I know that well."

Yep, if there had been something he and his brothers had never been good at, it was lying to his mother. But that didn't mean it had always come easy. When they were teenagers, she'd become adept at wrangling out the truth, one morsel at a time.

"Mom, it's really good to see you and Dad, but I have to be honest with you—it's thrown me for a loop."

"Should we have stayed away?"

"No. It's not that. I love seeing you."

"But—"

"But I'm embarrassed." He shrugged. "Here you haven't seen me in years, and I'm hiding out in the middle of Crittenden County. My face is multicolored, I've got bruises everywhere."

"Not to mention your tattoos and long hair."

"I'm not the boy you raised."

"Maybe not. But it sure seems like you've become a man to be proud of, though." Reaching out, she smoothed a wrinkle from his shirt. "It's hard to believe that you've been undercover so long, fighting so many bad things. It's a wonder you haven't been hurt worse."

"I've been careful."

"Are you sure you have to leave tomorrow?"

"Yeah. I do."

"I'm going to miss you." She squeezed that pillow a little harder.

"I'm going to miss you, too." So much. So much that it hurt.

She blinked rapidly, clearing her throat. "What about Beth?" She lifted a hand, stopping any sort of objection on his part. "And don't you start telling me that she's nothing to you. I may not be a DEA agent, but even I can tell when two people care about each other."

"I love her." There. He'd admitted it.

"And how does she feel?"

"She feels the same way."

"And there's nothing you can do about it?"

"You've seen her, Mom. She's pretty much perfect. I am definitely not."

"What if she wants you and not perfection?"

"I don't want to ruin her life. She needs someone different." Someone who wasn't very likely to be killed in the near future, he added silently.

"I see." After carefully setting his pillow back in its place, she stood up. "We better go see your father and brothers. I'm sure they're going to wonder where you've been hiding."

"Thanks for coming up here. And for listening."

210 • *Shelley Shepard Gray*

She curled her hand in the crook of his elbow, just as if he were escorting her down the aisle at a formal affair. "Chris? One last thing."

"What is that?"

"It's been my experience not to try to live other people's lives. It was hard to let you go on your way. To let you do things we never raised you to do. It was hard. But we were stronger than we thought."

"And?"

"Perhaps you need to let Beth be strong, too. She's going to do what she wants. You need to be strong enough to let her make the decisions. Don't make them for her, Christopher."

"I hear you."

Now the only question was what to do about it.

Ever since they'd returned from the prison, Jacob had felt listless and depressed. He felt bad about it. After all, he knew Deborah was suffering in her own way.

She was missing Perry, and even if she wasn't exactly missing the person he'd become, he knew she was missing the person he could have been. The brother she'd grown up with.

As always, it didn't escape his notice that the loss was entirely his and his father's fault.

But still, he was dealing with his own grief. It was hard to see his father in that environment. Hard to come to terms with this new reality that was theirs. Imagining what his father's life was like in prison was no comparison to how it really had been.

After walking through the empty store to make sure everything was as it should be, he wandered back into their home and found Deborah making a cake in the kitchen.

She looked charming. A swipe of flour was smudged across her cheek. He picked up a dishcloth and carefully wiped it away.

She froze at his touch. "What's wrong?"

"Nothing. Merely a bit of flour that didn't make it into your mixing bowl." He set the cloth down, then clasped his hands together. Otherwise he knew he'd be tempted to brush her face with his fingers. Anything to relieve the worried expression in her eyes. "I didn't think we were going to cook today."

"I wasn't planning to cook."

"But?"

"But I felt like I needed to do something."

"Deborah, did visiting the prison upset you? I know it was a scary place. Should I have gone to visit my father without you?"

She set down her wooden spoon, left it in the batter where it slowly sank. "I'm not upset with you, Jacob. After all, it was my idea to visit your *daed*. I've pushed and prodded and begged you to do this for months."

"You did prod and push and I'm grateful. I am. But it was hard to see my father in his prison uniform. It seemed to make the pain of what our family's gone through fresh again."

"I felt the same way. I had pushed so much of it away, I'd almost forgotten what Aaron must be going through." She looked down at her batter, fiddled with the spoon for a bit, then eyed him again. "May I be honest?"

"That's the only way I want you to ever be with me."

"Part of me has been glad he's been in prison. Even though him being in jail wouldn't bring my brother back, I didn't want him here, living his life while Perry was buried in the ground." She winced as she said the last few words. "I'm sorry. You must think I'm full of vengeance."

"I don't think you're like that." Unable to resist, he reached out and pulled him to her, then gently tilted her chin up to meet his gaze. "I could never think that."

"Sure?"

"Positive. I've felt that way, too. But now I hate to think of him suffering."

"Me, too."

"So, Deborah, do you wish we would have stayed home? Do you blame me for ruining our first Christmas together?"

"It's not our first Christmas together. We've seen

each other many times over the years, and I imagine, God willing, that we'll be able to spend this blessed day together for many years in the future."

Her words were sweet. But they hadn't answered his question. Not really.

He'd known Deborah all his life. Sweet Deborah, so strong, yet so timid in so many ways. She was giving him a way out. Glossing over her own discomfort so he wouldn't be hurt anymore.

But he loved her too much to continue in that vein. And so he pressed. "Deborah, how are you feeling?"

"Oh, I'm sad. And worried about you. And, to a certain extent, a little angry."

"Angry?"

Looking chagrined, she said, "Do you ever look around at some of the other families in our town and wonder why God decided that your family couldn't be like them?"

"What do you mean?"

"Why did I have to have a brother like Perry? Why did I get a selfish, drug-dealing brother? I would have loved to have had a relationship with him like Lydia has with her brother. Why do my parents still insist on mourning him, so much so that I often feel like an afterthought in their lives?"

"I don't know those answers. Perhaps He gave you a family like that because He knew you would be strong enough to bear their burdens," he said softly.

Taking care with each word, he added, "You know what I've decided? Christmas is bigger than all of us. It's bigger than dinners or stockings or trips to the mall. It's bigger than fancy meals and even visits to see family.

"At the heart of it, it's all about a baby. It's all about God coming to us in our form. It's about miracles and promises and faith. It's about finding peace in a life that isn't too peaceful. About finding peace in a world that isn't always good or perfect or fair."

Quietly, he finished. "And that is what Christmas is to me. I don't need gifts or presents or music. I just need to remember what it is all about. I need to remember what is important. And, you, Deborah are mighty important to me. You will get through this, you are strong enough to get through it all just fine."

"Do you think I'm strong, Jacob?" She bit her lip, then blurted. "Really?"

He took her hands. "I think you are the strongest person I've ever met, Deborah."

Little by little, her worried expression eased and her lips tilted upward slightly. "I love you."

"I love you more." Gesturing to the batter, he said, "How can I help?"

"Jacob, you can't help me cook."

"Sure I can. Cooking makes you happy and being with you makes me happy. Therefore I will cook, too."

She laughed. "Get out a cake pan, then, husband. We'll make a cake, and then maybe even some sandwiches and soup."

"And after our supper, I want to sit with you in front of the fire and give thanks."

"That sounds like the perfect way to spend the rest of our Christmas."

Chapter 22

Jesus was born in a manger because there was no room at the inn, you see.

BETH BYLER

Beth had acted like a coward and had stayed on the sidelines.

Oh, she'd smiled and chatted to his brothers and parents. But Beth didn't need to be older or wiser to know that it was far more important for them all to get to spend time with Chris.

More than once he'd looked at her, almost said her name. But then he would get pulled into yet another conversation and that moment would be forgotten.

After a lovely supper and many laughs in the kitchen while everyone insisted on helping clean up, Beth said she was tired and went to her room.

She didn't get ready for bed, though. Instead, she wrapped a quilt around herself, sat in the big, cushy chair near the window, and looked out at the moon-light glistening on the snow.

When she heard the light tapping at her door, she almost didn't answer it. But then her wish for the day to last a little longer outlasted any desire to observe propriety.

As she'd feared and expected, Chris was at the door.

She opened it a crack. "Chris, do you need something?"

"Yeah, I wanted to talk to you."

"Now?"

"Yes, now."

She shouldn't let him in, but where he was concerned, she had no choice. Not really. "What will your parents say?"

"Nothing, because I don't intend for them to see me visiting you in the middle of the night."

"Come in, then."

Chris came in, closed the door behind him, and then leaned against it. "What a day, huh?"

"Yes. It's been a *wonderful-gut* day."

"The best."

It hadn't been one of the best for her. She'd been too aware of his impending departure to be completely happy. But she did know that it was one of his best days. "Yes."

"I owe all of it to you."

"You owe it to yourself, Chris. You are a *gut* man. You are a very good man. Your family loves you, as they should."

"I don't want tomorrow to come. I don't want to leave them, or leave you. I don't want to leave this life."

She sat on the side of the bed and tried to imagine what it must be like to leave one's identity behind. Especially to leave one's identity behind in order to adopt such a bad one. "Is it hard, becoming a criminal?"

He smiled. "Yeah. I used to kind of like it. It was an adrenaline rush. Constantly being on edge, living in fear. Plus, I knew I was good at it. Not everyone can be so good at pretending to be bad."

"I imagine not." She couldn't help but smile at the thought of trying to assume someone else's personality.

"But Beth, now? I'm dreading it. I don't want to continue to be someone I've grown to hate, not even if it's to the benefit of the greater good."

"I'm dreading your leaving, too. And hating the thought of you having to give yourself up again."

"You are?"

"Chris, I meant what I said this morning. I've fallen in love with you. Even though we're not meant to be together, there's a part of me that's always hoped that we could."

"If I had you, I couldn't live this way. I couldn't live in hiding. I'd be too worried about you. I'd want to always be with you."

"Truly?"

"Definitely."

"I'd want to always be with you, too."

"Beth, tell me, why haven't you joined the church yet? Have you ever thought about not being Amish?"

"I love my faith. I love my way of life. But these past few days made me realize that I haven't completely embraced it. I've enjoyed my English babies and families. And with everything with my mother, I've needed to be a part of that world, too. I guess I've always had one foot in another world."

"Do you think we'd have a chance together?"

Hope filled her, but she forced herself to tamp it down. "How would we even know if we did have a chance? You're leaving."

"You're right." He cleared his throat. "I guess I just wanted to take a second and tell you thank you. For taking me in. And calling my family. For making this a Christmas that I'll always remember."

"You're welcome."

"Well, I guess . . ." His voice caught but he stumbled on. "I guess I'll head off to bed. Good night."

As he quietly opened and shut the door behind him, she lay down on the bed and cried.

The knock on the door came before eight in the morning.

Still feeling protective over Beth, Chris opened the door with a jerk, then felt his stomach drop when he realized it was Taylor. "You're here already?"

"Yep." In typical Taylor fashion, she walked right in, her manner as no-nonsense as ever. When her phone beeped, she lowered her head to read the message, talking at the same time. "How long are you going to take? I've got to get you out to St. Louis, dump you in a halfway house, and try to get back to watch my sister's kid's wrestling match."

"St. Louis, huh?"

Taylor was busy texting on her phone. "Yep. I'll fill you in on the drive." Glancing up, she looked at Chris critically. Then her eyes widened a bit. "Chris, look at you. I haven't seen you look this good in months."

He knew she wasn't joking. "Thanks," he said as he fingered the still fading bruise on his cheek.

"Listen, don't take a shower. You're supposed to be down on your luck."

"Sorry; all my clothes are clean."

"Don't worry. I've got the clothes you'll be wearing in the car." She wrinkled her nose. "They're pretty ripe."

Slowly, Chris became aware of the crowd of people behind him. All in sweats or jeans or robes and pajamas, everyone looking at his partner with somber expressions.

Taking in the crowd, Taylor looked slightly chagrined, like she suddenly remembered that she was
supposed to have better manners. "Hey."

Out of the crowd walked Beth. As usual, she
looked perfect. Neat as a pin. And completely welcoming.

"Won't you come in for a little while? May I make
you some breakfast? Or pour you a cup of coffee at
least?"

Taylor's eyes widened as she shoved her phone
into a pocket of her wool coat. "Oh. You know what,
thanks. Who are you?"

Taylor had always had the manners of a guinea
pig. "This is Beth," Chris answered. "She's . . ." His
voice drifted off as he realized that there was only
one answer. "She's my girlfriend."

Beth froze.

As did his family.

But Taylor? She just looked amused. "Yeah, right.
You don't date, Hart."

"I do now."

"Besides, she's Amish. I've seen them on TV."

Chris knew his partner well enough to know
that she wasn't trying to be rude or dismissive.
That was just how she was. She thought about
work, that was it.

But as he watched her check her messages once
again, he knew he couldn't go with her. He didn't

want to go put on smelly clothes, live in a halfway house and assume yet another fake identity.

He couldn't walk away from everyone in the room who meant so much to him.

Turning to Beth, he said, "I wanted to ask you this last night but I didn't know how. Would you start over with me?"

Her gaze met his with utter confusion. "I don't understand."

"I don't want to become another person. I don't want to do things I'm embarrassed about, say things I don't mean. Be a person my family is afraid of. But most of all, I don't want to be alone. I want to be with you, Beth."

Not giving her a chance to argue or protest, he reached for her shaking hands, then wrapped his hands around her waist. "I'm better with you," he murmured. "Please, let me be with you."

As she stood there stunned, obviously shaken, he started talking faster. Eager to say or promise whatever it took to make her his. "Beth, I'll live here with you and your mom. Or I can get a job somewhere and she can live with us. I don't care what we do, or where we'll be. As long as I get to be me, and that I'll get to call you mine."

Her facial expressions had gone from stunned to amazed to joyous to teary. "Chris—"

"Chris? What is going on?" Taylor blurted.

"Looks like you'll be leaving on your own, ma'am," Kevin rasped from his spot next to the stairwell.

Ignoring everyone else, Chris looked directly into her eyes. "Beth? What do you say?"

To his surprise, she pulled out of his embrace and slowly looked at his family behind him. Glanced at Taylor. Then finally reached up to him and rested one hand on his cheek. Right in the spot that was still swollen and black and blue.

"Yes," she whispered. "Oh yes."

Chris smiled. He ached to kiss her. He ached to pull her into his arms and tell her in a thousand ways how much she meant to him.

But all he did was raise his hand and place it over Beth's on his cheek. Keeping it in place. "Taylor, I won't be going with you."

Though her phone was buzzing again, she ignored it. "You can't just quit the DEA," she said, her voice incredulous.

"Sure he can," his father boomed. "Now come and get some breakfast."

Taylor kept looking around at the lot of them, just like she'd entered a crazy house. "I don't want to interrupt—"

"We insist," Kevin said, ushering Mike, Becca, and their parents into the kitchen. "Haven't you heard? It's Christmas. Join us."

And Taylor, his tough, heroic, somewhat reserved

partner, melted a bit and smiled. "You know what? Thanks. I . . . I'd love to join y'all."

When they were finally alone, Chris gathered Beth close and held her tight. "You, Beth Byler, are a miracle worker. You've changed my life in ways that I didn't think possible."

"It wasn't so hard. All I had to do was say yes."

He laughed. She was right. All it really took was a will to change, and change did occur.

Right there in Amish Country. In a tiny, bright yellow inn. On a beautiful, very special, very blessed Christmas.

Epilogue

New Year's Day

Beth Byler shifted her tote bag into her right hand before opening the door to Schrock's Variety Store.

The store was officially closed for the holiday, but Jacob and Deborah had decided to host a party for their friends. Actually, they'd wanted to host the party in their home behind the store. It had been Walker Anderson who'd asked that the location be changed.

"Beth, you finally made it," Frannie called out from one of the brightly painted rocking chairs that they'd arranged in a circle at the front of the store.

Leave it to Frannie to never hold her tongue. "I'm not that late," she said as she set her tote bag down next to a card table laden with food.

"Thirty minutes late." Her face breaking into a bright grin, she said, "Care to tell us the reason?"

Trying to ignore everyone's chuckles, Beth shrugged off her coat and hung it on one of the half dozen coat racks out for sale. "Chris called." For a moment, she tried to act nonchalant about her new relationship, but she quickly gave up the fight. Looking around the room, she met all of her friends' smiles as she felt her cheeks heat. "Chris wanted to tell me happy New Year. He's up in Chicago, you know."

Giving her a quick hug, Lydia said, "I bet that wasn't all he wanted to tell you."

Beth smiled. It wasn't. Chris had given her an update on how his last days of working for the DEA were going, and how his recent phone conversations with his parents had gone.

And then he'd told her how much he loved her.

"When will you see him again?" Walker asked, coming to stand by his fiancée.

"Hopefully next week. He said he'll be done with his work soon, then he's going to spend a few days with his parents and brothers. After that, he'll head out here to Crittenden County."

"He's going to stay at the inn," Frannie announced, looking very pleased.

"He's looking forward to it," Beth said.

Thinking about their plans, Beth let her mind drift once again. Chris was going to stay at the inn while she was going to be at home with her mother. But they'd already planned lots of things to do. Beth was mighty sure they'd spend every moment they could together.

Though they hadn't talked about marriage yet, she knew Chris well enough to suspect he was ready to broach the subject.

"I'm anxious to see him . . . and eager for you all to get to know him." Turning to Deborah, she winked. "But at the moment, I'm more anxious to see how Jacob is doing."

Jacob, who had been busy pouring sodas, paused. "What are you talking about?"

Deborah looped her arm around Jacob's elbow. "Beth's wondering what you think about our new *hund*."

His eyebrows rose. "What dog?"

"This one," Luke said, coming out from the back with a beautiful Irish setter. "Jacob, meet Ireland."

Beth stood next to Frannie and Lydia as Jacob stared at the dog in shock.

"Where did he come from?"

Luke rolled his eyes. "It's a *she*, Jacob. She's a rescue. Someone dumped her on the side of the road, and one of the patrolmen at our station found her shivering in the snow."

"She was abandoned? That's terrible." Jacob walked closer to her, slowly held out his hand for the dog to sniff. Ireland sniffed his hand carefully, as she stared at him with a wary expression in her dark brown eyes. They softened when he gently patted her.

When her tail started to wag slowly, Luke stepped

away, letting Jacob and the dog get to know each other.

Still petting her, he said, "I don't understand why you brought her to me."

"It's for the store, you see," Frannie said. "Everyone misses the animals. Since you don't want to sell pets, we thought she could come to work with you each day."

Deborah crouched down next to Ireland and petted her, too. "When Luke and Frannie called me about Ireland, I thought it would be the perfect solution. Folks could come in, see us, and see the dog, too. But she wouldn't be all the work that your father's pets for sale were."

Still hardly looking away from the dog, Jacob said, "It's a *gut* idea, for sure. But I don't know if we need a pet, or if the store does."

"Trust me," said Walker. "The store does."

"How about this?" Deborah asked. "Maybe it doesn't matter if you need her or not." Gesturing at the dog, who now was lying down on a little rug, looking happy and at peace, she said, "I think she needs you. Is that enough?"

As Jacob pondered that, Beth looked at their little group. At Frannie and Luke, at Lydia and Walker, at Jacob and Deborah, too.

Then, she smiled a bit, realizing that very soon she, too, would be a part of a couple.

Her friends were *wunderbaar*. Surely, some of the best friends in the world. The friends who had been there for one another through thick and thin.

And she realized that Deborah had made a very good point—they all needed one another.

Luckily, Jacob Schrock agreed. "Deborah, you're exactly right. Needing to be needed? Needing to be loved? It's more than enough for me," he said. "It is more than enough for anyone, I think. I do believe I have a new dog."

Pleased about Jacob's decision, Beth knew exactly the right thing to say to break up their serious moment. "Who's hungry?" she asked. Pointing to her tote bag, she smiled brightly. "Guess what? I brought snacks."

As expected, her announcement brought a chorus of groans and more than a few derisive jokes. And a whole lot of laughter.

Soon, Beth knew they'd all be having babies, and most likely she and Chris would be moving somewhere else.

Who knew what else the Lord had planned for them?

All she did know was that this moment was just about perfect. They were happy and healthy, and had each found someone who needed and loved them. They had found *peace*.

And that, indeed, was good enough.

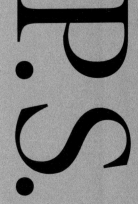

About the author

About the book

Read on

Insights,
Interviews
& More . . .

Meet
Shelley Shepard Gray

The New Studio

I GREW UP IN HOUSTON, TEXAS, went to Colorado for college, and after living in Arizona, Dallas, and Denver, we moved to southern Ohio about ten years ago.

I've always thought of myself as a very hard worker, but not "great" at anything. I've obtained a bachelor's and master's degree . . . but I never was a gifted student. I took years of ballet and dance, but I never was anywhere near the star of any recital. I love to cook, but I'm certainly not close to being gourmet . . . and, finally, I love to write books, but I've certainly read far better authors.

Maybe you are a little bit like me. I've been married for almost twenty years and have raised two kids. I try to exercise but really should put on my tennis shoes a whole lot more. I'm not a great housekeeper, I hate to drive in the snow, and I don't think I've ever won a Monopoly game. However, I am the best wife and mother I know how to be.

Isn't it wonderful to know that in God's eyes that is okay? That from His point of view, we are all exceptional? I treasure that knowledge and am always so thankful for my faith. His faith in me makes me stand a little straighter, smile a little bit more, and be so very grateful for every gift He's given me.

I started writing about the Amish because their way of life appealed to me. I wanted to write stories about regular, likeable people in extraordinary situations—and who just happened to be Amish.

Getting the opportunity to write inspirational novels is truly gratifying. With every book, I feel my faith grows stronger. And that makes me feel very special indeed. ∾

Letter from the Author

Dear Reader,

Have you ever spent a Christmas that wasn't all that festive? That was our Christmas in 2012. After my twenty-year-old daughter suffered through a series of increasingly bad bouts of strep throat, it was decided that her tonsils needed to come out during Christmas break.

She had the procedure on December 14, right after she finished finals. We had been warned that the recovery might not be easy for her. In truth, it was very difficult. As the days passed and we all grew exhausted, I stopped thinking about Christmas and only thought about taking care of her.

She was better by Christmas Eve, but only marginally so. My husband, son, and I went to church on Christmas Eve but came home directly afterward since my daughter was still in too much pain for us to leave her alone at the house for long.

On Christmas morning we opened the presents that I had bought months before, wrapped, and put under the tree. Then my son left for his girlfriend's house—her family was hosting a lovely dinner. Tom and I? We ate soup and sandwiches and continued to hope and pray that our daughter would feel better soon. And then . . . right around New Year's Day, she did. Just in time to go back to college.

After she left, I put away the decorations and reflected on the holiday. For a moment, I was even tempted to call it the Christmas That Wasn't! And then I remembered that Christmas isn't about parties and being around lots of people. Or about perfect decorations or lovely meals. It really is all about remembering a baby being born in a lowly manger . . . and everyone celebrating the miracle of His birth.

I have a feeling we might always remember the Christmas of 2012 with a bit of fondness and maybe a grimace, too. I know I never want to open a can of Campbell's chicken noodle soup again! But I bet years from now Tom and I will probably smile when we remember that that Christmas reminded us that the holiday is really all about love and faith and hope. Last Christmas we certainly had those in abundance! If those things are present, not much else is needed.

I sincerely hope you enjoyed *Peace*. I loved writing about two couples experiencing a somewhat difficult Christmas Day, and becoming happier and stronger because of it.

Wherever you are, I hope you will have a Merry Christmas! And if it doesn't happen to be quite so "merry," I hope you will find comfort in celebrating the joy of His birth!

With my thanks to you,
Shelley Shepard Gray ∾

Questions for Discussion

1. At the beginning of the novel, Chris reveals that he came to the Yellow Bird Inn because he had nowhere else to go. Do you think this is correct? Should he have gone somewhere else? Or, do you think he came to the Yellow Bird Inn for a far different reason?

2. At first glance, Beth Byler seems to be an extremely sheltered young Amish lady. But what experiences has she faced that might have prepared her for a relationship with a DEA agent?

3. How did you feel about Jacob's refusal to read his father's letters? Why do you think forgiving his father was so hard for him?

4. The visit to the prison was a life-changing event for everyone involved, certainly for both Jacob and Aaron. How do you imagine their relationship evolving? Have you ever had a rift in your family that you had to struggle to reconcile?

5. Beth's decision to contact Chris's family could have been a huge mistake. Chris's family could have been angry; it might even have brought more danger to their lives if their arrival put Chris is jeopardy. So, was it a mistake . . . or the right decision?

6. The two Christmases portrayed in the novel were definitely not the usual Christmas settings. Have you ever had an unusual Christmas? How did taking you out of your familiar setting allow you to see the gifts of the season in new ways?

7. Obviously, characters finding "peace" was a recurring theme throughout the novel. For each of the main characters, finding peace was not simple or easy, because they each had to overcome many emotional hurdles. Can you recall a time when you, too, had a hurdle to overcome?

8. Discuss how "Though he fall, he shall not be utterly cast down: for the Lord upholdeth him with His hand" (Psalms 37:24) relates to the characters in this book. ∽

A Sneak Peek of *Hopeful*
The First Book in Shelley Shepard Gray's New Series, *The Return to Sugarcreek*

SHE WAS LATE.

Holding her canvas tote bag in one hand and a box of oatmeal raisin cookies in the other, Miriam Zehr exited her house, darted down her street, turned left on Main Street, and almost ran down old Mr. Sommers.

With a grunt, he stepped to the side, his garden hose spraying a good bit of water onto her skirts before settling back onto his daffodils.

She skidded to a stop. "I'm sorry, Eli."

He merely raised one eyebrow. "Late again, Miriam?"

"*Jah.*" As discreetly as possible, she shook her blue apron and dress a bit. A few drops flew from the fabric, glinting in the morning sun.

He shook his head in exasperation. "One day you're going to injure someone with your haste."

She winced. "I know. And I am sorry, Eli."

Looking at the box in her hand, his voice turned wheedling. "Those cookies?"

"They're oatmeal raisin." When his eyes brightened, she set down her tote and carefully opened the box. "Care for one?"

After setting the hose down, he

8

reached in and pulled out two plump cookies. "Girl who cooks as *gut* as you should be married by now."

She'd heard the same refrain almost as often as she'd run late to work. "I've often thought the same thing," she said as she picked up her tote again. "But for now, I must be on my way."

"Have a care, now." He shook one arthritic finger at her. "Not everyone's as spry as me, you know."

"I'll be careful," she promised before continuing on her way to work.

Once at the Sugarcreek Inn, she would put on a crisp white apron, then divide her time between baking pies and serving the restaurant guests. The whole time, she'd do her best to smile brightly. Chat with customers and her coworkers. And pretend she didn't yearn for a different life.

But first, she had to do her best to get to work on time.

"Going pretty fast today, Miriam," Josh Graber called out from the front porch of his family's store. "How late are you?"

"Only five minutes. Hopefully."

He laughed. "Good luck. Stop by soon, wouldja? Gretta would love to see you."

"I'll do my best."

Now that the restaurant was finally in view, she slowed her pace and tried to catch her breath.

As she got closer, she forced herself to look at the building with a critical eye. There were places where the building needed a bit of touching up. A fresh coat of paint. One of the windowsills needed to be replaced. ▶

9

A Sneak Peek of *Hopeful* *(continued)*

The landscaping around the front door was a little shaggy, a little overgrown. It needed some sprucing up, a little tender loving care.

Kind of like herself, she supposed. Now that she was twenty-five, she was tired of biding her time, waiting in vain for something to happen.

Perhaps it really was time to think about doing something different. Going somewhere new. For too long now she'd been everyone's helper and assistant. She'd watch her best friends get courted, fall in love, and get married. Most were expecting their first babies. Some, like Josh and Gretta, already had two children.

Yes, it seemed like everyone had moved on with their lives except for her.

And the sad thing about that was there was no need to stay in Sugarcreek any longer. She had plenty of money saved and even her parents' blessing to go find her happiness.

So why hadn't she done anything yet? Was she afraid . . . or still holding out hope that a certain man would finally notice her and see that she was the perfect girl for him?

That she'd actually been the perfect one for years now?

Pushing aside that disturbing thought, she slipped inside and prepared to offer her excuses to Jana Kent, the proprietor.

Jana was just inside the front door, standing by a pair of bookshelves, unboxing more of the knickknacks she'd recently started selling in an attempt to drum up a bit more business and profit for the restaurant.

Her boss paused when she walked by. "Cutting it close today, Miriam."

Glancing up at the clock over the door, Miriam winced. It was ten after nine. Jana had long since given up on Miriam getting to work early or even on time. Now she merely hoped Miriam wouldn't be too late. "I know. I'm sorry."

"What's today's excuse?" Humor lit her eyes, telling Miriam that while Jana might feel exasperated, she wasn't mad.

Usually, Miriam came with an amusing story or fib. Over the years, earthquakes had erupted, washing machines had overflowed, and ravenous dogs had invaded her yard.

Today, however, her mind drew a complete blank. "Time simply got away from me this morning."

Jana looked almost disappointed. "That's it?"

Miriam shrugged weakly. "I'll come up with a better excuse tomorrow, I'm sure of it."

"Miriam Zehr. You are one of my best employees and one of my hardest workers. You always offer to help other people, and you never mind staying late. Why is it so hard for you to get here on time?"

There were all kinds of reasons. Miriam wasn't a morning person. She seemed to always sleep in. But deep ▶

11

down, she feared it was her somewhat irrational way to rebel against the continual routine of her life. Sometimes her frenetic morning's journey to work was the biggest excitement of her day.

Inching away, she mumbled, "I'll go put on my apron and get to work."

"Thank you, Miriam."

Hurrying toward the back, she scanned the tables. Quite a few were empty.

And then she noticed He was there. Junior Beiler. All six-foot-two inches of brawn and blond hair and perfection.

Junior, the object of too many of her daydreams. The boy she had a crush on. The man she yearned for to finally notice her.

Miriam kept walking, trying not to look his way. Trying not to stare. But she did. And as she did, she noticed that he was staring right back at her. More important, she was sure that something like interest glinted in his blue eyes.

Feeling her cheeks flush, she darted into the kitchen. But the moment the doors closed behind her, she let herself smile.

Maybe today, at long last, something would start to happen in her life.

The moment Junior Beiler saw the kitchen doors swing shut, he grinned at Joe. "You were right, Miriam Zehr works here. I just saw her walk by."

Joe looked around the restaurant dining room. "Are you sure?"

"I'm positive. She just went into the kitchen." Drumming his fingers on the table, he murmured, "I hope she comes out again soon."

Joe chuckled. "And when she does are you actually going to talk to her about what's been on your mind?"

"Absolutely." Noticing that his buddy's expression looked skeptical, he straightened his shoulders a bit. "What's wrong with that?"

"Junior, you can't just go asking women about their best friends and expect to get information."

"Why not?" It made perfect sense to him.

"A woman isn't going to give you information if she doesn't know you."

Junior scoffed. As usual, Joe was making too big a deal over nothing. "I've known Miriam for years. We both have, Joe."

"*Jah*, we went to school with her, that's true. And we're all in the same church district, too. But let me ask you this, when was the last time you actually talked to her?"

"I'm pretty sure I said hello to her at church last Sunday."

Joe tilted his head slightly. "Did you? Or did you walk right by her like you usually do?"

For the first time, Junior felt vaguely uncomfortable. He was one of eight kids, and he was sandwiched between two girls in his family. Because of that, he'd ▶

learned a thing or two about the female mind over the years. "I might have only thought about saying hello," he said grudgingly.

Joe looked triumphant. "See?"

Okay, Joe probably had a point. But his inattentiveness didn't mean he didn't like Miriam. He just had never thought about her much.

Until he realized she was best friends with Mary Kate Hershberger. Beautiful Mary Kate Hershberger.

Joe grabbed another hot biscuit from the basket on the table and began slathering it with peanut-butter spread. "I still think you should get your sister Kaylene to introduce you. After all, Mary Kate is Kaylene's teacher."

"*Nee.* Kaylene is having trouble in school." Lowering her voice, he said, "Actually, I'm not even all that certain Kaylene likes Mary Kate."

"Don't see why that matters."

"It just does." His youngest sister was eight years old, and the apple of his eye. There was no way he was going to use little Kaylene in order to get a date.

"Why?"

Luckily, the kitchen doors swung open again, and out came Miriam. She had on a white apron now, and was holding a coffeepot in her right hand. Seizing his chance, he turned his coffee cup right side up, waited until she was looking his way, and motioned her over.

Joe raised his brows. "Impressive," he muttered.

When she got to their table, her cheeks were flushed. *"Kaffi?"*

"Jah. For both of us, please."

After she'd filled both their cups, Joe gave him a little kick.

Thinking quickly, Junior asked, "So, Miriam, how have you been?"

She looked a bit startled by the question. "Me? I've been just fine. Why do you ask?"

"No reason. It's just that, well . . . I mean, I haven't seen you around lately."

She looked at him curiously. "Where have you been looking?"

"Nowhere. I mean, I guess I haven't seen you anywhere but at church. And here," he added, feeling like a fool.

Joe groaned as he took another bit of biscuit.

"Why were you looking? Did you need something?" Miriam asked.

His tongue was starting to feel like it was too big for his mouth. "Actually, ah . . . yes!" Seizing the opportunity, he added, "I've been wanting to talk to you about something."

She set the coffeepot right on the table. "You have?"

"Yes. When do you get off work? Can I stop by?"

"You want to come by my house? Tonight?" Her cheeks pinkened.

"I do. May I come over?" ▶

"You may . . . if you'd like. I'll be off work at four."

"*Gut.* I'll stop over around six."

"Do you need my address?"

"No, I know where you live. I'll see you then."

Miriam picked up the coffeepot, smiled shyly, then walked on.

When they were alone again, Junior picked up his coffee cup and took a fortifying sip. "That wasn't so hard."

"That wasn't so *gut.*"

"Really?"

Joe leaned back in his chair and folded his arms across his chest. "You, Junior, are an idiot."

"What are you talking about? I'm going to go over to Miriam's house tonight and talk to her about Mary Kate. It's a might *gut* plan. Perfect."

After making sure Miriam wasn't nearby to overhear, Joe hissed, "Miriam doesna think you're coming over to ask about Mary Kate. She thinks you're going courting. This is not good, Junior."

Warily, Junior glanced in the direction Joe was looking and spied Miriam.

Noticed that she was standing near the hostess station. Her light brown eyes were bright. She was smiling softly.

Meeting her gaze, he felt his neck flush.

He had a sudden feeling that Joe was right. And that was not good. Definitely not good at all. ∾

16

TAKE IT TO THE PEOPLE

Take It
to the People

New Ways in Soul Winning—
Unconventional Evangelism

Howard E. Mumma

THE WORLD PUBLISHING COMPANY
NEW YORK AND CLEVELAND

Published by The World Publishing Company
2231 West 110th Street, Cleveland, Ohio 44102
Published simultaneously in Canada by Nelson, Foster
& Scott Ltd.

First Printing—February, 1969

Manufactured at World Publishing Press, a division
of The World Publishing Company, Cleveland, Ohio.

Library of Congress Catalog Card Number: 68-26844

PRINTED IN THE UNITED STATES OF AMERICA

For
Elizabeth
and
the girls —
Sally, Julie, Kathy

Foreword

BOOKS have sundry beginnings. This one was born out of the vision and the will to bring the Christian message to people where they are. People are on the move particularly in the summer time. Religion must catch up with them wherever they go. These are the facts from which this book emerges.

It all began because of the fact that in the summer people defect from the church to the brookside, the lake, the amusement park, the drag race, the drive-in, or the front porch. The elect—the churchgoers—as well as the indifferent join the dispersion.

Unconventional Evangelism began with a religious service in a drive-in theater early Sunday morning—a simple service, a brief, straightforward message, an appeal to commitment. The idea worked. In one place 40 per cent of those attending such a service had not been going to church.

The idea grew, the movement spread, the Unconventional Evangelism began to function in state parks, at county fairs and on the beach. People listened and liked what they heard. What's more, they were challenged by the message. Many of them enlisted in the work of the Kingdom.

There are four observations to be made about Unconventional Evangelism (someone called it "unfashionable evangelism"):

1. It turns the summer season into a thriving experience for religion.

2. It takes the message out of the pulpit to where people are.

3. It courageously invades the secular wilderness of the nonchurch population.

4. It compels the speaker to talk religious sense and reality.

The author, Howard E. Mumma, is not merely reporting a phenomenal venture; he brought this movement to a high and notable level of fruition. It was his enthusiasm that gave the enterprise its momentum. It was his devotion that made possible the training of hundreds of ministers and laymen to do this work adequately. He has led the way in the accomplishment of a mobile gospel for a mobile people.

BISHOP HAZEN G. WERNER

Contents

Introduction

EVANGELISM has never been easy to define. There has always been considerable confusion, vagueness and frustration on the subject. Denominational leaders hold divergent views on the meaning of evangelism, and many laymen look with suspicion on the word.

With all its troubles and advantages, "evangelism" is a very old and familiar Christian word. Its roots touch upon New Testament documents, and Greek everyday use before that. Through the years it has acquired shallow and distasteful connotations, but it has somehow managed to rise above and survive the distortions. Every denomination is now convinced that evangelism is far from being a specialty of professionals or an elective in the purpose of the church. It is, rather, the central and supreme mission of the church. The church is here to evangelize the world, to make Christ known to all men.

In the words of the Madras Foreign Missions Council: "Evangelism is to present Christ Jesus in the power of the Holy Spirit so that men shall come to put their trust in God through Him, to accept Him as their Savior, and serve Him as their King, in the fellowship of His Church."

What do these words mean? They do not mean that
men are to organize their religious life exclusively around
a personal encounter with Jesus Christ, which gives them
assurance of forgiveness and renewal, yet permits them
to ignore the issues of community life. Evangelism so
defined implies that society can be saved only by saving
individual souls. Corrupt morals, crooked politics and
evil social customs then will automatically correct themselves. This is simply not so.

On the other hand, the Madras statement does not
mean we can define evangelism exclusively in terms of
correcting social issues. Some highly energetic people
want to center their Christianity exclusively on the great
social wrongs of modern life. This reduces religious
faith to a purely social and philanthropic concern. It
may lead to a humanism that holds positive ethical
values, nevertheless it is agnostic.

Finally, evangelism must never be equated with
church membership. Some have defined evangelism primarily as a verbal surrender to Christ. A proposition is
accepted (such as "Jesus Christ is Lord"), a card signed,
a prayer said—and a church receives a new member.
True evangelism must mean far more than this.

Basically, evangelism should be seen as the work of
God. Past, present and future, God came and yet comes
in Christ to save men from their sins. He gives to men the
gift of salvation through trust, which establishes their
rightful relationship with Him.

Evangelism, then, begins with man's vision of the nature and activity of God. Evangelism is the Good (mar-
velous and unexpected) News that the God of our Lord
Jesus Christ is not dead, but is alive and essentially personal. He is a conscious Being who is intelligent, moral
and unselfishly interested in human beings and devoted
to their highest good. He is the living God who is in con-

stant relation to the world and the affairs of men. He is purposely acting and seeking that which is broken, separated and lost, and is attempting to bring life into a new pattern of meaning and wholeness. The God who is doing this in and through Jesus Christ and His church is the basis of all evangelistic work.

Basic, too, is the fact that when men have been saved by Jesus Christ they find themselves to be members of a fellowship whose chief calling is to proclaim His gospel. Such people have a message and a claim. They claim the world for Jesus Christ.

Such people live by the power of the Holy Spirit. They know and depend on the God who goes forth as life-giving Spirit, "The divine presence in our lives, whereby we are kept in perpetual remembrance of the truth of Christ and find strength and help in time of need." To Christians the reality of Christ is not simply a brief event in history. The Spirit affirms that God is continuously at work among men, leading them into new truth, strengthening, guiding and inspiring new life and hope.

But something more than vision and knowledge of God's work is needed to produce evangelists. There must be response, involvement, commitment and an active witness. This is produced by the inner compulsion to spread the Good News. Every Christian ought to have this knowledge and this experience so that he motivates men to take a decisive step, to choose sides, to choose Christ. Such "reached" people enter into a solemn covenant with God which makes everything different for them from the inside out, from their private meditations to the farthest reaches of their social relations, from now to eternity. *This is evangelism.* To such a task God is summoning the church anew today.

In conclusion, I wish to express my appreciation to several hundred ministers and laymen throughout the

United States who have helped write this book by sharing with me their experiences in evangelism. I am greatly indebted to Bishop Hazen G. Werner and the Rev. Lyle Schaller for their constant help and encouragement, and to Mrs. Dorothy Mallone for her help in typing the manuscript.

HOWARD MUMMA

Chagrin Falls, Ohio

1. Is Protestantism Failing to Reach People?

IT was intermission time at the drag strip on a Sunday afternoon in a little Minnesota town. Very unexpectedly the public address system blared out this unusual announcement: "For the next few minutes our friend, Bob Brown, will speak to you on the subject 'The Race of Life.'" Bob Brown, a drag-stripper, gave a simple testimony and his witness of what Christ meant to him. Every Sunday afternoon in the racing season Bob confronts the thousands attending or participating in the races and bears witness to his Christian faith, showing how it can help in the race of life.

Unusual? Yes, by traditional practices, but the church is now taking Christ's message to the people *where they are*.

In an Ohio factory, the employees gather once a week before work for a worship service conducted by a local minister. This short service includes prayer, reading of the Scriptures and a brief meditation. After the service the minister is available for counseling.

Religious service in a factory? Without a worship center? Without music? Yes, but not without success in taking the message to people where they are and at a time convenient to them. The church is solidly established on its corner; but it is also mobile in its mission to people who are mobile and frequently unconventional.

American churches face a serious dilemma. While they provide their members with excellent opportunities for worship and spiritual growth, those same churches are doing very little to reach the outsider. It is hard to deny that today's churches are achieving a degree of success and vigor never before attained. At the same time there are evidences of abject and decisive failure. Failure in the midst of apparent success is twofold. First, clergy and laymen fail to reach the persons outside the organized church with the Christian message. Second, they fail to recover, restore and renew those who have strayed from membership and participation in the church.

The numbers of lapsed and indifferent are increasing with an affluent society's strong competition for the leisure time and also with the fragmentation of society into distinct social, economic and racial groups. Unless these failures are checked and their causes corrected, Protestants could become an eccentric minority within a generation or two.

The indictment of "failure" of American Protestantism is very likely to be protested, appealed and even denied. The defender will protest, "Look at our churches. They are prosperous, have plenty of members, hold more and better properties than ever before. What do you mean Protestantism has failed to reach people? We never had it so good."

It is true that statistically American Protestantism "never had it so good"—record memberships, record attendance, record budgets and record holdings. More than 63 million Americans are members of Protestant churches of all types, from the Society of Friends to the high-church Episcopalians. Approximately 35 per cent of all Americans over fourteen years of age have membership affiliation in Protestant churches. Comparing these statistics with the total population and with the membership of other religious groups, Protestants remain the dominant religious group in the United States.

Certainly, the Protestant churches of today have a tremendous popular appeal. Merely belonging enables people to make new acquaintances, and the church is easier to join than a civic or fraternal organization. In many sections of the country, church attendance is breaking records. American churches appear to be better organized to offer a wider range of activities for people of all ages than at any time in the church's history.

Protestantism has grown financially in the United States. Voluntary giving to all churches in 1967 approached five billion dollars.

Religious education efforts are expanding. Religious education programs include all age levels but the growth is more evident among those for children and youth. In many cases church schools do not have space for adult classes.

In higher education Protestants are working effectively in operating more than five hundred church-related colleges and universities. Over 250,000 children and youth are studying in Protestant church-related elementary and secondary schools.

From the outside, the church appears to be thriving. What is actually going on inside? Here, too, there are positive signs. Renewed interest and concern regarding religion are evidenced in the small-group movement taking place in many churches. Significant numbers of laymen today are participating in study groups where they are seriously considering the basic tenets of the Christian faith and its application to daily living.

Is this vitality real, or is it superficial and shallow?

The American church has traditionally been closely related to the business and social life of the community, yet, in general, the churches have also criticized the American ways that are not in accord with Christian principles. In direct contrast to the state-oriented churches of Europe, American churches have developed as free institutions with strong lay leadership.

During the years of World War II, the Korean conflict, and the Vietnam struggle, and in the periods of adjustment necessitated by each, American churchmen everywhere have begun to ask new questions about the morality of war. A good example concerns America's participation in the Vietnam conflict. In matters of government the Christian is committed to the principle that in Vietnam and elsewhere people have the right to self-determination. We entered the war to help achieve that to which we had been committed. Now we face the question, "Am I my brother's keeper?" On the one hand, what can we do for people who seemingly do not know what they want? On the other hand, there is justice. Between them lies a great no-man's land of immorality; or, as some would want to say, amorality.

Thus, the Christian is caught on the two horns of another dilemma. What is just, and what is right? The great field of expediency which lies between is a dark gray, if not a black, market of conflict between the materialism of war and the spirituality of peace. Laymen are still searching and trying to decide what they believe and why they believe it. Many answers have been suggested, from holding aloof to cooperating wholeheartedly in Christian social action, which seems to compromise with the world. Somehow, somewhere, there is a way; and many churches are leading their members through programs designed to deepen and renew their faith.

Following the deeper conviction and commitment to

his faith in Christ developed by depth study and intro-spection, the Christian layman expresses himself in his way of life. He has learned the value of spiritual disci-pline. He has learned the value of Christian living. He admires the solidarity of the family at worship, work and recreation.

These are the things that are happening within the church. All of them are good and have definite value. They are hopeful signs, but the common characteristic of these things is that basically they concern those people *within* the church. There is not enough being done to reach those *outside* the church effectively with the gos-pel.

The churches will do well to ask themselves, "How about those in the secular society who are without the church? How about the persons—and here must be in-cluded a large proportion of church members—who do not read the Scriptures, do not attend worship, do not participate in prayer or depth-study groups?"*

The fact must be faced that on an average Sunday over three-fourths of American Protestantism is absent from worship services. Perhaps 60 per cent of the Protes-tant total will find their way to a church sometime during the month, but there still remains that challenging 40 per cent who will not go to church on any occasion during the month. The churches are missing these millions al-most completely.

It is not that the church is failing to reach many peo-ple. It is the failure of the church to reach *all* of the people, inside and out, with the gospel that should be the concern of Christians. The church's success has been a selective success. How to change this condition, reach

* For a more extended treatment of this point, see Daniel D. Walker, *Enemy in the Pew?* (New York: Harper & Row, 1967), pp. 216f.

the unreached, change the unchanged—these are the problems of the church today.

Who are these people not being reached by the church? Where are they? Why are they not being reached?

The largest single group of those not being reached is composed of the 10 to 15 million Americans over the age of fourteen not identified with any church. Ironically, they and many others would consider themselves Protestants simply because they are not members of any other faith. They compose that large segment of Americans who believe it is possible to be a Christian, moral and decent, without joining a church and worshiping "en masse." They believe that the individual can get close to God without benefit of clergy or institution.

Within the unchurched group are some who do not give the matter any thought at all, who do not care about being religious, decent and moral because they do not see that it pays.

There are always a few who have acquired some rather bizarre viewpoints and, having failed to find a church where this particular peculiarity is catered to, will shun all churches as being deficient or irrelevant.

Some men and women experience a certain amount of self-fulfillment in the church for a brief time, but their interest rather quickly falters and dies. These persons feel that they "tried religion" and it failed them. Whatever the cause, their brief experience immunizes them from any further religious experience.

Many of the nonchurched answer, "Methodist," "Presbyterian," "Baptist" or simply "Protestant" to interviewers, but they regard the church as only a place to go for baptism, marriage and perhaps burial. Their religious philosophy is "live only for the present and let the future care for itself."

A second large segment not being reached by the church comprises those 3,600,000 children now coming of confirmation age and not affiliating with any church or denomination.

Some of these youngsters come from the homes of the unaffiliated and some from homes whose parents are inactive although they are on church membership rolls. Typically, a child from these groups has had some church school experience. Perhaps a friend took him or one of his parents deposited him at the church door.

Frequently such church school experiences end when the child is capable of entertaining himself while the parents catch up on lost sleep. By this time the young person concludes that church school must be only for children. This has been taught him by the attitude of his parents. Many such children are lost to the church irrevocably.

Since the turn of the century there has been a reorientation of values within the family. Whereas once the family could be viewed as an integrated unit bound together by strong economic and other ties, it is now happiness-oriented, saying that each individual should be happy in his own way, living for the moment's enjoyment and, in many instances, without regard for spiritual values.

One mother of such a family, socially *up* but religiously *out,* frankly admits that she is advising her children not to bother with religion. She testifies that she gets along well without it. Her weekends are filled with parties, guests, bridge or golf. Sabbath means rest, rest means enjoyment, so the hard work is done on weekdays, and Sunday is for the joy of living. Golfers are a religious lot. They play their golf religiously—on Sunday. But there is the devil to interfere with God's good joys! The labor union gathers its membership to the joys of contract negotiations at 11:00 A.M. on a Sunday. The cleansing baptism of the family automobile is a Sabbath morning rite. And even the Christian fisherman is confused why a benevolent God should have created the bass for prime feeding time precisely during early rural worship services. How bleak, that all the worthwhile things give our heavenly Father such unremitting competition.

The children of these parents cannot be classified as neglected. They are well fed, well clothed, and by community standards they are loved and cared for, having "everything they need." These parents feel they can make their children happy by giving them things, for they themselves have found some joy in a new set of golf clubs, a bigger and better car, and more opportunity for socializing; rather than meditating on and enjoying the "finer things" of life. Is this the best thing for the children, making them carbon copies of themselves? The observing minister or clergyman must certainly be asking himself: "Who is wayward, the child or the parent? What kind of parents will these children become? What do these conditions forecast for our future?" In a broader observation, the inquirer must ask: "What relationship exists between Protestant Christianity and the moral standards and practices of much of America?"

Unless many unconcerned parents see the validity of the Christian faith to the extent of being committed to it as a style of life; unless the inactive members come to realize they are members of Christ's Body and called to live in relationship to God, these children will never know Christ and the joy of living a Christian life. It is not difficult to see them as much dissociated from the church as if they lived in Communist China.

Many Americans live in mobile homes, moving with regularity from one trailer court to another. Usually, these persons are not absorbed by the community or accepted as an integral part of it. Likewise, the mobile-home dwellers do not take the initiative to become involved members of the community. It is unimportant where the fault lies—the need is great. There are 16,000 U.S. trailer parks, with about 4 million persons living in mobile homes.

Among trailer dwellers the average head of the household is thirty-four years old or younger. This group accounts for 43 per cent of all mobile-home dwellers. The second largest age group, accounting for 25 per cent, averages fifty-five years or older.

The industry's trade group says skilled craftsmen account for 21.4 per cent of total family heads. The second-largest group, with 18.8 per cent of the total, is classed as "semiskilled operatives." The military service accounts for 7.8 per cent.

Why don't these people attend church? The truth of the matter is that church people equate the trailer with a boat moored to the dock. Untie the rope and the boat drifts down the river.

On the other hand, the trailerites, for the most part, feel they are only temporary or quasi members of the community, living in the "Trailer Park" rather than in the community. They are not likely to have any strong ties, including church connections. They are less likely to drive several miles to church than their permanently housed neighbors.

Local church members tend to look upon trailerites as migrants and different. They feel that the temporary nature of the service they can render to the local congregation is hardly worth the time and effort required for leadership training. It is true that the trailer fraternity is a "mixed" group. Some come and go, some young families live this way until they can get established, and some older couples decide to spend their retirement years in a trailer, as can be seen in Phoenix, Arizona; Omaha, Nebraska; and other towns from California to Maine.

Yet, the trailerite, when new in the community, may feel lonely, displaced, unhappy, homesick and bewildered. It is possible that he awaits the invitation to participate in community activities. Unasked, uninvited and unrecognized, trailerites are a group lost to the church.

Another fast-growing group, largely made up of those outside the church, consists of weekend campers. Camping can have far-reaching benefits on family life, but it can become highly competitive with the church.*

State park agencies in fifty states report a significant annual gain since 1958 in the number of persons using state parks. Tent and trailer camping saw approximately 5 million participants in the past year. Federal, state and municipal governments are expending more and more for park facilities (state governments alone spend more than $100 million annually for acquisition of land and for personnel compensation). With leisure time on the increase, more weekend and summer camping can be anticipated in years to come.

Recently a survey in six states showed more than 12 million persons utilized trailer-camping facilities. About 40 per cent of those camping on Saturday and Sunday were unchurched. The other 60 per cent, belonging to churches, were learning to get along without worship. In fact, church attendance among campers is rare. The requirement of dressing up (and they would not think of attending otherwise) to attend worship in a strange

---

* A Tabulation of statistics for the state parks of any of the fifty states—location, size, number of persons in attendance, as well as rules and regulations for meetings and religious services— is generally available from the Director, Department of Natural Resources, Division of Parks, State Capital.

church many miles from their campsite is a considerable obstacle.

Closely related to the campers is another segment of society that the church is not effectively reaching or serving. It is composed of the "two-house family" group, and has been studied by Lyle Schaller, director of the Regional Church Planning Board in Cleveland, Ohio.

Schaller reports how a well-to-do resident of a Cleveland suburb purchased land in the heavily wooded hills of western Pennsylvania and constructed an elaborate summer home. As soon as the weather turns warm, the owner and his family spend their weekends at the "second" home. When school is out, the wife and three daughters move to their Pennsylvania retreat. In addition to spending his month's vacation with them, the father commutes each weekend to his home in the woods.

This two-home family belongs to a large suburban church that maintains an excellent staff of ministers and provides a vital program of Christian education for all ages. They visit a quaint little one-room church in rural Pennsylvania, but the family seldom enters into the total life of that church or its community. Schaller closes this account with the pointed question, "Who is the pastor of this family?"

With the ever shorter work week, higher income levels, increasing emphasis on outdoor life combined with the increased automotive speeds and the completion of the $50 billion interstate highway system, Schaller states that the two-house-family concept is more than a Madison Avenue advertising slogan. It is already a reality for many thousands of Americans.

Reinforcing Schaller's observations, a senior minister of a suburban church of 1,800 members states that in his church from May 1 to October 1 the average attendance in the worship service and church school is under 300. This is markedly less than attendance during October to April. Many members in recent years are apparently vacationing, camping, weekending and temporarily joining the "unreached" groups.

The economic pressures of modern society have created another large group that is being lost to the church—those who find it necessary to work on Sunday. Big industrial enterprises know that Sunday can be just as productive as Monday. In some instances, even when regular production is suspended, Sunday can be utilized for servicing. For many factories and industrial operations, closing on Sunday is prohibitively expensive. A steel mill cannot cool its furnaces or leave them untended over the weekend.

An increasing number of workers are necessary on Sunday to provide Sunday entertainment. Weekend campers, boaters and travelers require many goods and services. The old blue laws which regulated retail merchandising activities on Sunday have been repealed, altered and ignored.

The families of Sunday workers are also affected. Sometimes the family car must be used by the working member, so that the mother and children cannot go to church. Considerable commercial pressure is felt nowadays to regard Sunday as no different from any other day, and this adversely affects church attendance.

Thousands of nurses, aides and orderlies are on duty in hospitals from 8:00 to 5:00 on Sundays to attend the sick. These servants cannot refuse to serve on the basis of religion; they have a religious reason for not being in church on Sunday.

What is the church doing for these people who work on Sunday? Does the church have a mandate to speak out against shopping centers remaining open on Sunday? Is there a responsibility to those who must work as long as the existing laws permit Sunday commercial activity? Every church needs to evaluate its beliefs and its service on this part of its social concern and witness.

Another group lost to today's churches is called "Protestants Anonymous." It consists of persons who have moved from home community and church membership. Statistics show that one of every five Americans changes his residency every year. Though it is actually a simple task to transfer church membership, in practice comparatively few do without considerable encouragement.

The following factual story could be repeated over and over again:

Mr. and Mrs. Anderson moved to another community. Mr. Anderson, a young schoolteacher, had been an active lay leader in his church. The inactivity of many of his fellow members had disillusioned him. By the time he moved he concluded that he needed a rest. In his new locale, the minister of the church he would normally have attended called on him at once, and made several follow-up calls as well. His new neighbors, members of the church, showed their friendship; but apart from two visits to the church, the Andersons made no more contact.

Later, the Andersons left the second community, total strangers to the church. If it was so difficult to bring this family back into the Christian fellowship, how much more difficult with those having less initial interest and contact! Then too, loyalties—to a pastor, to a building, to friends—are difficult to duplicate in a new situation. New churches are filled with strangers, and the churches are bewildering places with unfamiliar ways. It is regrettable that the loyalties to the Christian fellowship are frequently centered in a pastor, a building or some physical aspect of the church. In these cases, a shift in com-

munity or locality makes it extremely difficult to retain
such people in the church.

Inactive members, though still resident, are neglected by today's churches. Often these people resent
any suggestion that they are not loyal members though
they are rarely present in worship and do not contribute
either time or money. By and large, the average attendance of Protestants is around one third of a congregation's membership. Those churches who can count one
half of their members present on an ordinary Sunday are
doing well. Usually they are the rural churches. In many
churches the proportion of attendance is little better than
one fifth for most Sundays during the year.

The absentees include a large percentage (30 to 40
per cent) of those who attend so intermittently that their
names may annually be under consideration for removal
from the membership roll. At the annual meetings of
some of the larger congregations, members are asked to
vote out or drop from membership rolls as many as 200 to
300 inactives.

The complexities of college life have created still another group whose members are commonly not reached
by the church. It is estimated that only 20 per cent of
Protestant-preference college students, who are church
members, attend worship services. This is in spite of the
fact that the churches take great care to place ministers
of outstanding ability in college communities.

Many factors contribute to the weak college situation. One is the amount of study required of the young
people. This is usually more extensive than the student
has been accustomed to. Frequently, and often owing to
procrastination, the student finds that Sunday becomes
the last possible opportunity for study. Another reason is
that the student takes advantage of his freedom from
accustomed family pressures. In the absence of the

family he finds it easy to drift away from church attendance.

On some campuses, including church-related schools, churchgoing is viewed with sarcasm or tolerant amusement. Religion is called harmless at best, sentimental, emotional, and nonintellectual. These attitudes are more likely to prevail in tax-supported institutions where the intellectual adventure of physical and social sciences is represented as more stimulating and exciting than religious or philosophical pursuits.

Lastly, college life can be so busy—with double candleburning, late hours, new freedoms, fraternal and extracurricular activities—that Sunday morning may be an island of retreat, for sleep and for complete isolation. After four years of this program, the college graduate may be unmoved by conventional church methods.

Two other groups lost to today's churches are the large Negro population and the poverty-stricken white migrants. The truth of the matter is that the middle-class white urban congregation has failed to reach the newcomers from Appalachia and the Negro from the south. These two groups, similar in their meager earning power, can be found in ever increasing concentrations in the blighted centers of large cities. As the members of "old-line," established Protestant churches have moved to the suburbs, their churches have moved with them. The new city dwellers are left with a "store-front" operation.

Many problems here have not been defined, let alone answered. Can the spontaneous, down-to-earth service of the little white church in the hills be duplicated for those who have moved to the city? Can the poverty-stricken be made to feel at home in a "decent church atmosphere"? Can minority groups, ethnic or racial, be supplied with their culturally oriented biases?

The Protestant churches have always had to grow in

physical stature as their constituents have moved into
the middle class. Not only has worship become more
liturgical, but the organizational structure has increasingly become less personal. This program and secessional
change, so important in the task of maintaining contact with one segment of the population, makes it practically impossible to serve the groups with differing back-
grounds and needs. Even when invited to the established churches—and in some places color and cultural
resistance from within the church may inhibit such invitations—there are many reasons why these people may
not wish to attend.

First, the church may be a large and imposing structure, cold in appearance to these people whose tastes
are simple, and very different indeed from the one-room,
frame structure many knew as the "old home church."
Great courage is required even to enter such a place.

Suppose the Negro, the Appalachian white or the
minority representative makes the first giant step and at-
tends the church service. The service will seem formal
and cold to him. The music will be acceptable to the
members but either incomprehensible or lacking in "fire"
to the less sophisticated. Some of the hymns, chosen for
their appropriateness to the season, the service or the
sermon, may be unknown to the outlander. Certainly
they will lack the spark of enthusiasm he remembers as
being part of the singing back home.

The sermon, helpful, articulate, reasonable and
scholarly to the "regular," may have little meat for the
appetite of the visitor. It doesn't even sound "right." There
is no excitement, no shouting, no denunciations, no serious warning. Having ventured into First Church once,
the visitor will be unlikely to try it a second time.

In conclusion, Protestantism is reaching an ever nar-
rowing band of the total social spectrum in America. At

one end, the church is missing the persons who can afford to regard weekends as times for pleasure and recreation. At the other end of the spectrum, the church is missing entirely the people who feel repelled and left out by the middle-class trappings of many Protestant churches.

With the facts on the table, the churches need to ask some probing questions. Is there any way to reverse the trend? How can the Christian gospel be demonstrated and delivered as Good News to these people? Why are the churches failing to reach them today? Apparently, they were reached yesterday; they must have been or the religious growth after World War II could never have occurred. Is part of the problem the inadequacy or obsolescence of the church's methods of evangelism?

Can the trend be reversed? Any new method of evangelism must do more than merely engage people in humanitarian dialogue; it must reach them with the gospel, the central core of the Christian faith. We now have such a method. It is Unconventional Evangelism. Here is a new movement in which persons are engaging other persons outside the walls of the church. This adventure utilizes new styles of ministry, taking the gospel out of the regular structure of church activities and witnessing to people where they are, and how they are. It does not replace, it supplements. It is an effort on the part of the church to follow the people, to reach them with the gospel in the midst of their work and leisure.

This chapter has surveyed a cross section of persons being missed by the present Protestant church program. Before describing the new Unconventional movement, the strengths and weaknesses of the present forms of evangelism merit exploration.

2. Are Conventional Methods of Evangelism Adequate?

"IT was Sunday, July 5. I had just finished leading worship as an assistant pastor at the drive-in and at the regular downtown service of Trinity Church. I had an afternoon to myself and finally decided to go to East Harbor and see the commissary. This is a store where campers buy their food and I had been told there was a dance hall nearby. I walked through the store and into the hall.

"A small group of four fellows and a few girls were sitting around listening to a record player. I sat down, asked a few questions, and then inquired, 'How would you boys like to talk?'

"'What about?' they replied. I answered, 'About God.' Two of them got up and walked away. The other two just sat there; they were uncomfortable and they weren't going to move regardless of what kind of nut sat down beside them. I just sat there and looked and waited. It wasn't long before one of the immovables asked me if I thought it was all right to drive down the road ninety miles an hour and drag. Then another question came, and then others. Before long the purpose of living and where was God in my life became the questions, and within ten minutes those who had walked away returned.

"Three other fellows came into the hall, sat across the room and then joined us. For a while the conversation was general and then a number of the fellows and girls began to express some of their needs and uncertainties about the meaning and purpose of life. I felt that the Holy Spirit was working. When the discussion was ended, another was planned for the following Sunday afternoon."

This is from a report of a young student assistant in his first step in a program of Unconventional Evangelism—a program which reached youth on that Sunday afternoon.

Trinity's program, like that of many churches, had become standardized, providing only the regular church school and worship service. The church had seen its opportunity for outreach in a drive-in ministry early in the day, but had not visualized the possibility of a Sunday afternoon ministry at the resort area called East Harbor, where hundreds of young people gather over the weekend. Is the nearsightedness of conventional evangelism that it fails to seize opportunities for new outreach which may become vital ministries in themselves?

The traditional methods used by the church to confront numbers of people with the Christian message have been pulpit evangelism, visitation evangelism, and for the past one hundred eighty years, church school evangelism.

The enormous increase in membership of Protestant churches during the past quarter century has been, in large part, due to the intensive evangelistic thrust of these methods. Each of these three evangelistic approaches has its strengths and weaknesses, its successes and failures. Each has made, and is making, its vital contribution to the strength of the Christian fellowship. Today, however, these traditional approaches are no longer meeting the whole need.

A brief look at each of the traditional methods of evangelism will show some of the individual strengths and weaknesses.

Pulpit Evangelism. We can trace the history of evangelism in America from the first Great Awakening of interest in religion between 1725 and 1750, with the preaching of Jonathan Edwards and George Whitefield, down through the years with such pulpit evangelists as Charles Finney, Timothy Dwight, Lyman Beecher, Dwight L. Moody, Gypsy Smith, E. Stanley Jones and Billy Graham. The Holy Spirit has used such men of power and message to win countless thousands to Christ and His church.

It is a fact, however, that even our best present-day evangelistic preaching within the church fails to reach the great mass of unconverted people, and the explanation is simple. Nonchurched people do not go to religious meetings in religious buildings. Even in the citywide crusades conducted by Billy Graham, the majority of those attending services are related to the churches.

In an article entitled "We Are Not Reaching the Unreached," published shortly before his death in 1964, Roy L. Smith stated his opinion that at least one half of our modern evangelistic effort is wasted. Some will say that the sermons preached are lacking in intellectual content or are uninteresting. Others may feel that the preacher lacks passion, or that the gospel is not stated in clear and meaningful terms. But this is not the case. The explanation is much more elementary. The reason is that the people who most need to be reached do not attend these religious meetings.

Fifty years ago, or even twenty years ago, when an evangelistic service was announced, a preacher knew in advance that from 25 to 35 per cent of the average assembly would be unchurched. Today, in the average evangelistic audience, it seldom runs as high as 2 per cent.

In a recent evangelistic effort, the pastor and laymen of a prominent church spent weeks in preparation for special services. A well-known preacher was engaged. On opening night the church was packed with over 600 persons. When the speaker asked the congregation for a show of hands to signify those who were already church members, almost every hand went up. When he asked those who were not members of *any* church to raise their hands, only three hands were raised. Of course, some people preferred not to make a public admission, and so it was estimated that approximately fifteen persons, or some 2½ per cent, in that congregation had never made a religious decision.

While many church members might have needed conversion—and they could have been helped that night —the unchurched were absent from the services. Yet, to reach this neglected group had been the purpose of the special evangelistic service. The pastor and his laymen were understandably disappointed.

Visitation Evangelism. A second form of evangelism which the church has used during the last ten years is visitation evangelism. Christian laymen go out "two by two" to call in the homes of the unchurched families. The method is based on New Testament records and the results of the first Christian evangelists. Jesus trained His twelve disciples and the seventy whom He sent forth, two by two. The contagion of one redeemed spirit spread to another, the touch of one life upon another life.

The early Christians did not set out primarily to establish churches. They did not plan to promote an institution or even to change the social order. They did all that, to be sure; they established a ring of churches around the Mediterranean, created a vital institution, and eventually changed the whole moral climate of the Roman Empire. But all these benefits were only by-products that came as indirect results of their major motive to make Christ known to all men. They went out to be witnesses to the life, death and resurrection of Jesus Christ and to bring all men into a saving relationship with Him. Every Christian was an evangelist.

For the first Christians and for us, the ideal place to witness is in the push and pull of everyday life. Wherever one life touches another life, in the market place, the busy street, the college campus, the business office, at home, there is an evangelistic opportunity. Evangelism at its best is not easy here, but in this kind of school, practice and learning take place. The sharing of God's Good News cannot be left to the ordained minister alone, for there are too few of them. Furthermore, every Christian is under the imperative to bear witness to the faith.

A most hopeful movement in these days is the rise of lay evangelism as part of the lay movement. Christianity began as, and still is, a layman's movement. Christ's disciples were not clergymen but laymen. The people upon whom the Spirit descended at Pentecost were laymen. Lay evangelists carried the Good News in the first century. Dr. Halford Luccock once christened them "inspired amateurs." Just as the clergy resent the designation "professional," so intelligent laymen today resist being put in the amateur category. The fire of vital faith makes authentic their witness. Laymen can win persons to Christ! The most capable and dependable members of the church should be engaged in this work.

Laymen involved in evangelistic efforts have discovered new dimensions of relationship. This work has been one of the most rewarding experiences of their lives.*

A minister tells how a small group of men in his church became involved in person-to-person evangelism because they grew weary of their spectator roles. So they set to work, beginning with their own colleagues. They were a bit awkward at first and operated with considerable hesitation. They did not have a formal theological approach. They did not have the ecclesiastical prestige of the minister. They knew nothing about statistics. But they knew Christ and they talked about Him, what He meant to them in their lives, in their homes, in their business, and what it meant to them to be a part of the ongoing Christian movement. By the freshness and spontaneity of their approach, they infused others with a new spirit.

American churches are beginning to realize that the time has come to broaden their ministry through the enlistment of laymen who dare go past the marginal to the heart of Christianity. Many laymen are living under the compulsion to "Seek ye first the kingdom of God and his righteousness; and all these things shall be added unto you" (Matthew 6:33 KJV) and they see "all these things" as including church members.

The power of strong lay witness cannot be overestimated. In a midwestern church having a vital program of visitation evangelism, two well-trained young businessmen called at one home. Before they walked up to the front door they both prayed that God would use them in this visit. When they were invited into the home they recognized two young girls of the family as regular

* For a more extended treatment of this subject see Leighton Ford, *The Christian Persuader* (New York: Harper & Row, 1966), pp. 61f.

attendants at the church. The two visitors explained to
the parents that they were making friendly calls and inquired concerning their church membership.

The father replied that he had not belonged in recent years simply because, as a boy, he was forced to go
to church twice on Sunday as well as to the midweek
service and he had resented it. Furthermore, he had
known many hypocrites in the church and was completely disillusioned, so he had his own private religion.
As various criticisms were brought up, each of the
callers, in a quiet way, witnessed to his faith in Christ
and the fellowship of the church. When the criticism of
"hypocrites in the church" was raised, one visitor said,
"Yes, I suppose there are a few in every church, but the
vast majority of the members are sincere, honest people
trying to follow the Master." When the argument was
raised that as a boy the father was forced to go to church,
the caller replied, "Yes, but you must admit that your
Christian parents thought that they were doing the right
thing."

Again and again, each criticism of religion and the
church was sincerely met, not with argument but with
personal testimony. The callers had a deep concern for
the winning of this family. They felt themselves under
the guidance of God's Spirit and kept the conversation
Christ-centered. They cleared up misconceptions with
patience, friendliness and a sincere concern. The only
decision made that night was that the three families
would sit together in church worship the following
Sunday. Several weeks later the family became a part of
a "seeking research fellowship group" where, together
with eight other couples, they became followers of Christ
and eventually united with the church.

But despite the effectiveness of visitation evangelism, it has been qualified by three continuing weaknesses.

First, many churches give inadequate training to their callers. Laymen are sent out with little understanding of what they are to do. Their instructions may be like this: "*First,* when you enter a home, take an interest in the family; pay particular attention to the children. You may observe flowers or some object in the home which you can admire. *Next,* learn and use the ten effective talking points. *Finally,* when you feel that the prospect is ready to make the decision, take your pencil and the decision card which contains the form of three decisions—the Christian life, church membership and transfer of church letter. Check the decision you want him to make. Hand the card with a pencil to the prospect and ask for his signature." Such instruction doesn't even mention the nature of Christian commitment.

One Sunday morning a pastor announced that volunteers were needed to make calls on prospective members. That evening a husband and wife, after receiving the basic "training," took a set of cards. The first call they made was upon a woman who had recently moved into the community. They gave her the "sales pitch." Her answer was that she did appreciate their visit and she did promise to attend the services the following Sunday. Imagine her surprise when she heard the minister read her name on Sunday morning and announce that she was being received into the church membership. She was so embarrassed that she left the church after the service and never returned.

A second weakness is best stated in the form of a question. Have we been so eager to have a good program of visitation evangelism that we have uncritically used people who have little to offer in genuine Christian witness? It is not always that they have lacked training in technique or even that they have been ignorant of their faith. They have simply lacked a personal spiritual experience, a compulsion to witness; and in consequence, while their friendliness may have won new members, it has won them on terms which have not been decisive in a Christian sense. Too often Christianity has been offered as a palatable sauce to pour on the American way of life. Seldom is Christianity presented as a commitment to a relationship with God that may require a radical change in a person's life.

The third weakness of visitation evangelism is that it usually does not reach the unreached. The average "prospect list" consists of a series of names of those who have already manifested at least some small interest in religion and the church.

It is possible that too much has been done in organized visitation evangelism and too little in terms of encouraging those who have some understanding of the spiritual relationship to use every day and every opportunity to make their witness. After all, the unreached are those who work next to Christians, shop with them, camp with them, live with them. It cannot be said that personal evangelism has failed; it can be said that it has barely been attempted.

Church School Evangelism. The third major evangelistic method in America is church school evangelism. Shortly after the advent of the Sunday school in the 1780's, the adult members came to realize that the educational effort could also be used for reaching the unchurched.

The purpose of church school evangelism is to lead every person into a saving knowledge of God through Christ. While the church school is known as an instrument for Christian education, it was from the beginning an organization used by the church to reach unchurched children and their parents.

In 1780 a Christian layman, Robert Raikes, printer by trade, became deeply concerned over the sad condition of the children of his native city, Gloucester, England. They were ragged, dirty, profane, delinquent, underprivileged and ignorant. After experimenting with ways of improving their condition he decided to gather them together on Sunday, because it was the only day of the week they were free from work. He visited each one of them personally, invited them to his home, and began to teach them the real truths of religion, and he taught them Christ!

Despite determined opposition, Raikes's venture was successful. Within five years the Sunday School Society of London was organized. In Philadelphia, the movement was organized as the First Day or Sunday School Society. By 1817 there were about one hundred schools in the United States, but they were not without their troubles.

In 1787 George Daughaday, a Methodist preacher in Charleston, South Carolina, was drenched with water pumped from a public cistern, "for the crime of conducting a Sunday School for the benefit of the Negro children of the vicinity."

A young girl in Connecticut who, about 1820, gathered a little Sunday school group in the church gallery was forbidden by the church authorities to continue on the grounds of its desecrating God's day and God's house.

Even so, this new service to people was recognized by leaders of the Wesleyan revival and made into a powerful evangelistic tool. Circuit riders, missionaries and laymen carried the new Sunday schools to the American frontier with evangelistic passion.*

By the beginning of the twentieth century the use of the term "church school" rather than "Sunday school" sig-

* For a history of the Sunday school movement, the reader may wish to consult Paul H. Vieth, *The Church and Christian Education* (St. Louis: The Bethany Press, 1947).

nified that this instrument of evangelism and education was an integral part of the church. Each congregation recognized that it must make provision for a well-organized program of graded instructions, with suitable buildings and equipment, and with lesson materials to develop the Christian life.

Early Sunday schools were strongly evangelistic in character. In more recent times the educational method has been emphasized. There are some who feel that the evangelistic purpose has suffered because of this emphasis. A sound Christian education program will lead persons to a better understanding of Christian living and to the understanding of the relevance of Christianity in their lives today, but the Church school should also be effective as an evangelistic tool. We should make certain that the Good News does not become submerged in planning and procedural techniques.

Today evangelism and education are married. Christ's great commission is: "Go therefore and make disciples of all nations, baptizing them in the name of the Father, and of the Son and of the Holy Spirit, teaching them to observe all that I have commanded you; and lo, I am with you always, to the close of the age" (Matthew 28: 19-20, RSV).

The first imperative of Christ's commission is to make disciples of all men, to convert them to the Christian faith, which is the evangelistic task of the church.

The second imperative of this command is to instruct the new convert. This is the educational task of the church. This procedure was followed by Paul, who not only established new congregations, but selected capable men of outstanding faith who were to provide for the continued nurture of the church.

This bond between evangelism and education was in evidence during the "Great Awakening" in the ministry of such men as John Wesley, Jonathan Edwards, and in more recent times in the ministry of Dwight L. Moody. These men were concerned not only with converting the "lost," but also with the nurture of the faithful. This is seen in Wesley's class meetings, in Edwards' concern for education, and Moody's founding of preparatory schools at Northfield, Massachusetts.

Thus, evangelism and education are not, and should never be, considered as competitors. The altar and the classroom are not foes. The revival meeting and the church school should never be thought of as rivals. Evangelism at its best must flow into instruction within the church; and education, if it is to remain Christ-centered, must issue in a life committed to Christ and His church.*

In our time we have seen a sharp decline in church school enrollment and attendance, and a gradual disappearance of adult classes. In the frontier days church gatherings were a vital community activity. The church's educational pattern took its momentum from the "little red schoolhouse." When the "little red schoolhouse" changed, the church school changed; and with it came a whole new emphasis on adult education. More adult classes came into being. Larger groups were amalgamated into even bigger ones, which required skilled teachers. The minister often found himself preparing an elaborate church school lesson for his Bible class of several hundred as well as his morning sermon.

With the coming of World War II and the exigencies imposed upon our people, a notable decline occurred so that many large adult Bible classes have all but disappeared in several sections of our country.

* The reader interested in a fuller discussion of the many interlocking functions of evangelism and education is invited to read Donald Stewart's lucid Chapter 5 in *Christian Education and Evangelism* (Philadelphia: The Westminster Press, 1963).

Nevertheless the church school has been the single most important source of new church members. For the past twenty years, more new members have come into the church each year from the church school than from all other organizations of the church put together. The work which it does to prepare young people for church membership must not be overlooked, for we should ensure that a child who has attended regularly will at age twelve have a fair knowledge of the Bible, basic Christian doctrines, their denominational emphases and church history.

But, however great these values of Christian education are, it must also be realized that church school has some real limitations as an evangelistic tool.

First, it must be acknowledged that something more than Christian education is needed. To know all these things is not to enter into a saving knowledge or relationship with God through Christ. Understanding and information may pave the way, and undoubtedly they often do. But knowledge *about* God must not be confused with *knowing* God. There must come the time when a person comes to know God other than by hearsay.

For example, a minister helped conduct a Junior High Summer Camp session. He and other leaders found that these young people had been taught nothing of what it means to commit their lives to Christ. An attempt was made to teach them what this meant. A final consecration service closed with a personal invitation. In the invitation it was clearly stated that only those who were sure this was what they wanted to do should come to the altar and respond, and the rest would be respected for their honesty. Over two thirds of the youngsters and several of the adult counselors responded. For the first time in their lives the God they had learned about and read about in church school became a real Person who transformed their lives.

This leads to a further shortcoming of the present situation in church school evangelism. Teachers are failing to lead their students to the point of decision. This may be true for several reasons. Primarily, many teachers do not feel that this is their task. They see their task as teaching the lesson rather than assisting their students in decision-making. The latter is to be left to the individual and his parents, or to the pastor's class. And sadly, there are many teachers who themselves are ignorant of the meaning of making a decision for Christ.

Some may object to this criticism. Does a commitment always need to be expressed outwardly? Can it not be an inward acceptance? There are many forms of conversion. In fact some think that a child brought up through church school does not need conversion. He or she can be a child of God all along.

Finally, many pastors and those in charge of the teacher-training programs are failing to instruct teachers in the meaning of conversion and how to lead their students to decision.

To summarize, the church school is in a unique and strategic position to be an effective agency for evangelism. For one thing, it is usually the church's primary point of contact with the community. When a new family moves into town, the parents, even if they themselves are not church members, want at least to send their children to Sunday school.

Young married couples, with little money and perhaps a big mortgage, hunger for fellowship and find the young adult class meeting their needs. Older people, looking for companionship and friends, are looking for opportunities for activity, and many church schools are providing a program that attracts these "golden-agers." Somewhere in the church school there can be a place for each and every one associated with the church. Little wonder, then, that it is the chief source for the winning

and recruitment of new members. The figures for most
of the major Protestant denominations show that the
majority of the members received into the average congregation come directly out of the church school.

In 1964–65 Methodist churches received by transfer
260,000 members from other Methodist churches; 100,-
000 transferred from other denominations; 20,000 were
restored to membership; and 300,000 were received by
profession of faith. At least one half, and perhaps two
thirds, came from the church school. Thus nearly 600,000
of the 700,000 "new" members came from within "the
family."

Available figures for Lutheran, Evangelical United
Brethren, and Presbyterian churches indicate that they do
little better than Methodists on adult evangelism. For
other denominations, somewhere between 70 per cent
and 85 per cent of the persons who join the local church
come from within "the family"—children of members,
transfers, those restored to good standing, etc. As many
as 75 per cent of the new members of any major denomination come from within "the family." Thus, most of our
Protestant evangelism efforts have been directed toward
winning new members from among those persons already
related in some way to the church family.

Thus we have arrived at a crucial hour in the evangelistic enterprise of the Protestant church. We have
come to that place where the three conventional methods
of evangelism—pulpit, visitation and church school—are
no longer touching the lives of the vast numbers of the
unchurched.

The day when the evangelistic campaign at the
local church was the only event in town has long since
passed. Today if we are to speak to these people we
must move out to those busy areas where they are and
interest them. Helmut Thielicke holds to the view that

we should get the people to listen outside that they may by and by worship inside.

We must realize our current cultural changes and patterns are being determined by, if not unchristian, at least non-Christian values. This is an age which many men like Martin E. Marty, associate editor of *The Christian Century,* have already referred to as the Post-Christian Era. Has not the church come to the place where it must admit that conventional methods of evangelism are inadequate to meet the needs of the most needy segment of our society?

The outreach of any church, whether it follows conventional or unconventional patterns, must be undergirded by a strong evangelistic emphasis from the proclamation in the pulpit. For Protestants, preaching has been the foundation stone upon which all else is built and from which all else receives its potency. It was so in the first century. The Christian Church got its start with a sermon, for on the day of Pentecost Peter stood up to preach (Acts 2:14); and Paul wrote, "It pleased God by the foolishness of preaching to save them that believe" (1 Corinthians 1:21b, KJV). Preaching is central to the witness of the Christian Church. There will never be a substitute for this—the mystic call of the divine Spirit coming through a human voice. If there is a strong strain of evangelism from the pulpit, laymen will be encouraged and assisted in their efforts in visitation and the church school program.

Likewise, it is only through a strong visitation program that many inactive members will ever be reached with the gospel and won for Christ. Further, only through a strong educational program which leads our young people to that point of commitment will many of them be won. Our youth do not become Christian either by heredity or by environment (attending church school regularly) but by decision (an act of the will), which may grow out of the other two. Each new generation must be won afresh for Christ and His church.

However, if our laymen are not being moved to perform these vital ministries of winning others for Christ, it may be because their pastors are not moved by the importance of this task. If laymen do not reflect a passion for the lost, it may be because their ministers do not preach and lead with this passion and concern. Certainly there is no cause which receives so vast a hearing, week after week in this nation, as does the gospel of Christ, preached from the Protestant pulpit. If the churches and communities are not stirred by its claims, it can only mean that there is a failure to take full advantage of this opportunity.

As important as conventional methods are, the day has come when these alone are not enough. Something additional is needed.

Dr. Truman Douglas, vice president of the Board of Homeland Ministeries for the United Church of Christ, in an interview said: "We must have creative ministries. The first thing we have to do is take people seriously as they are and where they are. That means we have to do an awful lot of listening before we do much talking. We have to persuade people to talk with us and bring us the questions they have. We have to convince people we are dealing with them as persons, not as stereotypes for conversion. Take them as they are. I think we have to consciously get into some of the subcultures where we are dealing with people who represent forms of human life to which the church is likely to be a stranger. . . . We want to learn what people are saying to us, and we want to take the church's message to them."

Bishop Hazen G. Werner of the Methodist Church has commented, "It is now time to take the church and the gospel to the people wherever they are." This means reaching them on street corners, in shopping centers, at county fairs, in parks.

Dietrich Bonhoeffer made the point that the exciting age of church history was neither the sixteenth century nor the fourth, not the Middle Ages nor even the early church; the golden age of the church is directly before us. The church should die like her Lord to the redemption of the world. The task of the church is not to save her own life; it is to go out of the temple into the world of workers, citizens, businessmen, and scientists, and offer the good news of God revealed in Christ.*

Perhaps that is what Jesus meant when He said, "New wine must be put into fresh wineskins" (Luke 5: 38, RSV).

* For a more extended treatment of this point see Frederick K. Wentz, *The Layman's Role Today* (Garden City: Doubleday & Co., 1963), pp. 17f.

3. Something New Has Been Found

THE energetic minister of a three-hundred-member church in Minnesota, Bob Brown, mentioned in the first chapter, became interested in Unconventional Evangelism. He was convinced that the church should reach out to more people to tell about Christ and His teachings. He had read about services in drive-in theaters, shopping centers and resort areas. But in his little town there was no drive-in theater close by; there was no lake or resort area; there were no factories. The only unusual feature of the town was a racing drag strip. Every Sunday afternoon around five thousand persons came to this race. For miles one could hear the roar of the powerful engines as the drivers tuned them and warmed them up.

The minister prayed to discover how he might be used. He thought, "Five thousand people—what a congregation!" He was led to call on the owners of the drag strip. He was cordially received. He asked what happened between races. The answer was that canned music was played over the loudspeakers. Surprisingly enough, they told him that next Sunday afternoon there would be a fifteen-minute intermission and that he might say something.

The following Sunday afternoon he drove out to the ninety-eight-acre strip. The vehicles were shrieking around the track emitting bursts of acrid fumes. It was noisy and it was smoky. Most of the spectators were young people and friends of the drivers. Some were race-car enthusiasts. When it was time for the intermission, the owners of the track said, "For the next few minutes our friend Bob Brown will speak to you on the subject 'The Race of Life.'"

Later the minister said, "I was scared. I did not know what to say. I had never spoken to five thousand people before and I had no idea what their reaction might be; but I began to think that there is a race of life to be run and won, and God is in the driver's seat. He can guide our lives in this race."

He started to speak and although he was nervous, he made a simple testimony and witness as to what Christ meant to him. Because it was Mother's Day and national family week he said that one thing that Christ had given him was a Christian home and family. That was what Christ meant to him—a mother who brought Christ down out of theory into everyday life, and revealed His spirit in her own personality—who never altered in her expression of His love, mercy and tenderness. He said that however normal he was today was due to the fact that he was reared in a home where there was love and harmony and not dissension and discord. To his surprise, the majority of the people were attentive.

Later as the pastor was walking through the crowd a young couple approached him. The man said, "Pastor, I was not reared in that sort of home and the scars of friction are still with me. What can Christ do for me?"

The pastor replied, "If you let Christ have His way in your life, if you will receive Him fully into your heart, He can overcome and obliterate all the wounds which an unhappy past may have left upon you. Furthermore, if

you two are looking forward to establishing a home of
your own He can make it possible for you to establish
the kind of home where there will be love and understanding."

This young couple wanted to be married. They
faced family difficulties and were of different faiths.
They wanted to know if he would see them again. A date
was set and the minister had an opportunity to help two
very confused young people.

Now, for twenty Sunday afternoons a year, during
the intermission, this minister uses the public address
system to speak to a large crowd about the race of life
and how the Christian faith can lead and guide them in
that race. More people see the religious literature rack at
this one drag strip on one Sunday afternoon than see one
in the local church building in six months. As they come
in and go out of the race track, they have an opportunity
to take copies of *The Upper Room*, a self-interest ques-
tionnaire, a booklet entitled *How to Pray* and family
studies. Hundreds of these are taken each Sunday. Jesus
communicated the gospel wheresoever and to whomso-
ever. Does not this illustrate Jesus' approach when He
said, "No one puts new wine into old wineskins; if he
does, the new wine will burst the skins and it will be
spilled, and the skins will be destroyed. But new wine
must be put into fresh wineskins" (Luke 5:37–38, RSV).

Jesus is saying that there must continually be fresh
and vivid ways found to reach the lives of men and
women. There must never be a static church. If the
church is not advancing, decay has already set in; if it is
not going forward, it is going backward. There must be
continued discovery of new modes for expressing the
Christian gospel and new techniques whereby to take
the gospel to the people.

During the past few years a new wineskin has been

discovered. It has been named Unconventional Evangelism. Unconventional Evangelism is an adventure into the use of creative and unusual ways of taking the gospel out from the church building and witnessing to people where they are. It is an effort on the part of the church to follow the people—to minister to them where they work and where they play.

This new cutting edge of the churches, Unconventional Evangelism, has these distinct features:

1. It is a program of religious contact with persons in unconventional places.

2. It calls for unconventional preaching and unconventional orders of worship in unconventional settings.

3. It is an evangelistic program which seeks a commitment to Christ and to the Christian way of life.

4. It requires practical planning like any other program.

5. It is designed to supplement, and not replace, all other forms of evangelism utilized by the church.

Unconventional Evangelism is attracting wide attention across the United States. For several years ministers and churches have been conducting drive-in services and with the prospect of reaching some of the ten million campers in the state and national parks, a number of ministers are setting up services in or close to these parks. Still others are conducting informal and simple services at county fairs, shopping plazas and in factories. Many laymen are being enlisted to serve as ushers, distribute song sheets, and sing in quartets and choirs. Leaflets and notices are printed, advertising the services, and are distributed at the fairgrounds or the campsites on Saturdays by Boy and Girl Scouts. Women set up coffee stands at the close of the services. As to dress, the emphasis is placed on "come as you are."

Other pastors have sought permission of factory

managers to hold ten-minute services once a week in factories. Some pastors have tried brief services in shopping centers, leading people in repeating the Twentythird Psalm. Brief prayers are offered for families, the nation and the people of the world.

Ministers are reporting that these projects are the keys to new life. A few of these reports follow:

"One night at our park service, a small circus was camped on the side of the grounds. We sent our men through the circus tents to witness to the circus people. At the close of our meeting, the leader of the group sought the minister and asked for help. The man had lost his wife by death, and in his heartbroken experience he came for new life in Christ. This was real victory."

Holding services at a drive-in theater area led to this episode: "The two helpers [employees of the theater] required to be present had to be back at the drive-in by 7:00 A.M. after working until 3:00 or 4:00 o'clock in the morning. One of these men was an alcoholic and a victim of many effects of drinking. His life was touched with a new power. He has given up the use of alcohol. He has become associated with a church near his home and has spoken to the people with whom he works about the change Christ has effected in his life." This is real evangelism.

This is a time of tremendous novelty so far as the methods of reaching spiritual lives of men and women are concerned. For example, a minister in New Jersey after attending a one-day workshop on Unconventional Evangelism two years ago, went home and wondered how he could carry the gospel out of the church building into the open.

The following Saturday evening he accompanied his wife to the grocery store at the shopping center. As he was walking from the car to the grocery, he thought, "What a wonderful audience; if I could only reach these

people with the Good News of the gospel!" The following week he thought about it again and again. Every day
he walked through the shopping center, thinking about
how he might reach some of these people. He got the
idea that he would simply stand in front of a busy grocery store in the shopping center, and begin to talk to individuals about their relationship to Christ.

All week long he thought about his message, and
then on Thursday morning he "got cold feet and chick-
ened out," as he put it. On Thursday evening as he attended the choir rehearsal in his church, he recalled that
four members of the choir also sang as a barbershop
quartet. After the rehearsal, he took these four men to
the parsonage to have a cup of coffee and shared with
them his idea of witnessing in the shopping center. He
asked if they would be willing to go with him and hold
him up if he fainted. The four men said, "Yes," and he
then asked if they would be willing to sing a church
hymn. They replied, "Fine."

On Saturday evening at seven o'clock the members
of the quartet and the pastor went down to the shopping
center, and the quartet sang several hymns. No one
stopped except a few curious boys.

As a result, before the pastor even got ready for his
message, he was so discouraged that he simply turned
to the four men in the quartet and said, "Fellows, we
have bitten off too much. Let's just call it quits and go
home."

But the leader of the quartet replied, "Well, all right,
pastor, whatever you want. But before we leave, would
you mind if we sing a couple of barbershop numbers?"
You can imagine what happened. Within the next five
minutes, more than fifty people stopped and listened to
the singing. Then, at the signal of the leader, they went
from the barbershop number into a spiritual often sung
at church camps, "We Are Climbing Jacob's Ladder."

At the close of their singing, the newly inspired minister stood up and said, "Friends, we are from the local neighborhood church and we've come out here to hold a brief service. I'd like to ask you a simple question. How many of you would like me to offer a word of prayer in your behalf?" A number of hands went up. Then he asked, "How many would like for me to pray for your families?" and more hands went up. Finally he asked, "How many of you would like to join in praying for America and world peace?" He said every single hand in the crowd went up.

The minister offered prayer in the manner he had promised. Following the prayer no one seemed to want to leave. In about five minutes this minister gave a testimony and witness as to what Jesus Christ meant to him in his life.

He said that Jesus had revealed to him the meaning and purpose of life. There is so much cynicism and frustration in our world today, so much unhappiness and despair, and much of it is due to the fact that few of us have ever learned what life is for. We have been filling our time with the trivial and inconsequential. When Jesus said, "I am come that you may have life and that you may have it more abundantly," He was not saying, "I am going to discover what you want most and give it to you." He was saying, "I am going to lead you into participation in the Kingdom of God, and as you serve your fellow men, and give yourself to the needs of humanity, you will discover what life was meant to be. Then all the satisfaction and joy of life will be yours as by-products."

Later, one of the members of the quartet spoke briefly on what the Christian faith meant to him. He said, "Although I was reared in a Christian home and given every spiritual opportunity, I soon discovered that I was a sinner in need of a Savior, and that salvation does not come through the civilizing influences of education, social opportunity, and all the rest of the things which some men are privileged to enjoy. Salvation comes through a personal surrender of one's life to God through Jesus Christ. I found it much easier, for instance, to lie than to tell the truth. I found it much easier to be selfish than to be unselfish; to become impatient and irritable instead of being calm and considerate. I found it much easier to be small and picayunish than to be magnanimous. I discovered that I need Christ within my being to make those necessary changes possible. Paul speaks of it as 'Christ in you the hope of glory,' that mystical union between the believer and his Savior. We are not only to stand at a distance and imitate Christ; we are to open the doors of our hearts and take Him in, and let Him live in and through us, revealing Himself to all mankind. This, and infinitely more, Christ has done for me. What has He done for you? He will do all that you will permit Him to do. He will give you all the peace that your soul requires; all the strength that you may need in the tempting hours; all the companionship that your loneliness may long for, if you will open your heart and take Him in."

Following this layman's testimony the barbershop quartet sang:

> Jesus is all the world to me,
> My life, my joy, my all;
> He is my strength from day to day,
> Without Him I would fall.
> When I am sad, to Him I go,
> No other one can cheer me so;
> When I am sad He makes me glad,
> He's my Friend.

The pastor closed with a prayer of commitment and dedication. He then invited the people to come to church to worship the next morning.

But that is not the end of the story. One man in the Saturday-evening crowd took the invitation seriously and came to church. Some weeks later he began meeting with a fellowship group in the church where he joined others in seeking to determine what it meant to be a Christian. Several months later he became a member of the church and now is one of its officials.

The minister and the quartet repeated the shopping-center service for a number of Saturday evenings. This pastor has said that sharing with people on the street what Christ and the gospel mean to him has done something for him and his ministry. He has shared his wealth with others and in turn found himself enriched. He has found that this is the way Christianity works.

The Church of the Good Shepherd, Glen Burnie, Maryland (United Church of Christ), has leased 1,500 square feet of space in a shopping mall. The church center includes a reception room, a chapel, a conference room and a kitchenette. It is staffed by trained lay persons who seek to face the real issues confronting the individuals who stop in. Among the ministries are courses of study in parenthood, family financing, Christian faith and the Bible; a religious lending library; a ministry to young people; and a counseling service.

On Chicago's west side, Msgr. John J. Egan, pastor of Presentation parish, estimates that there are 42,000 people living within the parish boundaries. His question: "How do we reach each and every person in a meaningful way, on a basis of friendship and confidence?" Months of thinking, talking and struggling with this problem produced a plan which he calls "Operation Saturation," which follows three steps:

He enlisted sixty priests, seminarians and nuns who agreed to devote at least two full days a month in the parish community. Each was assigned one city block with

full responsibility. Their task was to get to know everybody and about everything on the block—the youth, the
sick, the lonely, the unemployed. Also they were to seek
out and help develop the lay leaders who could assume
their rightful responsibilities in carrying out projects in
their own block. Together the priests, seminarians, nuns
and trained laymen are witnessing to Christ in love.
They are loving, serving and saving. They are working
with children, meeting the teen-age gangs and visiting
in the homes. These inner-city workers possess a social
conscience and are dedicated to the cause of social justice. They are relating God and the church to the people
and the people to the church.

In 1967, according to an official count of the Federal
Government, 8,905,100 persons visited Lake Texoma.
This was the third year that the number of weekenders
and summer vacationers topped eight million. The
twenty-two-year-old man-made lake between Texas and
Oklahoma is a particularly powerful magnet for residents
of the Dallas–Fort Worth and the Oklahoma City–Tulsa
metropolitan areas.

Some visitors make the effort to attend worship services in one of the towns within easy driving distance,
but those who do are rare. Most of Texoma's relaxing
millions, says a local pastor, do not have churchgoing
clothes with them or time for a trip into town.

For nearly two years now the interdenominationally
sponsored Lake Texoma United Ministry has been
bringing the church to the people. In 1967, 2,950 men,
women and children attended the worship services,
Bible studies, or other programs provided by the United
Ministry. During 1968 thirteen services each week were
held, along the lake, in a lodge and under picnic shelters.
Ed and Alice Edwards, who manage a resort on the lake,
believe that the Texoma United Ministry has "taken

Christianity out of the dress-up fashion category and given it back the down-to-earthiness" of its Palestinian beginnings. "Never before have we heard of the church's coming to the people," they say.

A pastor in Indiana uses another approach. On Sunday morning at seven o'clock fifteen laymen of the church begin preparing a nearby drive-in theater for a worship service which will begin at eight o'clock. They set up the portable platform and pulpit. A truck arrives with the portable organ. The men make a final check of the electrical system, and at twenty minutes of eight the cars begin to roll in.

One Sunday, by five minutes of eight there were one hundred and seventy cars with five hundred and thirty-two men, women and children present. As the cars arrive, the minister and his wife go from car to car shaking hands and welcoming the people. When eight o'clock comes, the pastor steps to the microphone and invites persons to leave their cars and come to the platform to join the quartet and become a choir. One Sunday morning twenty-five persons volunteered for this ministry of music.

The drive-in service is simple. It consists of an opening prayer, the singing of a hymn, the reading of the Scriptures, and a fifteen-minute sermon, followed by a benediction. The sermon is always closed with a period of quiet, followed by an invitation to make a decision while they are sitting there as a family in the car. Commitment cards read: "(1) I wish to make my commitment to Jesus Christ and His way of life. (2) I should like to have a call from the pastor. My name, address and telephone number are_____. (3) I am interested in preparing myself for church membership."

The pastor stands at the gate, and as the cars come out, each slows up and those who have commitment cards hand them to him. If they are from nearby summer homes, the pastor and trained laymen visit them. Person-to-person contacts are very important.

A unique community situation and need was discovered and responded to by a minister in Iowa. About two miles from the village in which he is pastor, there is a mobile-home park. It started with four families a year ago, and now eighty families live there in trailers. When the pastor and the membership and evangelism committee realized this, they immediately took an interest and made calls into each of these homes.

Several of the trailer families came to church. They were of the lower economic class and were somewhat defensive. Efforts to make them feel at home were unsuccessful. The pastor came to the conclusion that instead of trying to get the mobile-home people into the church building, perhaps he ought to take the church to the people.

The owner of the trailer park had just completed an all-purpose building which had folding chairs, kitchen and toilet facilities. When he was approached by the minister, he said that the minister could use the building any time on Sunday. The pastor then secured six teachers who volunteered to go with him on Sunday afternoon to start an outpost Sunday school.

On the Friday and Saturday preceding the first classes, the pastor had the Boy Scouts and the Girl Scouts distribute simple announcements to each of the homes, and on Sunday afternoon twenty-five of the children met together in the recreation building. They had a song service, then divided by age groups and the various teachers taught the classes. Today they are averaging thirty to forty children and youth each Sunday.

Eventually, the time came when this pastor felt that instead of bringing the teachers from the church, perhaps he could set up a teacher-training class for the parents of the children right there. So while the children were studying on Sunday afternoon, he conducted a teacher-training class.

Now all the teachers are drawn from the park itself. The pastor continues to give leadership and is planning a service of worship as well as the church school.

In Bethesda, Maryland, there is a Presbyterian church that discovered a number of retarded children in their parish who were being deprived of Christian education. "Retarded children are people just as you and I are. They need the opportunity to learn about the gospel too," says the Rev. David V. Voss, minister of education at Bradley Hills church. This church along with other churches across the nation has found that not only do special classes convey the gospel to retarded children, but they also serve as channels of evangelism. Open to children of any faith or none, the Bradley Hills class has attracted eight families with no church affiliations to participate actively. Presbyterian and Lutheran churches in such cities as Fort Worth, Texas; Cuyahoga Falls, Ohio; St. Joseph, Missouri; and Burlington, New Jersey, are now providing classes for some of the nation's 2,500,000 retarded children, many of whom have no church school to attend.

Another experiment occurred in Ohio when a new seminary graduate was appointed to his first full-time charge. It was the first time the church had ever had a full-time ordained minister and the people were worried about the rundown condition of the parsonage. After some discussion they decided to rent another home.

Failing to find any property for rent in the small town, they leased a dwelling in a new housing area a little over four miles from the church. The minister and his wife were quite disturbed because they had to be so far away from the church. The housing development had three hundred homes with a population of twelve hundred. They were downcast about moving into this situation.

On the second day they were in their new home, a neighbor rang their doorbell. The conversation went something like this: "I am your next-door neighbor. For the last twenty-four hours the word has spread around the community that a minister has moved into our midst, and I am the first one to have enough courage to come and inquire if this is true." Assuring her that it was true, the minister and his wife invited her in for coffee. Their neighbor said that almost every morning a group of women got together over coffee and had discussions on many different topics. Some of the questions pertained to religion, and she wondered if the pastor and his wife would be willing to come over the next morning to take part. They agreed to do so.

The next morning there were a dozen women present. The children were put out in the backyard to play, and for the next two hours the minister was besieged with all kinds of questions. He said later that he might have sat back and tried to answer them one at a time, but he decided to rephrase the questions and throw them right back in order to draw out from the individual persons what they thought. They had a wonderful time.

Again that very evening the pastor was invited to a get-together with the men of the community and another fine discussion and conversation period followed. His experience brings out the fact that the way to reach people is through person-to-person contact.

The pastor was not surprised to learn from the juvenile and welfare authorities of that county that this new housing development was the source of many of their problems. Many families were young, in their twenties or early thirties, with two to five children. Many had been teen-age marriages. Both man and wife were still very much in the process of making adjustments to married life and were trying desperately to discover guidelines for life. A deprived community, it had no schools, no churches, no park for the children and no community spirit.

The young pastor estimated that less than 10 per cent of these people attended church. This was a special concern, since roughly 70 per cent of the families who lived there were Roman Catholic and they constituted almost all of those who attended worship.

One plan the pastor entertained was to gather groups in homes and lead them from their discussions into directed studies (perhaps Bible reading and prayer), and then from there into a sense of Christian commitment. As he says, "There is something in the New Testament about the church in the home." This minister, who initially resented to some degree his appointment to this charge, says he feels that in addition to his church in another community, he has a great opportunity among twelve hundred persons in these three hundred homes.

Another interesting situation involves a factory in Ohio, briefly mentioned in the first chapter. The Cobey Manufacturing Company of Bucyrus, which manufactures farm tools, employs between three and four hundred men. The factory is next door to a church. For some time the president, who is Jewish, and the plant manager, a Protestant, had felt that they wanted to do more for their employees. They had a genuine interest in the men and wanted them to have a larger and broader interest in life.

After consultation with the union management, the two executives approached the local Protestant pastor with the question, "Wouldn't you like to share your life and ministry with all of us?"

Eagerly assenting, the Rev. Glenn Lockard and his successor, the Rev. Norman Prichard, have each carried on a genuine ministry to the management and employees of the Cobey Manufacturing Company. This is the way it works: every Monday morning all employees are invited into the sheet-metal department at 7:00 A.M. This is before the machinery is started. Those who do not care to participate remain in other departments of the factory.

The service begins at 7:00 and closes at 7:30 A.M. There is no singing. An opening prayer is followed by the reading of the Scriptures and this is followed by an extended period of silent prayer, each person being invited to pray from his own heart and in his own way. Then the pastor leads in prayer for the individuals present and their families, for America and for world peace. Following this period of prayer he gives a brief meditation based upon the Scripture reading. After the service the pastor is free to visit throughout the factory. He discovers all sorts of personal matters, and person after person is invited to the pastor's study next door after work to talk further.

It must be stated that it was not easy at first for the pastor to win the confidence of the men. They thought that the worship service was a scheme promoted by the management of the company, but the employees of the factory have learned to trust the pastor and feel free to go to him for discussion or counseling.

Each day during a county fair in Iowa, some local ministers hold daily services in a seventy-five-seat tent on the fairgrounds. They rented this tent from the officials of the fairground. There was a large sign over the entrance, "Come in and Rest Awhile." Several things claimed the visitor's attention. First, there was a ten-gallon jug of ice-cold water and paper cups. There were plenty of folding chairs around a large literature table.

From morning until night the tent was a busy place.

During the morning and afternoon there were religious motion pictures and slides provided by a group of churches. At 7:00 P.M. there was an evangelistic service with altar calls. People decided for the Lord. Then at 10:00 P.M. there was a prayer service for the employees. From thirteen to twenty persons attended this night prayer service. Throughout the week about five hundred persons entered the tent and participated in services.

An altogether different approach in Unconventional Evangelism was used at the DeQuoin, Illinois, State Fair. It was sponsored by a group of DeQuoin churches in conjunction with national boards of evangelism, social concerns, and lay activities. It was decided to name the project "the Fish," borrowing the ancient fish symbol, or *Ichthus*, used by early Christians. Space was rented at a prime location on the fairground where hundreds of people passed every hour. An outdoor platform was erected that could hold groups of ten to fifteen persons plus a piano and organ.

Throughout the day and evening a rock 'n' roll musical group, the Vincels, performed. In addition to secular music, they played such numbers as "The Battle Hymn of the Republic" and "He Has the Whole World in His Hands." Folk music and spirituals were played and sung. Every hour or two something unusual was done to attract a crowd. For instance, an enthusiastic master of ceremonies announced: "Ladies and gentlemen, in just a few moments Joe Hale will attempt a daring straitjacket escape hanging from this boom! Please stand by!" A crowd moved toward the outdoor platform which stood four feet high and was covered with bright red, white and blue cloth. They looked at the sign above the canopied platform, and wondered at the Ichthus symbol. A young person reached for a cup to draw water from a cooler that bore a sign: "Ice water given in the name of

Christ." On the platform, the Vincels were performing.
A large number of youth gathered around. Some looked
in wonder as the groovy sounds came from a Christian
pavilion. Others examined the display of great Christian
paintings on wooden racks outside the canopy. A young
person handed them a mimeographed sheet explaining
the history of the paintings.

Beside the platform was a tent with flaps up. You
could see the daylight screen and chairs. A young person handed out the booklet "One Way for Modern
Man"—the Gospel of John in a contemporary transla-
tion—and a card which explained the program of the
Fish.

The announcer spoke above the movement and
noise: "Welcome to the Fish. This program is free and
open to all. We are Christians here to have a good time
and to share our witness and faith with others. In a
few moments, we will have an opportunity to see
Parable, an eighteen-minute film from the New York
World's Fair. Right now we welcome Joe Hale, nationally
known escape artist and illusionist!" Joe Hale, at the
microphone, talked for a minute about the history of
strait-jacket escapes and then called men from the
crowd to place him securely in that article of restraint.
He was lowered from the platform and tied by the feet
to the lift.

A drum rolled slowly as the lift took Joe up, up, into
the air. "Are you ready, Joe?" the announcer asked. "Get
ready, set, go Joe!" . . . Five seconds . . . ten seconds . . .
twelve . . . the audience watched spellbound. Joe, swing-
ing by his feet, attempted to get out of the strait-jacket.
In just thirty seconds amid the clashing of cymbals, he
was free.

Joe Hale came quickly to the microphone. "I want
to tell you about a man who did not escape," he was say-

ing. "He wanted more than anything else to help people. He reached out His hands to bless people. When He drew them back, they were bleeding. He smiled at people and they crushed on His head a crown of thorns. I am here because that man has made life different for me!" A hush came over the audience. Many seemed moved by this expression of faith. Some walked on; some stayed to see and hear more of the program.

The announcer invited the people into the tent to see *Parable*. Throughout the day young people walked through the fairgrounds with cardboard signs hanging around their necks which read: "Special notice. Worship service Sunday morning at 7:30 A.M. and 9:00 A.M. Come as you are. For people of all churches. Paul Leaming will speak here on the subject, 'The Day the Lord Visited the DeQuoin State Fair.' "

How effective was it all?

Two opposite views were expressed as people visited the Fish at the DeQuoin State Fair last fall. One man said, "You certainly cannot call this evangelism." A woman replied, "I think this is wonderful. These young people are able to perform and express themselves. I wish the church had been willing to let my son be a part of something like this. Maybe we could have kept him in church."

The directors Paul Leaming and James Nettleton think about the things they saw: young people singing and speaking about their faith; the entire youth group of St. Matthew's Church from Bellville, Illinois, marching up the main street of the fair singing spirituals; the stranger who came up to Joe Hale, asking, "Can you help me? I am an alcoholic," and they move to one side as they engage in conversation. The question comes again: How effective was it all?

Of one thing, they are sure. At least the people at

the fair had been reminded again that God is concerned with persons wherever they are, and that He is seeking them even in the circus setting of life. One thing is sure— the church belongs where people are.

When *Time* magazine described Ocean City, New Jersey, as a place with the wildest reputation, a group of Drew University seminarians led by Professor David Randolph decided to start a project of Christian evangelism. Headquartered in "the Open House"—a summer home whose doors were never closed to those who sought conversations in the Christian faith—and distinguished outwardly by its use of the surfboard, the group made an effort to reach out for the interest and allegiance of the college crowd which was determined to find fun and avoid serious thought.

The aims were (1) to provide a place for young people to meet, and to engage in open discussion, creative expression and Christian witness; (2) to lead persons through individual work to appropriate Christ as Lord of their lives; (3) to develop a community of faith in which Christian responsibility could be developed.

During the first summer their ministry was primarily on one beach populated mainly by older youth and college students. Every approach was attempted during the summer months. Brief services of worship were held on the beach; "happenings"—dramatic events which pose a question or suggest an answer—were performed to large crowds on the beach; films were shown under the boardwalk and in the Open House; discussions were held on the beach, probing contemporary problems; informal discussions were held wherever contacts were made; and "sing-alongs" often led into informal discussions. Invitations were extended to the Open House to those who were having fun and wanted more, to those in trouble looking for a way out, and to those who wanted to deepen their understanding of life. That first summer the Open House was visited by hundreds of youth, dozens of whom wanted to seek further the meaning of God for their lives.

Whereas in the summer of 1966 the beach and the boardwalk were the setting for their public proclamation, the city commissioners prohibited this in 1967 under a new ordinance. Thus it was necessary to create within the Open House itself a public gathering place. The first floor largely became an auditorium in which young people could gather nightly to hear live music, poetry, discussions and Christian witnessing. It soon became one of the most popular gathering places for the young people in Ocean City. Good music, lively discussions, poetry and frank Christian proclamation drew crowds regularly. It was a rare night when the house was not packed.

Consequently, the difference between the first summer and the second should not be exaggerated. The place of witness was changed from outdoors to in, but the pattern was still the same: Christian proclamation in a public place by further conversation and often commitment to the community of Christian faith.

Inevitably the question must arise: Did the project achieve its purposes? What were the results? Well over five thousand persons visited the Open House during the second summer. The average attendance was more than one hundred persons for more than fifty nights. More than five hundred counseling sessions were carried on by staff members.

Randolph states:

> The crucial test of a project such as the Open House is the new life which is or is not lived by those who take part. The Open House is a project of Christian evangelism. What matters is the life of those persons who, looking back on their Christian experience in the

project can say, "Once I was blind, now I see." When this happens, it is the greatest reward that anyone can know and I thank God that it has happened again and again at the Open House. Perhaps the testimony of persons who have had this experience themselves is the best way to share it.

There is Jimmy. After listening to a sermon on the sand, he came to one of us and said, "I know there is this Jesus who is real for some of you. How can He become real for me?" That night, Jesus of Nazareth became real for Jimmy.

There is Bob, the playboy. Sensual, careless, flagrant. But the Open House at least opens up an option for him, an option for the best. And late one evening, sitting in his apartment, we are strangely moved as Bob reads with great sensitivity about the meaning of the Incarnation of Jesus Christ in W. H. Auden's great poem, "For the Time Being."

There is George. Strong, brilliant, articulate. In the beginning, he "knows" that God is dead, the Church defunct, Jesus a phony. At the beginning of the summer, George stands on the boardwalk and questions. But conversation ensues. Persons meet George at the Open House. We talk through the night. Later, we talk through another night. And another. At the end of the summer, George stands on the sand, and preaches. A girl passes by and, recognizing him, cries out, "I thought you were an atheist!" "I was," replies George, "but I have changed."

There is Susan. Full of promise, and of fear. Talented, and troubled. She joins the Open House and finding acceptance she begins to give the fullness of her joy and the richness of her talent. She looks like a new person. She is.

There is Carol. She visits the Open House. She must call her grandfather who is to visit her soon. While she is actually talking to her grandfather on the telephone, he dies suddenly. One of the staff sees her to her dorm, talks with her through the dark hours. Later Carol tells how that moment of concern and assurance held her life together when it was at the breaking point.

There is Bernice. She is in town for only a few days. But on Saturday night passing the 11th Street pavilion she listens to a song, hears the word of witness. She is struck. She writes to tell about the difference that made to her understanding of the Christian witness.

We could go on, filling in those faces in the crowd that light up the summer and make it glow with meaning. There may be cynics who sneer, "It's only for a moment." But no one who was there can believe that. This is real, and it is forever.

If out of the whole summer, just one of these miracles had taken place it would have been more than worth all our efforts. For now we know unmistakably that Christ stands by the Sea of the Atlantic as He did by the Sea of Galilee, and says still, "Follow me." And scholars and skeptics, waitresses and cooks, swingers and surfers become disciples.

Also, here are excerpts from some of the unsolicited letters which came from young people who had been at the Open House:

From a college student in Ohio: "Just a note to say thanks for allowing me the privilege of knowing, living with, learning and worshipping with you. I was greatly changed for the better. I hope that the change stays with me."

From a high-school student in Philadelphia: "I had to write and tell you how much this summer has changed my life. I was so confused when I first came down. Slowly but surely, the Open House changed my life and unraveled my tangled mind. I've really got to hand it to you. You've really got what it takes. . . . I know that no matter how hard I try, I'll never be able to put my feelings into words, but one thing you can be sure of is that if the Open House is open next year, I'll be there."

From a college student in New Jersey: "I want to tell you how much I enjoyed that Sunday service I attended. It made me think that formalized, ritualistic services seem medieval. I think the churches, especially mine, have a long way to go before they can reach the people—at least people like me. Most of all, I want to thank you for the Open House."

Young men and women recognize that God is the Giver of the new life they discover at the Open House. And many begin to walk with the One who walks by the Atlantic as He did by Galilee.*

In the present renewal of the church the parish has received slight attention. The updating of the parish is far down on the reformer's list of priorities. One of the new forms of evangelism that is attempting to utilize the strength of the local parish in reaching people in the inner-city is called STEM—Short Term Evangelistic Mission. While still in the experimental stage, it has met with some success in Harrisburg, Pennsylvania, and Akron, Ohio. The purpose of STEM is to enlist and train members of the local congregation to become involved and render a ministry to people in the inner-city. It has a three-point program. It seeks to enlist church members in a lay academy. Here through the study of Scripture and prayer along with the basic principles of sociology they learn how to relate the church to the needs of people in the local community.

Here is how it worked in the Centenary Church, Akron, Ohio. Centenary Church has about four hundred members and is situated in the inner-city of Akron. The majority of the members are middle-class Negroes living in the better Negro neighborhoods of Akron. The church is located in the ghetto near the urban renewal project and near a large metropolitan housing project. One hun-

* From an unpublished statement by David Randolph. A full account of the Ocean City ministry is available from the Board of Evangelism, The United Methodist Church, 1908 Grand Avenue, Nashville, Tennessee 37203.

dred twenty-five laymen in the church enlisted in the
lay academy. They pledged three nights a week for three
months to involve themselves in making contacts with
the church's mission outreach. This mission commitment
was expressed in the following ministries:

Pastoral Care
   Counseling
   Social welfare
   Senior citizens
   Juvenile offenders
   Street and night encounters
Youth and Young Adult Groups
   Coffee house
   Work projects
   Drama clubs
   Athletic teams
   Study hall and tutorial services
   Dialogue groups
Social Action
   Community organization
   Employment
   Housing developments
   Poverty

This unique three-month ministry involving one
hundred twenty-five persons had the following results:
The people in the ghetto community have had a completely changed attitude toward Centenary Church. The
people are beginning to realize that the church is interested in them. They are beginning to come to the church
for aid and they often see the pastor and the lay ambas-
sadors on the streets of the neighborhood. The church's
mini-bus often carries children to church activities or cultural activities in the city. They are aware that the
church is present in their community.

The STEM experiment has been a "revival" in the true sense of the word, because many of the church members of Centenary are more "alive" and involved with the work of the church as a result of the experiment. The experiment is the best of evangelism, since it gives a "wholistic" approach to the message of Jesus of Nazareth. Rather than being divided into social concern, education, missions, etc., the STEM experiment proclaimed the gospel in its wholeness on the streets of the ghetto, in the bars, before the altar, in the classroom setting, and everywhere. STEM did not openly proclaim civil rights or integration, but the experiment was conducted by a Negro missionary and a Caucasian pastor in a largely Negro neighborhood and sponsored by a predominately white annual conference Board of Evangelism. Tremendous interracial and intercultural action and progress was made. One result is that the white minister is now much better understood and accepted because the young Negro missionary and he proclaimed the same message in a united effort.

In the relatively short span of five years, more than one hundred churches, mostly campus churches and foundations, have opened the doors of a "coffee house." They are to be found in almost every section of the country. There is "The Ship's Mast" in Fitchburg, Massachusetts; "The Exit" in New Haven, Connecticut; "The Potter's House" operated by the Church of the Saviour in Washington, D.C.; "The Edge" in Bryn Mawr, Pennsylvania; "The Two Little Fishes" in Geneva-on-the-Lake, Ohio; "The Pipe" in Flint, Michigan; and "The Precarious Vision" in San Francisco, California. Although varying in purpose and method, they are all efforts to relate Christianity to a certain segment of society which is outside the organized church.

Typical of this new form of ministry is "Le Rapport"

coffee house in Seattle, Washington. This unconventional
development grew out of the couples club meetings of a
Presbyterian church. Discussions of contemporary novels,
paintings and films brought about many questions on
the meaning of life and the relevance of the Christian
faith, questions which seemed to confront both Christian
people and those outside the church. It was decided that
a coffee house could serve as an ideal place for such discussion, with people who might "come in off the street"
for refreshment.

Implicit in the decision to establish the house was
the belief that Christians are called to listen to and understand the beliefs and values that are most important
to the lives of their brothers outside the established
church. Why not meet them where they are, in an atmosphere of openness?

The enterprise soon got under way when the club
rented quarters next to the Ridgemont Theater in Seattle. (It has since relocated near the Seattle civic and
cultural center.) Inside the building, a large room serves
as an art museum, attracting people from all over the
Greater Seattle area. The main part of the coffee house,
dimly lit and furnished with small tables, has a wide
variety of enticing snacks available at moderate cost.

The programs of the coffee houses are varied, but
most include group discussions of contemporary ideas,
art exhibits, jazz and folk-song performances, dramatic
and poetry presentations, and film showings.*

The unique thing about the "Le Rapport" program is
its regular public discussions on weekend evenings. Most

---

* For a full description of this type of ministry see Elizabeth
O'Connor's two books, *Call to Commitment* (New York: Harper
& Row, 1963) and *Journey Inward, Journey Outward* (New York:
Harper & Row, 1968), and John D. Perry, Jr., *The Coffee House
Ministry* (Richmond: John Knox Press, 1966).

of these discussions begin at 10:00 P.M. and continue into the early morning hours. Lively and significant discussions have been held on such issues as civil rights, liturgical jazz, love and marriage, existentialism, the draft, disarmament, Christianity, the Bible, and modern science.

Coffee houses draw a varied clientele. Some attract mostly college students, while others attract young business and professional people. The difference depends largely on the location. Many unchurched persons take an active part in the discussions. The number of participants varies between twenty-five and two hundred.

Taking stock of this venture, a few observations can be made. First, the very fact that church people are involved in such an enterprise has been a strong witness to the church's concern to be relevant to the contemporary world. Christian people and those outside the church are sharing their ideas and feelings and listening and learning from one another. More than one person has remarked, "I never thought the church had it in itself to do such a thing."

Again, real dialogue and encounter between individuals is taking place. Very often, long after the public discussion has ended, small groups and couples will continue to discuss the issues on a personal level. Much friendship and understanding have been experienced over a cup of coffee.

Finally, the coffee house provides a place where Christians can witness to their Christian beliefs. Sometimes in a theoretical way, sometimes in a practical way, but nearly always in a decisive way, the nature of the Christian life and its challenges can be made clear.

From all the experiences described in this chapter, two factors merit special attention.

First, the importance of person-to-person contact stands out. Lyle Schaller's surveys have shown that fully one half of the persons who have been won to Christ and His church have named some form of person-to-person contact—influence of parent, spouse, friend, church visitor, pastor—as the single most important factor in making their commitment. If the Christian witness is to be expressed, Christians must be present and express it. Christians need to seek ways of sharing the Christian life. Each individual must seek creative ways of communicating the faith.

The second factor that merits special attention is that the time is past when it is possible to think that the needs of people can be met with three hymns and a sermon in a building at 11:00 A.M. on Sunday. They are the old wineskins and Christ has told us that our task is to find new ones. This new form of evangelism may be considered the new wineskin, and a worthy supplement to the conventional methods already being used.

There is now a mobile gospel for a mobile age. The message can be transported. The church need not stay in the safe sanctuary, which has become a ghetto to many. The church which is primarily concerned with its own support can now move out into the highways and byways to bring the message of God to man.*

* For further reading on this subject the reader may consult Hans Jürgen Schultz, *Conversion to the World* (New York: Charles Scribner's Sons, 1968), pp. 74f.

4. Preaching in Unconventional Places

Hymns, prayers and a brief sermon for those who will stop and listen are provided by the First Congregational Church of Washington, D.C. Services are held at noon on the corner of 10th and G streets. Laymen always participate in the services. Often a layman will make a personal testimony as to what the Christian faith means to him. Commenting on the services, a neighboring pastor said: "Two facts impress me about such an outdoor service. We actually have so much more opportunity to praise and witness for God by what we do and by what we are when we are outside a church building. The religious teaching that goes on inside even the best of churches is secondary to the learning that takes place in our business relations, in our homes, in our day-by-day conversations on busy streets. An outdoor service is a needed symbol that authentic religion belongs on the streets of the city, permeating our busy, hectic life. The second fact that such a service symbolizes is that each of us inevitably makes a testimony to the faith we live by. Sometimes we do it formally by a sermon, or the teaching of a church school lesson. More often and more persuasively we testify by the exhibition of our unstudied and casual revelation of how much the love of Christ is reflected in our own affection and attitude toward one another."

Most Unconventional Evangelism takes place outside the church building. Preaching in the open under the skies is as old as preaching itself and is thoroughly biblical.

The Old Testament is filled with many instances. When Enoch preached, his pulpit was a hillside; and Noah spoke in the shipyard while his ark was being built. Moses and Joshua addressed vast assemblies in the open air. Samuel closed his sermon in a field at Gilgal amid thunder and rain. Elijah stood on Mount Carmel and challenged the vacillating nation with "How long halt ye between two opinions. If the Lord be God, follow Him; if Baal, then follow him." Jonah gave his warning in the streets of Ninevah. He was heard by multitudes who would never had known of his existence if he had hired a hall.

In the New Testament, we have John the Baptist crying in the wilderness and lifting his voice along the river's bank. He awakened an interest which never would have been aroused had he remained in the synagogue.

Jesus began His teaching in the synagogues of Galilee, but before long the opposition and the hatred of the orthodox religious authorities of His day had shut the door of the synagogue against Him and He was driven out to the roads and the hillsides and the seashore. By far the greatest part of His teaching and preaching was done in the open air.

The disciples preached in the court of the Temple, and, with equal earnestness, in every house they sought to teach and preach Jesus Christ. From city to city they proclaimed everywhere the Word of the Lord.

During the Dark Ages the itinerant friars and founders of religious orders such as Berthold and Bernard, who preached and taught in the open air and in homes, kept the faith alive. It would be accurate to say that revivals of religion have usually been accompanied, if not caused, by a considerable amount of preaching in unconventional places. The first avowed preaching of Protestantism was almost necessarily in the open air, or in places not dedicated to public worship. Would there have been a Reformation in the sixteenth century if the preachers had confined themselves to the churches? Would the common people have heard the Good News of the gospel if it had not been for the traveling evangelists who went to the market places, the burial grounds, and the hillsides, to proclaim the Good News, where the common people heard them gladly?

It was a great day for England, and the world, when John Wesley took up Unconventional Evangelism. It was not easy for him to do this. He writes in his *Journal*: "Saturday, the thirty-first [March 31, 1731]. In the evening I reached Bristol, and met Mr. Whitefield there. I could scarce reconcile myself at first to this strange way of preaching in the fields, of which he set me an example on Sunday; having been all my life (till very lately) so tenacious of every point relating to decency and order, that I should have thought the saving of souls almost a sin, had it not been done in a church."

Again, he could write: "Our societies were formed of those who were wandering upon the dark mountains, that belonged to no Christian Church and were awakened by the preaching of the Methodists who have pursued them through the wilderness of this world, to the highways and hedges, to the markets and the fairs, to the hills and the dale, who set up the standard of the cross in the streets and lanes of the cities, in the villages, in the barns, in the farmers' kitchens and all this in such a way and to such an extent as never had been before since the apostolic age."*

The great benefit of preaching in unconventional places is that we get so many people to hear the gospel who otherwise would never hear it. In numerous projects as many as 40 per cent of those present never attend religious services in a church building. There are multitudes of men and women who will not be reached by routine sermons at 11:00 A.M. on Sunday morning.

Preaching outdoors is never easy. The speaker will be preaching the Word in unconventional places. He will be without the support of an altar and church surroundings. With the exception of the drive-in services, the people will be those who did not come to hear him preach, but who are seeking pleasure or business or whatever it may be that brought them into the area at that time. Something real has to speak out of a person's mind and heart as he presents God and Christ.

In regard to a message to these people, a speaker needs to be explicit in a good, homely, simple way, stating what a Christian believes. He needs to forget his theological terms. The theology will be there but he must not attempt to preach theology. He has to begin with people at the point where they are. He cannot tell them to come back to God when they have never been with God. The best of preaching is to pick people up at the point of their questions and continue from there. The message that he presents must be simple. What is God attempting to say to us? How does the Christian faith speak to us? What does a Christian believe? How can we

* *The Journal of the Rev. John Wesley, A.M.,* ed. Nehemiah Curnock, Standard Edition (London, 1911), Vol. II, p. 167. For an account of the part played by the Religious Societies in the earliest periods of the Evangelical Revival see Vol. I, p. 198 *note,* p. 316 *note;* Vol. II, p. 71 *note,* p. 113 *note.*

receive God's help? How can we learn to pray? These are relevant questions and he should give answers and guidance.*

He will be talking with people who may think about God but who do not know Him. From the very beginning he needs to put himself in their place. After a church service one day, a member said to his pastor, "You preach always to us as though we are all Christians." He should have some way of explaining to these people who do not understand. He must be clear.

Harry Denman tells about the man who was at the Boston Airport when the lights went out. An expert was called in who checked the switch, cleaned it, and then all the lights went on again. This electrician then commented, "You need to keep your points clean."

A young woman told her father when he was coming to the college campus to talk to some young people, "Dad, don't horse around, get to the point."

The preacher needs to drop the conventional phrase and word, get rid of the generalities, be real, with no elaboration. He must preach in such a way that what he says will stick with the person even in the gray cold light of the next morning. He needs to preach so that people are changed, to preach as though he means it—because he does. He must preach as though it matters terribly what these people do about it—because it does.

Avoid the weary phrase and the complicated sentence structure. The phrase "we beseech thee" is totally alien to the unchurched. So is the expression "saved by Grace" without an explanation. Rufus Jones used to tell about a scientist on a lyceum circuit in a small town who started his lecture with the statement, "Now you all

* For a good example of a preacher facing these and other relevant questions, see Leonard Griffith, *Barriers to Christian Belief* (London: Hodder and Stoughton, 1962).

know what the inside of a corpuscle is like." Whereupon
he was interrupted by the chairman of the meeting who,
speaking for the group, said, "Yes, most of us do know
what the inside of a corpuscle is like, but I would suggest
that you describe it for the benefit of the few who have
never been inside one!" That is a parable with a moral
for those who would indulge in the old vocabulary.*

Sometimes the preacher needs to make people uncomfortable. Jesus was not all gentleness. Don't pull any
punches. Preachers will recall that Peter said, "Go away
from me, I cannot take it." The sin of some people is that
they think nothing is wrong with them.

Bishop Hazen G. Werner tells of an experience in
traveling overseas. He was approached by a man who
wanted to sell him some essence. The Bishop said that
he could get all the perfume he wanted in the United
States. The man then told the Bishop what perfume is
made of. "Its base is essence. Essence is the most important part of the perfume; it is what gives it its quality and
fragrance." This is true also in preaching. If one gives
the essence of the gospel to people, they will recognize
it for the real thing. He may not have the protective
background of an altar and a pulpit; but if he speaks in
the language they understand and is truly sincere, they
will get what he is trying to give them.

But a person cannot preach this way unless Christ
matters to him. The best preparation for this kind of
preaching is in the solitude of one's own self-examina-
tion, in his own petition to Almighty God for light and
understanding and in his own relationship to Christ. God
can make us able for this, and these people need the wit-

* For further reading on how to translate the Word into
concrete terms of Christian living and acting in the world, the
reader is referred to Reuel L. Howe, Partners in Preaching (New
York: The Seabury Press, 1967).

ness of our spirit. This is a great venture. The leader will find that it is not only inspiring, but also in this he will discover an experience that will renew himself. In this rediscovery he will begin to see men and women change because of his presence with them.

I heard the story of the successful finish of a drama that had been enacted one night. That night a little boy, five years old, was attending a picnic with his parents and wandered away. In panic the parents called the forest rangers. They in turn alerted the police, and five hundred persons, dismissing their own responsibilities and their need of sleep, tramped the woods because a boy was lost. In the morning the planes took off and continued the search from the air until the glad word came that the child was found. This tremendous outpouring of concern for a lost child exemplifies what needs to happen to us in this whole matter of evangelistic process.

5. Some Requisites and Observations

FOR some time now the church has recognized that more than the traditional "Sunday-go-to-meeting" service is necessary if the witness for Jesus Christ is to be made with penetration and force in our time. The church has been aware that she needs to find new and more adequate forms and structures through which she may witness her eternal concern for persons and that God's love become a prime mover in the hearts of people. This concern gave birth to the movement known as Unconventional Evangelism.

Unfortunately, Unconventional Evangelism is still too new to have developed planning principles that guarantee success, but it is time to systematize the knowledge we do possess about this form of evangelism and to begin to formulate some basic principles for implementation of the concept.

Some of the principles stated here may appear to be so self-evident that the reader will wonder why it is necessary to write them down. However, they are so important that they need to be mentioned so that they will not be overlooked when the actual planning is done.

FIRST PRINCIPLE

Unconventional Evangelism provides Christian encounter with people in unusual places. It differs from conventional evangelism in at least three ways.

First, one goal of conventional evangelism is to get people into the church building to hear the preaching of the gospel. Unconventional Evangelism is taking the gospel out of the church building to where the people are. It is taking the Good News to persons in state parks, recreational areas, county fairs, shopping centers, drive-in theaters, mobile homes and camping areas. It is an attempt to reach the multitudes of men and women who never come to a church building.

A second way in which unconventional and conventional evangelism differ is in the area of visitation. In a well-organized program of conventional evangelism the members of the church are trained and directed to visit unchurched families in their homes. This is not true in Unconventional Evangelism, with the exception of visiting families in the mobile-home areas. Any visiting that occurs in connection with Unconventional Evangelism will be done on the spot—in the county fair prayer tent, in the cars in the drive-in theater and in the tents of the recreation and camping areas.

Third, in conventional programs, while it is often announced that commitment to Christ and the Christian faith is the primary goal, the goal that is usually stressed is the uniting with the fellowship of the church. In the program of Unconventional Evangelism the primary goal is not the uniting with the church, although this may be one of the end results. The primary goal is twofold: a commitment to Christ and the Christian faith and an invitation to join an "inquirers" group where they become seekers and learners in the Christian faith. This is brought out more fully in the Fourth Principle.

Second Principle

Unconventional Evangelism requires understanding of the people to whom one witnesses. The person using the techniques of Unconventional Evangelism meets many kinds of people. He finds that many of them are negative in their thinking. They probably belong to that group of citizens who seldom, if ever, are in a church. Close to 40 per cent of the people in America are non-church people. Some have a remote religious history; and some, none at all. They have probably forgotten the name of the church they stay away from. Many never hear a spiritual word from one week to the next. They are uncommitted people. One has to go to them; they will not come to him.

Most of the people there did not come to hear him preach, but are seeking pleasure, or business, or whatever it may be that brought them into the area at that time. Many of the people he will be preaching to are materialistic, pleasure seeking and fatalistic. Many of them—as in the case of those reached through factory evangelism, drive-in services, and park areas—belong to the so-called middle-class. They include working mothers, union-minded fathers, dollar-seeking businessmen and pleasure-bent youth and adults—all of them thrust down into the very midst of life.

Essentially, this means that they will be thinking in terms of materialistic concerns. They are people who believe in success and who think that the sole answer to their need is affluence. These people are seeking life more and more but finding it less. "Sin is an attempt to

get out of life what God never put in it," said John Oman.
"The lives of such men and women are empty; they are
truly called the hollow people." Many are full of fear in
spite of the fact that they project an image of confidence.

There are, however, basically good things about
many people. Most demonstrate a loyalty to their country. They approve of conventional moral standards. They
love and have concern for their children. Many have a
nostalgic feeling about God. They are generous in respect to their fellow man. They want their lives to have
meaning. They have a desire for significance. Many
people are having a desperate time. We can address ourselves to all these concerns. We must bear all these things
in mind when we talk to them.

Today, many people are estranged from God. To
many, God represents a vague recollection of something.
The question is: Have we a gospel for these people? Is it
relevant? Will it meet their need? People are caught up
in a modern type of depravity. Moral decline is evident
in American life, like a plague of locusts. The mass of the
people never hear a spiritual message. Many are without
standards, they are without God. People are enduring
life as best they can. The only deity these people have
is the dollar sign—no Christian dreams or Christian idealism. People can hardly return to a God they have never
known.

These are the people whom we are to love. These
are the people for whom Christ is the answer. They are
rarely moved by the invitation, "Come to church and get
in with the right crowd." Many people know all too well
that the average church does not speak meaningfully to
their condition. They want to know where they can find
specific answers to the gnawing hunger of their hearts:
"Who am I? Where am I going? Why am I here? Upon

what or whom can I place my hope?" They want to know where they can find the answers to such fundamental questions.

Modern man has explored and exploited sex. He has floated his problems on a sea of alcohol. He has turned gregarious—joined the gang, the country club, the lodge, the bridge club, the poker gathering, or a labor union. He has participated in every kind of sport—yachting, fishing, golf, bowling and all the spectator sports. He has tried new cars. He has sought to escape from it all on weekends, near or on the water, or in parks and playgrounds. Yet, his deepest hunger eludes him, leaving him restless and choked with anxieties.

Our task is to take the gospel, the Good News, to such people.

THIRD PRINCIPLE

Unconventional Evangelism offers a unique opportunity for laymen to witness. Methodist Bishop Francis E. Kearns reminds us that the term "evangelism" does not refer to an office. Rather, it denotes a function which is the responsibility of every person who has committed himself to Christ and enthroned Him as the Lord of his life.

When Our Lord called His followers "witnesses," He made it clear that their place is in the world with people. The world is where the people are—in factories, shops, state parks and recreational areas. Whether we are passing out bulletins or directing people as they drive their cars into a drive-in service or giving a testimony in a county fair prayer-tent service or visiting in a crowded mobile home, our witness is to reach out to people, listen to them and care for them. A Christian witness is more than a mere person-to-person social contact. We are to relate ourselves intimately through His spirit with them. We are to understand them. Only as we demonstrate our concern for them as persons have we the right to speak to them of Christ.

This leads to the second step in witnessing. We may call it the sufficiency of a simple Christian experience. A leading businessman in one community said to a large gathering of churchmen, "I have served with you on every kind of committee—Red Cross, Community Chest, Chamber of Commerce, and Better Business—but I have never before had a chance to tell you about the most important thing in my life, Jesus Christ." And with that he launched into one of the most convincing testimonies ever heard from a layman. He witnessed to the central issue of personal redemption through Jesus Christ.

Some Christian people feel that they cannot be witnesses because they have nothing to tell others that is extraordinary or impressive. They have never had any great mystical experiences and feel that they have nothing to say. Christianity does not consist entirely or even primarily in such experiences. To be a Christian is not so much to have special kinds of experiences as it is to understand all the ordinary experiences of life in a new way.

The Christian, for example, sees God's goodness and mercy in the ordinary blessings and joys of life which others either take for granted or just set down to good luck. The Christian sees God's guiding and leading hand in all the opportunities that come for helpfulness and service; opportunities which others think of as burdens and responsibilities. The Christian sees God's disciplining and schooling in disappointment, suffering and loss; things which others regard as misfortunes or unlucky accidents. So a witness has eyes and sees the significant things that are happening, the meaning of the surface events which others miss. A good witness is not only one who is on the spot; he also gets the point. Our Christian witness most often consists in finding God in every one of our daily experiences and living in such an expectant and confident way that people begin to realize that we, indeed, have found Him there.

People will very largely make up their minds about Our Lord and His importance for life on the basis of our testimony—not just the testimony of our words but of our lives. If we see Him as secondary in importance to most other things in life, if we serve Him with the leftovers of our time, our money and our talents, if we never take any trouble to speak to friends and neighbors about Him and about the change He can work in life, the world will conclude that He is of very little importance after all, no matter what great things we say about Him in the Creed. Whether we are bearing witness consciously or not, what we do about Our Lord will be the weightiest kind of testimony—either pro or con—in the minds of a questioning and wistful world.

If we have really known the joy and the peace of being accepted by Him and loved by Him and of having all men as our brethren because of His love, then ought we not to move in the world as His witnesses, persuading others by word and by life that Christ is what He claims to be, the Savior and Redeemer of the world? *

* For further reading on this Principle, see John Macquarrie, *Principles of Christian Theology* (New York: Charles Scribner's Sons, 1966), pp. 374f.; Franklin H. Littell, *The Ministry of the Laity*, leaflet available from the National Council of Churches, 475 Riverside Drive, New York, N.Y.

FOURTH PRINCIPLE

Unconventional Evangelism calls for a threefold commitment. First, it seeks to enlist new persons wherever they are and establish them in the Christian faith. It seeks to take the gospel to the outsider in a way that will cause him to accept it. The task is to recreate persons individually and socially and to bring their lives into harmony with the will and purposes of God.

The unconventional evangelist tries to create such an environment that persons will experience God as the ground of their being—that they will be aware of Him as closer than breathing, nearer than hands or feet, and will recognize that they are alive by existing in Him.

John R. Mott has defined the task as "making Jesus Christ known, trusted, loved and obeyed." This states the task. How to accomplish it requires careful explaining.

This leads to a second element in commitment. The environment created by the unconventional evangelist needs to offer an invitation to discipleship, making clear how the invitation may be accepted. It does not seek a mere profession of faith upon the part of the individual. It is not an invitation to church membership.

Rather, the evangelist seeks to bring persons to commit their lives to God in joyful obedience. The best way to do this is to suggest that they join a fellowship group. Here they will make Christian friends, learn the fundamentals of Christian belief and practice, learn the meaning of worship and discipleship—all in the company of similar seekers. The experience of many unconventional evangelists indicates that uncommitted persons confronted by the claims of Christ upon their lives are much more likely to respond to an affirmative decision within a fellowship group than are persons who are confronted as

isolated individuals. Often persons experience the re-
deeming love of God within the sustaining fellowship
and are empowered to go into the world to witness and
to be salt and light.*

The third element in commitment involves the new
believer's witness in the world. The goal of Unconventional Evangelism is to prepare persons for penetration
into society, not to imprison the evangelized within the
church building. The purpose of evangelism is the preparation of the believer for Christian witness in the
world. This witness is to be measured by the quality of
one's love for persons. It is not enough to declare that
God is love; it is, rather, to declare that all our relationships exist on love. He who does not know and demonstrate love toward his fellow man does not know God,
says the apostle John.

Becoming a Christian is more than a commitment.
The commitment must be followed by a process of
growth.

FIFTH PRINCIPLE

*Unconventional Evangelism may lead to unpredict-
able results.* "God moves in a mysterious way His wonders to perform" certainly applies to Unconventional

* For a more extended treatment of this point see James E.
Sellers, *The Outsider and the Word of God* (Nashville: Abingdon
Press, 1961), pp. 27f.
For further reading: Stark and Glock, *American Piety: The
Nature of Religious Commitment* (Berkeley: University of Cal-
ifornia Press, 1968), pp. 11-21; a helpful discussion of the impact
of religious commitment in the lives of people. D. Elton Trueblood,
The Company of the Committed (New York: Harper & Row,
1961), pp. 22f. Hans Jürgen Schultz, *Conversion to the World*
(New York: Charles Scribner's Sons, 1968), pp. 95f.

Evangelism. The following demonstrates what can take place.

A disgruntled church member, who had not attended church for a couple of months because he was irritated with his pastor, was walking through a shopping center where his pastor and a quartet were holding a witnessing service. He paused to listen. Somehow the spirit of Christ spoke to him in a new way. At the close of the service he talked to his pastor and has been restored to activity in the church once more.

At a county fair there was a prayer tent set up under the auspices of the Council of Churches. Every evening at 10:00 o'clock, one of the pastors held a prayer service for the employees of the fair. One man, who ran the ferris wheel and who traveled from fair to fair, began attending these prayer services. At the close of one of the meetings, he came to the pastor, asking for help. Life had lost its purpose and meaning for him, and in this prayer experience he came to find life in Christ.

A pastor reports that after every service in a state park, two to five persons make appointments for counseling.

Another pastor says: "In our service at the county jail, we have many who ask for prayer. One man who was involved in a murder made a statement worth repeating. After hearing the claims of Christ, he said: 'I wish I had heard this message when I was seventeen.' He was twenty-four years of age."

The pastor of an outpost church school gives this testimony: "The elementary teachers, where our Central Avenue children attend school, remark that the children are cleaner and are much more regular in attendance. We hope to rent a larger building where we can care for more students."

Across the country many large churches are conducting projects in Unconventional Evangelism. One church of 1,800 members has four major projects they carry on: drive-in church, food tent at a county fair, state park services, and meditations at the local drag strip. Here is what the minister has to say about them: "Both my associate minister and I use the above-mentioned projects for personal work wherever the opportunity presents itself. At the drive-in church we hold a Fellowship Hour after the service, and serve coffee and doughnuts. This gives us an opportunity to set up counseling appointments. At the county fair we work full time in the tent, using every opportunity to talk to our own people as well as friends that drop in to eat. Increasingly we serve the carnival crowd and minister to them. At the state park we have many opportunities to speak to people in a relaxed way around their camp fire. Always we try to witness to Christ and the Christian life."

This minister has learned that evangelism is more than engaging people in dialogue. Christian witness is helpful and meaningful only if persons are confronted with the claims of God upon their lives. At this juncture of man's need and God's action in Jesus Christ, evangelism occurs.

SIXTH PRINCIPLE

Unconventional Evangelism must be led by people who dare to be event-makers. Admiral Halsey said there are no great men but occasionally a man rises from mediocrity to the challenge before him. This is not necessarily true, for heroes come in two classes. There are eventful heroes who have greatness thrust upon them, like the fabled Dutch boy at the dike. He happened along at the right time. Then there are those who seize events and through their imaginative use of talents and drive make such events servants of their personality, purpose and goal. Both classes of men are to be found in the ministry. Some move with the time or conditions of their church and often have greatness thrust upon them —such is often the case with ministers who have been assigned town or country parishes and have awakened one morning to find suburbia upon them. People have poured into their little churches to be served and the churches have grown enormously.

Unconventional Evangelism does not fall within this category. It can be said that a person engaged in Unconventional Evangelism is an event-maker rather than an eventful hero. As in any other area the success of the venture is bound up in the personality of the leader or leaders.

Let us take the case of Peter Parry, a second-year student at the Boston University School of Theology. His assignment was to hold dialogue with young people in a state park on weekends and to make a witness. Let him tell his own story:

"On the first weekend my main objective was to get into the state park, look at the place and make contacts. After looking around I decided the best way to get a group of young people together without causing suspicion or complaint was to have a ball game. I got a group of some twenty-two fellows together for about four innings. Some girls stood around. After the game the boys and girls dispersed as quickly as they had come. Sunday, I was to discover that the camping crowd was a very fluid society—the people were there only a day or two.

"The following Saturday I tried the same technique, with the same results. When the game ended, so did the group. At no time did I feel 'comfortable enough' or feel it to be the opportune time to make any religious witness or appeal. On Sunday I assisted in a drive-in service near the park and no young people were present.

"Next Saturday I started another ball game with the intention of keeping the group together somehow. It started to rain and I made up my mind that instead of growling at the weather, I was going to use it somehow. I followed the group over to a nearby social hall, just a large building that could be used for dancing, with a few chairs around. The boys and girls sat down and we began to talk about life in general. After asking a few questions I then said, 'Do any of you ever pray about the problems that you are facing?' One boy said, 'Pray. To whom?' I said, 'Have you ever prayed to God?' One girl said, 'I prayed when my mother died, but that was years ago.' Another boy said, 'Science seems to have an explanation for everything. I am wondering if there is a God.' One question after another came, and before long they were talking about the purpose of life and one asked what God meant to me. I began to feel God's spirit was working among us. Some sixteen of us were beginning to dig into something other than 'rock 'n' roll' and cigarettes.

"When I went into the hall on the following Saturday afternoon, I was amazed that the kids there were almost the same gang I had the previous Saturday. They were eager to jump into another discussion, and afterwards they begged me to come on their safari with them (a safari is a big necking party in the picnic pavilion about a half-mile from the social hall). I decided to join them, so at 9:00 P.M. we were off for the picnic pavilion. Not everybody had a girl, so I wasn't alone in my bachelorhood. When we got to the pavilion I told them a story about a dangerous hunt; they enjoyed it, but were frank enough to inform me not to lengthen the story and take all their romantic time away, for they had to be in by 10:30.

"On Sunday afternoon at 2:15 the gang was at the hall ready for the planned discussion on 'sin.' The discussions were good, and I drove home one point more than any other: 'God has a purpose for your life; why don't you ask Him what it is and follow it.' It hurt to say goodbye to those kids because we shared a lot together in a few days. They liked me, I liked them, and I knew next week I would have to start all over and form a new group for a discussion.

"The following Saturday night I went to the social hall to see what I could arrange for Sunday afternoon. Much to my surprise, one of the fellows was there from last week's gang and he had been going around telling all the kids that there was going to be a great discussion Sunday afternoon. It was good to see one of the boys recruiting. On Sunday afternoon the discussion was held —twelve were present, all new except one. These discussions went on all summer.

Each time there is a discussion the kids don't want me to leave, not always because they want to discuss more but sometimes because they like what I stand for. I make this observation to show you that these kids— rough, at times crudely frank in their comments to both girls and boys—are hungry for something that they don't know how to find, and they need courage and encouragement to seek the living God. At least 85 per cent of them never darken a church doorway but I knew at the end of the summer they were really thinking and wanting something that lifts men from what they are to something much greater.

"At the same time I was working with the youth, I was developing an adult interfaith program among the trailerites, but this is another story."

Such a summer experience as Pete Parry's breathes new life into the ministry. In ministering to those young people in pre-evangelism he had no neat solutions, but he was there, in Christ's name and spirit, exploring and experimenting, ever seeking new and relevant approaches in the midst of young people who have forsaken the church and who, in too many instances, have been forsaken by the church. As Pete began this ministry, the youth were not tuned to hear the message of God's forgiveness and acceptance. Now he has helped them to a place where they are open to the life-changing Word which has yet to be spoken. We need event-makers like Pete Parry.

SEVENTH PRINCIPLE

Unconventional Evangelism is effective in areas of neglect. Obviously, one needs initiative in the task of finding places to carry on this ministry.

About four miles from Rootstown, Ohio, there is a mobile-home area called Valley Hills Mobile Home Park. It consists of sixty trailers and is a community within itself. It has electricity, sewers, water and a recreation building. It also has a laundromat, small restaurants, stores and a beauty parlor—everything but a church.

One day the Rev. Mr. Wagner and Mr. Albert Jones, church school superintendent, visited the manager and confronted him with the possibility of a church school in his development. The manager was not optimistic, but he said, "You may feel free to visit the families and, if there are enough interested, you may have free use of the recreation building." After one evening of training, some members of the church called upon the occupants of the sixty trailers and found the majority of the people to be Baptists, Congregationalists and Methodists. Without exception, they were delighted with the possibility of a church school. The people were neither rich nor poor—they were average-income people. About a third were of retirement age. Many of the others had children. The husbands worked on construction and as truck drivers.

A committee of interested parents was set up. In the home church, a meeting was called for the committee on education. Committees were chosen to obtain equipment and personnel. At first the teachers came from the church, but several weeks later the interested parents at Valley Hills took a course in teacher training. They conducted church school amid billiard tables, pingpong tables and the like. Today there is a thriving church school.

This is a good illustration of a man's imagination and recognition of need.

EIGHTH PRINCIPLE

Unconventional Evangelism requires a definite purpose and a clear goal. If you plan to set up a project at a county fair and call it a prayer tent, your committee ought to know its objective long before the project gets under way. Of course, one can say we already have an over-all purpose in our theme, Unconventional Evangelism, to reach persons for Christ. With that we can agree, but we must be more specific if we are to present an effective picture to the persons who have absolutely no interest in religion. Also, we can't forget those who feel that the tent at a county fair is simply reverting to the "old-time religion" of their grandfathers and the "sawdust trail."

For this particular project we get a clear-cut clue to the objective or purpose for the designation "prayer tent." If we are going to call it a prayer tent then it ought to be just that. It should serve as a sanctuary where people from all walks of life enter to pray, reflect and meditate in private. It should serve the people who are not only visitors to the fairgrounds, but also those who are employed by the fair board and the many who are there to display their goods, wares, livestock, etc. Further, the purpose ought to be to expose persons to some of the finest devotional literature the church produces, so that Christ may speak to them through the words of others in print.

It is important for the leaders of such a project to realize that just setting up a tent with background music and being hospitable is not evangelism. Everything within the tent—the conversation of friendly hosts and leaders, the atmosphere created, music and physical articles such as pictures, altar, etc., as well as the opportunities for prayer and meditation—must be conducive to the presence of God's Spirit seeking those who enter.

NINTH PRINCIPLE

Unconventional Evangelism must not assume a flash-in-the-pan character. The proposed project should be thoroughly studied and analyzed before one attempts to put it into operation. A clear division of purposes should be formulated, even though they may change as the project progresses. Evaluation procedures should also be planned, not only at the close of the project, but also at a midpoint so that reorientation may be accomplished, if necessary.

Integration of the project into the official program of the local church is essential if the church is to benefit. Surely the minimum would be reporting through a committee to the official organization of the church so that the church would be aware of what is going on.

Thorough study is required of cooperative ventures to be conducted by councils of churches or neighborhood groups of churches. In one state, the Methodist bishop called for volunteers who would be willing to go out and make a Christian witness in factories, shopping centers, drive-in theaters, and state and municipal resorts. Fifty-two ministers and laymen attended a one-day workshop. Experienced leaders in various areas held training sessions on how to set up the programs. Guidance was given on the type of messages to be presented. In each instance, responsibility was checked so that the reality of the message was effective and in good taste. In many activities the responsibility was centered in the individual minister and church. As a matter of experience, Unconventional Evangelism at the local level needs the active participation of many laymen.

Speaking in a more personal vein, it is necessary that every person seeking a total commitment to Christ and the Christian way of life be assimilated into the life of a worshiping community. The best way to grow in the life of commitment is to participate in the community of fellow seekers. One cannot do this alone. There is no such thing as a solitary Christian. A Christian is a person who participates in the church because he seeks a living fellowship where he may both receive the spirit and presence of Christ and share it with others. To claim to walk alone outside the company of other seekers after Christ is pure self-righteousness. One can no more think of an independent Christian than he can think of a finger or an ear existing by itself.*

The purpose of the church is to encourage a person in his spiritual growth and development. By being part of a group and engaging wholeheartedly in worship and

* For a more extended treatment of this point see D. Elton Trueblood, *The Company of the Committed* (New York: Harper & Row, 1961), p. 49.

study, such a person stands a much better chance of advancing in his own personal knowledge and strength than if he goes it alone.

TENTH PRINCIPLE

Unconventional Evangelism should avoid gadgets, gimmicks and sensationalism. Gadgets, gimmicks and sensationalism may work effectively in advertising but they are not the answer to promoting a project of Unconventional Evangelism. Churches that have tried to build an appeal to their constituents through gimmicks may have succeeded in attracting a crowd for a time, but in the long run they have lost their audience as well as the confidence of the people they have been seeking to reach.

One such church had on its lawn a ten-foot cross of rugged timber. A tattered white garment with red spots floated from it in the breeze, and below the garment were propped a spear and an oversize pair of dice. At the base of the cross rested a sign: "Is it nothing to you, all you that pass by?"

Another church runs large newspaper ads emphasizing the healing services. Great emphasis is placed on the miraculous power of the oil that is used in the healing service. Promises are made through newspaper ads that "If you bring your sick and maimed, God will perform a miracle."

In another church there is an enormous backdrop of the Sea of Galilee with a spout of water gushing out. Such gadgets and appeals detract from the central message of the gospel. Unconventional Evangelism's keynote is not toward such spectacular, bizarre and "far-out" symbols.

During the past five years an interesting experiment has been conducted during Easter vacation at Daytona Beach, Florida. One year a caravan made up of Christian athletes and ministers drove up and down the two miles of sand at Daytona Beach entertaining thousands of college students. Members of the caravan at the same time reminded the students of the week's religious significance and told them of their own Christian faith.

"We're trying to let them know the church cares," said one clergyman. "We like to believe that if they were home, they would be attending Holy Week services. They can't be in church here, so we're taking the 'church' to them."

The caravan traveled the beach for two or three hours each afternoon, stopping for thirty minutes or so at heavily populated spots. A brief jazz concert attracted hundreds, sometimes more than a thousand, to the two trucks in the caravan. A weight-lifter performed, showing his physical prowess by lifting a table of eight husky collegians and invited aspiring musclemen to work with him later in the afternoon. An artist drew chalk pictures of Christ; sometimes he added a few words on the Holy Week theme. Professional athletes, their names and teams stamped on their sweatshirts, mingled among the crowd to establish personal rapport, then climbed to the platform to explain why they were there.

Reactions among the students were varied. Some considered the Christian "pitch" an intrusion on their one week away from the pressure of college.

Another complained that the athletes were cheapening religion. "It's just like one of these guys going on the tube and proclaiming he uses a shaving cream or a hair lotion," he said. "The scene just doesn't seem right."

Surprisingly few displayed disgust. "Most waited in boredom until trumpeter 'Doc' Evans and banjo artist

Marvin Montgomery gave them what they wanted to hear."

Many others found themselves for the first time engaging in meaningful dialogue with Christian athletes, whom they highly regarded.

Having pointed out some of the results of the spectacular, it must be added that the abilities and the personality of the conductor of any project of Unconventional Evangelism must be taken into consideration. One man's strong point is another's downfall.

ELEVENTH PRINCIPLE

Unconventional Evangelism contacts are frequently made through regular church programs. The community religious survey by telephone makes contact with unchurched people living within a reasonable distance of the local church. Such a survey may be conducted cooperatively by a council of churches or by an individual church. If it is conducted by a local church it will take about six weeks to discover where the people are and to ascertain their interest in church.

When Broad Street Church, Columbus, Ohio, decided to have a Spiritual New Life Mission, members felt they had two alternatives: first, the members of the church could go from door to door, asking where the residents worship and extending an invitation to the local church; second, they could try using the "survey by telephone." They decided on the latter.

Two months before the survey, the geographical area was determined. This normally falls under the work of the Membership and Evangelism Committee. They secured a street-address telephone directory, found the number of phones within the given area, and determined how many workers would be needed to reach this number. A budget was established which included the installing and rental of twelve telephones; the purchase of two street-address telephone directories (in some situations these must be rented); the preparation of call sheets which had the name, address and telephone number plus space for "no answer," "busy response" and "comments"; cards on which to write the names of unchurched families and pertinent information concerning them; and survey posters. The governing body of the church gave its unanimous approval to this budget.

The phone survey was highlighted in worship services in the church, and volunteers were asked to sign up on a chart placed at the rear of the sanctuary to work specific shifts. A two-week schedule was provided. Organizations of the church were urged to take over entire shifts, providing twelve operators. These shifts, which had been established by consultation with the telephone company, began on Monday and ended on Friday of each of the six weeks: shift 1, 10:00–11:30 A.M.; shift 2, 1:30–3:00 P.M.; shift 3, 3:30–5:00 P.M.; shift 4, 7:00–9:00 P.M. The men and working girls of the church were urged to sign up for the evening shift. Space was provided on the charts not only for the name of the caller but also for his report, which consisted of calls completed and unchurched families found. The charts thus served as a progress report. A summary chart kept the congregation informed and advised them of its completion.

The phones were set up around one large table, which became the communication center. This simplified the supervision of the telephoning (some churches have farmed out numbers to be called by individuals from their homes, which has proved unsatisfactory). A second advantage was found in the camaraderie and encouragement shared about the table. Another advantage was that the people were gathered in one place for one task, and this led to efficiency in that it curtailed much telephone gossip.

An average call went something like this: "Mr. Jones, I am calling from Broad Street Church. We're taking a local church survey. Are you an active member of a church?" If the answer was Yes, the caller said, "Thank You" and hung up. If no, then he continued: "A member of our church would like to call in your home soon." (This statement should always be in the affirmative; people will hasten to tell you if they are not interested.) The pertinent information was written on a prospect card. The telephones were used by 121 persons to make 6,658 calls and recorded 403 interested families. Actual telephoning lasted for two weeks.

The second phase of this survey was the two-week visitation of the families who expressed interest. Calling teams visited in the homes, shared mutual family experiences and discovered spiritual needs.

The third and final phase featured five nights of special worship services. The unconventional thing about this final program was that the prospects, who were first contacted by telephone and who committed themselves to participate in the services, were given the opportunity to witness. They sat with the persons who had visited them in their homes. The sense of interest and concern by all—the telephone callers, the visitors, the church members, and new folks contacted—made the witnessing experience real and vital.

Two important goals were reached by the Spiritual Life Mission: (1) several hundred members of the church participated in the program, and (2) hundreds were eventually won to the church fellowship.

TWELFTH PRINCIPLE

Unconventional Evangelism needs to employ mass communications. It is important that church leaders keep alert to the field of mass communications so that they may use all the media available to tell the Good News of the gospel.

Radio, the most widely used mass medium of Unconventional Evangelism, has not been utilized by the large denominations to the extent that it has been by sects, independent groups and smaller denominations. Noteworthy exceptions include local councils of churches that sponsor news and similar broadcasts. Other radio programs profitably used are those sponsored by large congregations as well as those presented by Bishop Fulton Sheen and Dr. Norman Vincent Peale. Included in the former are "live" worship services, in whole or in part.

Examples of unconventional radio programing might be noted:

Pastor's Study

This involves questions that are phoned-in to a special telephone number and the format may include a single pastor, a panel of ministers or representatives of the major faiths. Programs may be sponsored by a council of churches, a single church, or a public-spirited business firm or individual. Where these programs are adequately produced, great numbers of people respond, especially in the area of group counseling. Where the religious or theological position is clearly stated, differences among the members fairly presented, and a thoughtful, realistic approach to personal problems is offered, some programs have been popular two years or more.

Teen-age Programing

"What's Bugging You?" is the title of a religious program slanted toward young people, especially teen-agers. Air time is often on Saturday but may be on another day, for instance 4:00 P.M. weekdays, when teen-agers are listening; it is usually inserted between two favorite music sessions. Panels of young people are sometimes invited to sit in and help answer questions oriented to child-parent conflicts, ethical behavior and personal adjustment problems.

Crisis Telephone Ministries

Here the telephone is the key to the program, and the calls come from people representing the whole range of human need from simple loneliness to suicidal despair. Critical problems concern alcholics, unmarried mothers, compulsive gamblers and drug addicts. These "life-line" phones are always attended and arrangements are made to offer answers in depth to all who turn there for help. Professional people, doctors, psychiatrists, lawyers, businessmen and personnel from church-related homes and hospitals, together with other agencies, assist as needed. Group therapy is also attempted when personnel is adequate. The Life Line Movement, a "Discipleship in Depth," is not primarily an organization, but a fellowship of people who have made a commitment to Christ and His church. It begins with a serious call to personal holiness, continues with growth in Christian faith, and results in a dedication to the service of mankind and a Christian witness to society. The heart of the program, together with its purpose, is summed up in the saying of Jesus, "I am come that they may have life . . . in all its fulness" (John 10:10, NEB).

Dial-a-Prayer

These programs operate on the same principle as weather information or time service given over the telephone: when a person dials a number, a recorded message—in this instance a prayer—is transmitted. In some instances jamming of the trunk-line phone circuits has made this method of therapy impractical.

Some short-term projects of this nature have proved relatively successful. One dial-a-prayer program ended with these statements: If you would like to receive help in living the life of a Christian, please dial the following number ———. If you would like to know more about the Christian faith, please dial the following number ———. If you want to receive help in your personal problem, please dial the following number ———.

Another recently reported program was the Supportive Telephone therapy offered to those who had attended a four-day clinic to break the smoking habit. Here the clientele was limited and the purpose definite. The simple technique used consisted of a temporary private line set up with a recorder that had twenty messages which were transmitted to the dialer. This method has been used by some individual churches with special emphasis, and it suggests the possibility of opening up a whole new area of Unconventional Evangelism.

Life with its varied problems is forever in a state of movement: change, with possible personality and character deterioration or, on the other hand, creative growth. Mass media with their multiplicity of known techniques offer the church a working tool of Christian faith which can help make Christ known, loved and obeyed.

It must be pointed out that simply reaching people and getting them to listen is not evangelism. Evangelism is engaging people with the gospel. One of the pitfalls that must be avoided is permitting communication with people to deteriorate into purely humanistic dialogue. This approach to people will be helpful and meaningful only if it includes the gospel.*

THIRTEENTH PRINCIPLE

Unconventional Evangelism provides numerous forms of experience and growth. INPOST, downtown religious center established cooperatively by a group of Akron, Ohio, churches, is a church outpost in the center of the city providing worship, counseling, reading, discussion and meditation for those who work, shop or live in the downtown area. It is staffed by a group of volunteers who are trained to greet visitors and direct them to trained ministers who are on duty to offer emergency help. INPOST is an attempt to bring the church to where the people are in their daily lives downtown. Their motto is: "We do not seek to bring people to the church but to bring the gospel to the people."

"Catacombs" is the unusual name for an equally unusual project which seeks to reach the teen-ager with the Christian message. Located in a former ballroom, the Catacombs is a Christian coffee house for teen-agers of all religious persuasions. It is sponsored by the Men's Club of the Sharon Center, Ohio, Methodist Church. Activities include discussions, drama groups, combo music and planned recreational games. Among the sub-

---

* For further reading on mass media and Christian communication: James E. Sellers, *The Outsider and the Word of God* (Nashville: Abingdon Press, 1961), pp. 120f.; 184-192. Martin E. Marty, *The Improper Opinion* (Philadelphia: The Westminster Press, 1961), pp. 48f.

jects for discussion are "Dating," "The Age-old Problem between Parents and Youth" and "Christian Vocations for Young People." The discussions are led mostly by laymen. Talking about the young people's reaction to the club, one teen-ager remarked, "I didn't think at first they'd be for it, but they are." "The Catacombs provides a chance for us to express our own ideas," said another teen-ager.

Even calling the club the Catacombs has a significance for what the church is trying to do. The name is drawn from the burial place in Rome where first-century Christians met secretly while hiding from those who were persecuting them. During this time, too, drawings of fish were scratched on the walls. The club's symbol is the fish, which was the secret sign of recognition between Christians.

The need for such an organization in the community was expressed by its director, the Rev. Blair Stewart.

First of all, the club is an effective way for the church to reach teen-agers outside its own walls. Inviting young people to religious services just doesn't get much response anymore. The club provides a strong attraction for those youth who remain untouched by conventional church programs.

Second, there is a disparity between many young people's intellectual and Christian awareness. There are many youth, fourteen to seventeen years of age, who have a kindergarten knowledge of Christianity, but who are otherwise intelligent students. The church is trying to close this gap.

The leaders of the Catacombs are committed to making the gospel meaningful to young people today.*

* For a description of a similar youth center in Sydney, Australia, see Alan Walker, *A Ringing Call to Mission* (Nashville: Abingdon Press, 1966), pp. 63f.

FOURTEENTH PRINCIPLE

Unconventional Evangelism offers an additional opportunity to minister to the family. Almost any program of Unconventional Evangelism should concern itself with reaching the entire family unit.

At the services held in state parks, recreation areas, and in county fair prayer tents, up to 40 per cent of the persons attending are unchurched; 60 per cent of the total attending services are there as families. In drive-in services, 90 per cent are there as families. If these families were to become Christian, thousands of children of the future generation would grow up in the Christian way. The church dare not neglect family evangelism. When you evangelize a family, father and mother accept Christ and the Christian way of life; children become Christian. When you evangelize the family, you have an atmosphere of Christlikeness that will preserve and enlarge each individual commitment. When you evangelize the family, children grow spiritually while they grow physically and socially. The church will be wise to concern itself with the redemption of the family as such.

Any church participating in a program of Unconventional Evangelism needs to involve church members who have some aptitude for giving help and guidance to intelligently inform and counsel families about Christian living in their homes. Each counselor should be assigned to a certain number of families whom he will visit regularly. He should make arrangements for two to five couples to come together to work at the problem of actually being Christian in their families. Three or four such weekly gatherings would help to prepare people to live the Christlike way in their homes. Here full and free discussions can be held concerning what is a Christian home. The counselor and parents can discuss methods of helping children develop a spiritual life, Christian norms for decisions concerning right and wrong, and materials that can be used for devotions and prayers. Parents can be helped to answer the questions of small children about "Where is God?" and "How can He hear me pray?" If more parents could answer religious questions, they would develop more Christian persons in their homes.

Again, one family can visit or invite another family into their home. To be invited to a home—there is something special about that. "The Abernathys have invited a number of us to their home." This is a heart-warming experience to begin with, to be the guest in another home. With a minimum of self-consciousness, fathers and mothers can talk about the questions little children ask about God, about Jesus, the difficulties of having daily prayer, the same experiments in Christian family living. All of this and more flows into the give-and-take of an evening together on the part of four or five families meeting in a neighbor's home. These families can strengthen and give courage to each other. This, as a program, could revolutionize life in many of our families. If families were to move out to win other families for Christ, they would revolutionize the character of America.

These fourteen principles are presented, not as rigid rules, but as guidelines based on experience which may be useful to ministers and laymen who are committed to taking the gospel out of the church building to the people where they are.

6. Purpose, Plans and Program

UNCONVENTIONAL Evangelism is just beginning. The surface has only been scratched. It is hoped that the reader may be challenged to take hold and carry on. The work of evangelism is done only as friends of Christ are obedient to His call and leadership.

Unconventional Evangelism is most effective when systematically organized. Even though the setting of Unconventional Evangelism is often informal and may border on the far-out or bizarre, this does not imply that it must not be prepared for as carefully as any service held in the church. In fact, the casual observer on the corner, the worker in the factory, or the vacationist in the park may well be more critical of what you do than those in attendance at regular church service. Unconventional Evangelism stands a better chance of attracting the average man on the street if what is done has been carefully planned.

Though the setting calls for an extemporaneous service, making it appear spontaneous and fresh, this does not mean there should be no planning. Spontaneity *must* be planned for, prepared for and well thought-out; if not, rather than appearing fresh, alive, fast-moving and spontaneous, it will appear to be just what it is—slipshod, shabby and disorganized.

One must always keep in mind that because of the setting of most of these projects, one is competing with many other attractions for people's time and interest. What is to be done, therefore, must be done quickly; which means that one must know what he is going to do every moment, what comes next, and what he hopes to accomplish. To do this takes *planning, preparation* and *training.*

THE TRAINING

The best place for a person to receive training in Unconventional Evangelism is in a workshop. One way to start is to have the denominational executive officer or the state council of churches through its department of evangelism conduct a one-day consultation for interested ministers and laymen. The consultation should be an all-day meeting conducted by ministers and laymen who would be interested in working in the proposed project, whether it is in shopping centers, drive-in theaters, state parks, county fairs, factories, mobile homes, or on radio, telephone, television or drag strips. Fall and early winter are the best times to hold consultations. The following schedule may serve as a guide for these meetings:

I. Procedures:

1. Determine the areas of concern for new structures for ministry.

2. Enlist resource persons who are able to provide leadership in these areas.

3. Invite ministers and laymen from local churches to participate in one-day consultations.

4. Provide channels for *continued* (or follow-up) communication and support in each project initiated.

II. Set Goals:

1. Have a prayer tent in every county fair in the state.

2. Establish a drive-in open-air service in every community.

3. Have a planned witnessing service on Saturday night, Sunday morning, and Sunday evening, followed by discussion groups on different age levels, in areas close to every state, municipal and privately owned camp and park in the state.

4. Establish a witnessing project in factories.

5. Have a planned Saturday night witnessing program in shopping centers.

6. Establish church schools in every mobile-home center in which there are a minimum of twenty-five house trailers.

7. Provide services in homes in new housing developments in which no church buildings exist.

8. Provide brief witnessing services at all drag strips and speedways throughout the state.

9. Attempt evangelism programs for groups of civic officials, firemen, police and other city employees; also, teachers, attorneys, nurses, physicians, etc.

10. Begin all "seasonal" projects on Easter Sunday and run through October 1, wherever possible.

III. Suggested schedule for a "One-Day Consultation":

9:00 A.M.   Coffee. (Get acquainted. Visit displays of projects.)

10:00 A.M. Devotions.

10:15 A.M. Inspirational message by denominational executive. Subject: "Why Unconventional Evangelism?"

10:45 A.M. Brief previews of the various projects by resource leaders. "It Works for Us."

11:00 A.M. Consultations to answer "How?" questions. Persons divided into groups of their own special interest for simultaneous discussions.

1. Drive-in services.
2. State, municipal, private parks and resort areas.
3. County fair prayer tents.
4. Factory evangelism.
5. Mobile-home centers.
6. New housing development services.
7. Drag strip and speedway.
8. Open-air meetings—church lawns, shopping centers, etc.
9. Outpost church schools.
10. Vocational evangelism for state, county and city employees, teachers, nurses.

12:30 P.M. Luncheon. Testimonies from experimental projects. Visit displays.

1:45 P.M. Second session for consultations. Use films, records, demonstrations, etc.

2:45 P.M. "The Meaning of Commitment."

3:15 P.M. "The Call to Commitment"—the denominational head. Covenant to specific experimental ministries.

3:30 P.M. Benediction.
Now go do it!

PRACTICAL STEPS

I. You and Your Church:

1. Secure the support of your governing board and its committees, as many as possible—Evangelism, Education, Finance, Worship, Missions, etc.

2. Include a number of laymen from these committees in the planning stage of the project. They may have good suggestions and they will keep the project from being centered around the minister.

3. Any ministry which you carry out should represent the impact of your local church upon the persons that you are seeking to reach.

II. You and the Civil Authorities:

1. Get to know on a friendly, personal basis the following persons with whom you will be dealing:

   a) mayor

   b) police chief or officers

   c) property owners or administrators

   d) in a factory—the superintendent or manager of the plant

2. Know your existing laws and keep within them. Some municipal governments have restrictive laws regarding their community parks. Some state parks have stringent rules that must be followed.

3. Involve these authorities, if possible, in the early planning stage of the project—at least, seek their reaction to your plans. If properly approached, these persons are usually interested, cooperative and helpful.

III. You and the Service:

Establish a committee to plan the service. The committee should consider:

1. Time and place of the service.

In many recreational areas, for instance, short vesper services on Saturday and Sunday evenings from 7:00 to 7:45 P.M. are appreciated.

On Sunday mornings services from 8:00 to 8:30 have been popular. Following the worship service, discussion groups for different age levels have proved successful. In some places, perhaps an afternoon service would be best.

Care should be given to the selection of a place for the service. The location should be easily accessible, yet not in the way of other distracting, ongoing activities, i.e., a cleared area in a camp (not on the main walk or street area in a shopping center, but a roped-off area, etc.).

2. Plan of the service.

A number of laymen should be used in the service. They should be trained to create a friendly, warm and informal atmosphere.

Ushers and greeters are very important.

Your own church people can be of help in making up the congregation when you first begin.

It is most important that the people helping with the service dress informally. The minister or leader of the service should refrain from the use of a robe. White shirt with tie, and without suit coat, is in good taste.

A bulletin or plain sheet of paper with the order of service and hymns to be used is helpful.

Hymns should be well known. Singing in an outdoor setting is difficult. A choir or quartet will help a great deal in congregational singing.

Organs are available at varied cost. Field organs can be secured from army surplus for $20 or less. A music store may loan an electric organ for the sake of advertising.

People enjoy the informality of the out-of-doors. Use this spirit to advantage.

3. Purpose of the Service.

Involve the spectator in some way. Encourage his participation. Inquire who has traveled the longest distance. Ask the audience what states or communities are represented in the service.

Invite people to join the choir.

Do not invite laymen to take up an offering. If **an**

offering is taken, it should be minimized. Several students or Boy Scouts waiting at exits with plates as people leave will take care of your expenses.

Preach for decisions. Your preaching should be simple and direct, a message you can deliver without notes.

Make sure you know what you want participants to do. Make it clear and plain.

Know beforehand what goal you hope to achieve, what kind of response you hope for.

The type of response called for should be in keeping with the kind and location of the service:

a) In a park area you may want to give an invitation to those who wish to come forward and make a commitment, while others are dismissed.

b) In some places you may want to extend an invitation for further discussion after the service.

c) In other situations you may wish to conclude with the use of a "Response Guide." The use of the Guide may be preceded by this statement:

WHY CALL FOR A DECISION?

Many people become frustrated when they are challenged to make important decisions in their lives. They want to be left basically (and comfortably) the same people they were before the proclamation and explanation of the Christian faith.*

However, the hearing of the Good News *demands a response.* No person can sit idly by if he has really "heard" the message. He must accept, reject or distort it—along with his relation to the Lord who seeks men through that message.

* For a more extended treatment of this point, see Robert J. Versteeg, *The Gracious Calling of the Lord* (Nashville: Abingdon Press, 1960), Ch. 2, "The Structure of Decision."

The call is essential also because of one's very nature as a free person. Persons are not robots whom God can manipulate. For that reason, the *only way* to enter into a covenant with God, or into any specific aspect of the Christian life, is through *the free decision of one's will.*

In response to the nature of the gospel, to a person's nature as a human being, and in the desire to know the abundant life, we extend the Response Guide in His name. It covers the major relationships of life—God, church, other and self.

Notice the first suggestion pertaining to a personal basic relationship with Jesus Christ. All other decisions are secondary to that one. It must take prior claim in one's attention. If you have made it, then search the other areas of your life using this Response Guide.

Do *not* check something just for the sake of checking something, or because the person sitting next to you is checking his Response Guide. This calls for a sacred decision. God will hold each person responsible for the decisions that he makes.*

The Guide itself may be in the following form:

MY RESPONSE TO GOD

During this service I have made and now make the following decision(s). God being my helper, I look carefully at these important areas of my life and here *record* my covenant with God.

MY RELATIONSHIP TO GOD

———I desire to receive Christ as my Lord for the first time in my life, and accept the relationship of forgiveness and acceptance that God wants for me.

* For a more extended treatment of this point see James W. Kennedy, *Minister's Shop-Talk* (New York: Harper & Row, 1965), pp. 50f.; also Leighton Ford, *The Christian Persuader* (New York: Harper & Row, 1966), pp. 118f.

MY RELATIONSHIP TO THE CHURCH

———(For youth.) I commit my life to a full-time church-related vocation.

———I desire to be a part of a———prayer group,——— Bible study group.

———I will endeavor to attend church and Sunday school regularly.

MY RELATIONSHIP TO OTHER PEOPLE

———I will seek to follow Christ in loving all people.

———I commit myself to making my home Christian.

MY RELATIONSHIP TO MYSELF

———I will seek ways to serve God through my occupation.

———I will read the Bible daily to seek understanding for my life.

———I will practice daily devotions, using *The Upper Room* or some other devotional guide.

Name:————————————————————————

Address:————————————————————————

The pastor or leader should feel free to make additions or changes to the Guide.

In all projects of Unconventional Evangelism, you should be sensitive to the kind of people you are talking to, the environment, and the task at hand—telling people about the Good News of Christ and His gospel, witnessing to what it has done for you, and what it can mean in their lives.